FOURTH THOUSAND.

THE

SENATOR'S SON,

OR,

THE MAINE LAW;

A LAST REFUGE;

A STORY DEDICATED

TO

THE LAW-MAKERS.

BY

METTA VICTORIA FULLER.

SECOND EDITION.

CLEVELAND, O.

TOOKER AND GATCHEL.

1853.

Entered according to Act of Congress, in the year Eighteen Hundred and Fifty-three,

By TOOKER & GATCHEL,

In the Clerk's Office of the District Court of the United States for the District of Ohio.

WILLIAM H. SHAIN,
HUDSON STEREOTYPE FOUNDRY.

HARRIS, FAIRBANKS & CO.,
PRINTERS, CLEVELAND.

"Does our political party stand on rum? If so, let us be ashamed of it and quit it. But let us take heed lest our political party is soon in the minority, from its adherence to rum, for it surely will be. Degeneracy and subserviency to wickedness and debasement is not the spirit of the age. God will overturn, and overturn, and overturn, until temperance and truth are triumphant."

PREFACE.

It may perhaps be expected that a few explanations should be given for the publication of a new work of fiction. My attention was particularly called, during the past summer, to the fact that, in many States, there existed a strong feeling in favor of the general adoption of the Maine Liquor Law, as it is called; but so many of past usages and modes of thinking prevailed, that philanthropists have been unable, except in a few instances, to carry into effect an Act that must so clearly benefit all classes of society. The thought suggested itself, that if a new work could be written on this subject, sufficiently interesting to attract anything like general attention, it might perhaps turn the scale, now so nearly balanced, in favor of this noble end.

To do this successfully, one would be obliged to go out of the ordinary manner of treating the subject of Temperance. For long years, the most vivid descriptions have been given of the terrible sufferings and awful wretchedness that await the victim of Intemperance. Reason and judgment have been appealed to in vain. Thousands are at this moment reeling towards a drunkard's grave. Experience has proved that in no way can the evils of the heart or of society be shown so plainly and effectively as under the garb of fiction. Here, casting aside the dull argument and dry statistics, the subject is mirrored in its natural beauty or deformity, unobscured by the mists of custom or familiarity. We look beneath the smiling demeanor of vice, on the hidden agony gnawing at its heart-strings. We gaze with rapture on the pure, calm brow of virtue, radiant with happiness amid the clouds of adversity and the storms of misfortune. We behold the first, the secret inducement to crime, and shudder as we observe the terrible results that must follow looming up, black and threatening, in the dim and distant future. We see reflected in a new and vivid light evils of vast magnitude and extent, that were before trite and commonplace; and we see, too, divested of all expediency and sophistry, the true remedy to be applied. Hence, in all reforms this kind of writing will be found most effective. But it is only when some effort at human improvement is robed in its captivating garb that fiction should be tolerated. As in the spreading landscape, the ragged rocks, the majestic oak and the dark ravine, take a firmer hold upon the mind than all the gay colors of field and forest, so in this kind of fiction, while we cull its sweets, and linger entranced over its fascinating pages, the stern ideas of truth and right that meet us at every turn will gradually fasten upon our judgments, and linger in our memories, long after the sweet flowers that decked them have faded and been forgotten.

With such a desire have the following pages been written ; and though I have wandered in the luxuriant fields of the imagination to select colors for my theme, yet my aim has been to draw, with stronger outline and deeper shading, the mournful ruins of humanity, caused by Intemperance, and to place them in the foreground of the picture ; and if I should ever hear of one soul saved by its means from the dark and fearful gloom that hangs forever over the end of the drunkard, it would be more than payment for all my labors. Whether it is ever destined to accomplish even this much remains to be seen ; but its failure will not alter my faith in the ultimate triumph of the Maine Liquor Law, through the length and breadth of our fair land.

THE SENATOR'S SON.

A Story,

DEDICATED TO THE LAW-MAKERS.

CHAPTER I.

"Why do the ladies come away from the table first, mother? don't they eat as much as the gentlemen?"

"I hardly think they do, Parke," replied the lady with a smile: "but the gentlemen are not eating; they are drinking wine."

"Don't the ladies drink wine?"

"A little sometimes. But when papa and his friends have drank a few glasses, they become very sociable, and converse wisely upon politics and other subjects too abstruse for feminine ears."

"I don't think its very pretty," responded the little

fellow, not fully comprehending his mother's apologies. At the same time he made up his mind to see for himself what there was so fascinating in the dining-room; so stealing from her lap, in a few moments his bright head was peeping in at the door, where, finding himself unobserved, he walked in and hid behind his father's chair.

"Well! its mighty pleasant here anyhow," was his secret conclusion. There was a profusion of lamp-light, making the costly table-service glitter and gleam; Harry and White, the two black waiters, were busy uncorking dark, ancient-looking bottles; the cut-glass decanters and goblets sparkled only less than their contents. A dozen gentlemen, each smiling, affable, and witty, were trifling with some fruit, leisurely picking out the kernels from the almonds, and toying more or less fondly with their glasses. People, poetry, and politics were being discussed; old puns and new puns were received with equal good humor, and even some brilliant repartee flashed across the mahogany board.

"This wine is fit for old Bacchus' own use," said one of the number. "I propose that we drink the health of our host — a long continuance of his late success, and defeat to his enemies: may his brother senators receive him with merited applause, — may his country appreciate his services, — may his speeches be distinguished for their brevity as well as wit, — and may he be spared, after a successful session, to return to the smiles of his numerous friends and the arms of his truly lovely family."

The enthusiasm with which this toast was received was such that it came near to penetrating the sacred precincts of the parlors. Their host arose to make a few remarks, partly referring to his principles and party, but mostly personal thanks and sentiments of friendship.

He was a fine-looking man, speaking with grace and ease. His dark-blue eye sparkles with wit and fire; he had an open, generous brow, beautified by masses of brown ringlets, and a rich, persuasive voice. Upon this occasion he was more than usually animated.

He was giving a farewell dinner to a few of his friends, previous to his departure for Washington, whither the votes of his party had destined him; in their evident love and admiration was something to arouse his sympathies, and he spoke with eloquence.

The little intruder edges round to the side of the table, regarding his father with intense interest. He could not, of course, understand much of what he was saying, but the language of looks was not lost upon him. He, as well as the older listeners, was charmed with the brilliant smile and the graceful gesture; as Mr. Madison sat down, he looked around with a proud air, and his rosy cheek flushed as if it said —

"What man is there so wonderful as my papa?"

A guest caught sight of the triumphant look, and remarked with a smile —

"Your little son appears, like the rest of us, very much pleased with your sentiments."

The father's eye lighted on the eager, sparkling face.

"Here, Parke, my boy, is a glass of wine; we are going to drink to the memory of George Washington. You shall have the honor of proposing the words."

The child of four years stepped forward and seized the glass. Holding it as he had seen his father do, he spoke out boldly, — in his clear, baby voice, —

"To the memory of George Washington, the Father of his Country. First in war — first in peace — and first in the hearts of his countrymen!"

An enthusiasm befitting an older heart seemed to shine in the eyes of the boy, who had thus early caught his parent's words, and, almost, thoughts. Every man rose to his feet; and there was a momentary silence.

But a child's thoughts do not dwell long upon subjects so profound, and he whispered in his papa's ear, as the gentlemen replaced their glasses,

"I like the wine very much indeed."

It was meet that no other name should be crowned with rosy wine after that of Washington, and the gentlemen soon joined their fairer companions. Here, as everywhere else, Mr. Madison was the first object of admiration. Beautiful women smiled graciously at receiving his delicate and welcome attentions — they looked for his courtly glance, and listened for the changing flow of his discourse — now mirthful, satirical, pathetic — always that of a man of genius, with kindly sympathies, and a generous heart. His wife, a most lovely and graceful woman, moved quietly among her guests, with an unequaled tact and propriety, yet not the less conscious of her husband's gifts. Devotion and pride were in her aspect; as if not having anything but love in her own nature, she had yet learned to be proud of herself as a part of him. The thought that to-morrow they were to be separated for some months, was more to her than the brilliancy and triumph of the occasion; and now and then her glances meeting his would melt away into almost tears. Despite of this the evening could not but be very happy; the lights were so brilliant, the company so pleased, the music so sweet, and Mr. Madison himself, in one of his most fascinating humors.

There was but one fault to be found with him — he was too fascinating. For the winning flash of his eye, the quick beaming of his smile, the glow of his humor, the sparkle of his wit, had all borrowed a flame — beautiful but burning — a flame from the fire in the wine-cup. A suspicion of this had not as yet shaded the soft brow of the young wife, turned so reverently up to him.

"Why, Parke, I thought Margaret had put you to bed, long ago," she said in a low voice to her little boy, as he crept to her side, while one of the ladies was at the piano. "You'll not be awake in the morning to bid papa good-bye, if you sit up so long after your bed-time."

The boy looked at her with eyes unnaturally bright.

"Hurrah for my papa Washington!" he shouted, staggering away from his mother's caressing hand, and attempting to wave his little arm.

"Why, darling, what makes you so rude?" she continued walking after him to take him from the room.

"Hurrah for Washington! he's the man for senator," he murmured in a lower tone, as he fell over an ottoman, from whence he was lifted by his astonished parents.

"The child is in a fit," cried Mrs. Madison, turning pale.

"A fit?" said the father; and he laughed gayly. "The truth is we left him in the dining-room, and he must have been drinking some private toasts in honor of my departure. The little rogue! but he did not know any better."

The gentlemen joined in the laugh, and called him a brave little fellow; but the mother, who had summoned Margaret to carry him to the nursery, could hardly smile, for poor Parke's cheeks were already growing white.

She was obliged to excuse herself from her friends, who were already departing; and for more than half the night she had to watch by the sick-bed of the young patriot.

His sufferings at last over, he fell into a deep sleep that was not even disturbed by his father's parting kiss, three hours after day-break. When he did awake, his mother sat beside his little cot, weeping. The thought that his party had chosen her husband to represent their principles at the Capitol, although a proud one, could not suffice in the moment of parting to take away its bitterness. With his last kiss upon her lips,and the pressure of his hand yet thrilling her fingers, she stole to the room of their only child to comfort herself with the sight of his innocent face. And a comfort it was; for her loneliness began to divert itself with joyful plans of what she should do for his improvement, to surprise his father when he came home.

He should live mostly upon bread and milk, to keep his cheek rosy and his complexion clear; he should make astonishing progress in spelling, and be deep in primary geography; and she should embroider him the most exquisite suit of clothes to wear in honor of the absent one's return. With innocent mother-thoughts like these, she was beguiling her quiet tears; on and on her fancy flew to times when he should be grown out of his boy-jacket, and cap with plumes, and be a man, beautiful as his father, and like him honored and beloved. She smiled even while she wept, and Parke awoke to meet a kiss of yearning tenderness.

The first day was not passed, however, much to Parke's edification or that of his mother. The effects of last night's disobedience were pale cheeks and a very fretful humor.

The proposed bread and milk regimen, and a fine ride the next morning in the carriage, restored him to his wonted excellent temper.

As Mrs. Madison was laying aside her cloak after the ride, the cook told her that there was a poor woman in the kitchen who wanted to speak with her. Going down, she found a Mrs. Burns, who, in former times, had nearly lived upon her charity. But her husband, a hod-carrier, and dreadfully intemperate, had, for the last few months, reformed and provided comfortably for his family.

"How is this, Mrs. Burns? you look as if you were in trouble again," said the senator's wife, in her winning, sympathizing manner.

The woman glanced at her almost fiercely from the corner by the range, where she was standing, for she would not sit.

"Trouble! you may well call it trouble," she said briefly.

"Is your husband drinking again?"

"Aye! worse than ever."

"What a pity — what a great pity!"

"Yes! its a pity for him, and a pity for me, and a pity for the children; but its a pity, too, for them as has the blame of it — a pity and a shame!"

"Has any one the blame of his evil conduct, except himself?" asked Mrs. Madison gently, for she saw that her visitor was much excited.

"There are those, ma'am, whom God will not hold guiltless at the judgment-day. Fine gentlemen they are too, and fine speeches they can make about their principles; and your husband, one of them — he's one of them as has the faults of my poor man on his head."

"Hush, Mrs. Burns," said the lady, while the roses flushed out into her face, "you must not speak so in my presence."

"But I will speak so, ma'am, for I came here to tell you the truth. You are an angel, almost, I know; and have been good to me and mine; but that doesn't signify but that you are too good for *him*. There's no kinder man than mine when he's sober; and not a drop of liquor did he taste since last March, until 'lection day. He earned his dollar a day, and brought it home at night; the children had shoes and decent clothes, and Tom went to school; and you couldn't find a woman with a happier heart than mine. But election times must come, and my husband must have his say with the rest, and as he walks along the street towards the polls, Mr. Madison comes up and shakes hands, with his sweet smile, and says, 'Who are you going to support to-day, Mr. Burns?' So my husband tells him, and he says, 'You'll make a great mistake if you do that. Their party don't care any more for you or any other honest working man, than just to get your vote, and when they've got it, and got the power, they'll use it against you, and wages will come down, and the poor'll suffer,' or some other such kind of speeches. 'I don't believe it, Mr. Madison,' says my husband. 'Well, just step in and take a glass of some thing to make you more reasonable, and we'll talk it over, says Mr. Madison. 'I'm obliged to you, but I don't drink anything now,' says Tom. 'I'm glad to hear it,' says your fine gentleman, 'but just take a little to-day — it'll help you see clearer which of us is in the right.' The pleasant smiles and the fine words were more than he could resist, and he went in, and your husband treated him, and got his vote, and he came home drunk that night, and he's been drunk ever since. Not a day's work has he done — the little silver there was laid by has gone — the children are cold, and there is no fire; and he's warming himself by the bar-room fire, that's only better than the flames below."

She paused and stood looking gloomily into the range. Mrs. Madison could not say a word; in her heart she confessed the wrongs of the drunkard's wife, and was ready to shed tears over the thoughtless conduct of her own proud husband.

"He was carried away by the excitement of the occasion," she said to herself; "he forgot into what temptation he was leading this poor man," — but all sophistry of affection could not entirely excuse his selfish eagerness for the triumph of his party. "This must be the wrongs of suffrage instead of the rights," continued her thoughts. "Facts like these cry shame upon politicians — facts like these are soils upon the beautiful garments of Liberty!"

Mrs. Burns turned her face again towards the lady, it was a face that seemed to have been gentle and pretty enough once; now it looked cold and hard as stone.

"I am going to out with the worst, Mrs. Madison. Little Ann is dead."

"Why, Mrs. Burns! what was the matter with her?"

"Oh, she died," said the woman, in a voice made harsh by repressed emotions; "she died because somebody wanted her father's vote, and made him drunk. He must needs drink more and more, and grow worse and worse — Burns is a devil when he's drunk, peaceful as he is when he lets liquor alone — until he must go to abusing the young ones, and getting mad at me; and because I tried to keep his hands off the little girl — she was a delicate thing you know, and only two years old — oh! how I prayed to him upon my knees to let her alone! — he catched her away from me and shook her furiously, dashed her down over a chair, and went out the door with an oath. When I picked her up, I thought she was dead. But after awhile she began to moan, and every time she was stirred she shrieked — I think that her back was broke — and so she laid in my arms that night and the next day, and last night she died."

Her listener had sank half-fainting into a chair, with the tears rolling rapidly down her colorless cheeks.

"*I've* not shed a tear yet," continued her visitor, in the same constrained voice. "But I've had some awful thoughts. As I sat there so many hours, holding my poor darling, looking into her white face, with the black circles of pain around the eyes, and listening to her moans, I thought of your little boy, so rosy and so bright, and I came near cursing him for his father's fault."

"Oh, don't speak so, Mrs. Burns!" Mrs. Madison held up her hands appealingly, while a shudder went through her soul at the sudden thought of *her* beautiful child with a curse upon his innocent head. "No one can wish any ill to *him*," she said half-aloud.

"No! no one can wish any ill to him, for his mother's sake," said the woman, catching at her words. "But I'm afraid it'll come without anybody's wishing. 'The sins of the fathers are visited upon the children.' "

"Shall I go home with you, and do what I can for poor Annie?"

"If you will, ma'am; its little can be done for her now."

The carriage was still at the door, and Mrs. Madison told the driver to come around with it to Mrs. Burns', in half an hour; and the two mothers wended their way down the narrow alley leading to the desolate home of one of them.

The senator's wife was a lady of delicate nerves; but her nerves and her antipathies were under the firm control of her reason and benevolence. Her large charities had made her familiar with the houses of the poor; but her heart sank as she stepped over the threshold of this dwelling. A feeling that she herself was not wholly guiltless of the wretchedness which met her eye, could not be shaken off. A moment she stood silent, looking at the two shivering children crouched by the fireless hearth, at the empty cupboard, the broken windows, and, lastly, at the bed — where laid the corpse of the murdered child. Approaching, she turned back the sheet, and gazed at its little, quiet face, which she last remembered so pretty, blooming, and fair.

It was too much for her mother's heart. The miserable father — the mother who could not shed a tear — the innocent infant released from a world too harsh for its gentle endurance — the want — the wrong — the wo — came over her soul like a rushing cloud, and, sinking beside the bed, she sobbed aloud. Her weeping was contagious. It melted the icy grief of the mourner down to the level of natural expression; she threw herself upon the couch with cries and tears, kissing the cold hands of her darling, touching her flaxen curls, calling her, in accents of moving pathos, "Annie! Annie!"

The two boys, frightened and cold, drew closer together, looking on with wondering eyes. The carriage came to the door, and Mrs. Madison, controling her emotion, whispered,

"It will do you good to cry, I am glad that you can. I will go now and do what is necessary to be done, and then return." Food and fuel came in due time; lastly, a little coffin. With her own fair hands the lady kindled a fire upon the hearth, washed the faces of the children, brushed their hair, and helped them plentifully to the contents of a basket which had been well stored from her own pantry. Then she aroused their mother from her stupor of exhaustion; made her eat, drink a cup of tea, and warm herself.

Tenderly she placed the pretty Annie in her coffin, decked out in one of Parke's nicest baby-gowns, with some pale buds in her little hands gathered from the conservatory. The boys were told to kiss their dear sister for the last time before the coffin-lid was fastened down; then all got into the carriage and followed the hearse to the cemetery. All was well and quietly done. The grave was hollowed in a pleasant place, where roses would bloom in summer; now the wind blew drearily, and scattered flakes of snow portended the death of autumn.

The mother would have cast herself down upon her baby's grave and remained there; but with gentle force her friend compelled her home. It was late in the afternoon when they returned. Mrs. Madison went in a few moments to see that the children were left in comfort. While she was there, Burns came in. He was not drunk, for he was out of money, and could not get any liquor. He had not been home since that fatal night; it was the first time he had been sober for days and days. He looked pale, cross, and unhappy; his face flushed with shame when he met the eye of their visitor. His wife turned her face away from him, as he came in, without looking towards him. An ominous silence settled him; glancing around, he asked hastily —

"Where is Annie?"

Perhaps he had a recollection of his cruelty.

"She is dead," replied Mrs. Madison, gravely; "dead and buried."

"Annie dead?" he enquired with a bewildered air.

"Yes! Mr. Burns, she is dead. Do you remember your brutal treatment of her the other night? She died of that — you are her murderer!"

"My God!" burst from the lips of the miserable man, after a moment's silence. "No! I couldn't have killed her — little Annie! our only girl — our little Ann! — don't say so, don't say that!"

He sank into a chair, trembling all over

Soon the fear of a weak nature began to overpower even remorse.

"Does any one know it? Are the officers after me?" he asked.

"No one knows of it yet except myself, out of your family, and no one shall know of it, as long as you remain a sober, penitent man. Let this awful lesson be enough, Mr. Burns. Promise me never to taste another drop of ardent spirits, and we promise you to keep your terrible secret. But break your promise, and we give you up at once to the justice of the law."

"I promise you," he replied eagerly.

It was growing dark: Mrs. Madison was obliged to leave the unhappy man to make his peace with his wife, as best he could, and went away, leaving them with each other. Her beautiful mansion welcomed her home with its look of luxury and ease. She went to her room and sat down in her favorite easy chair, weary and dejected. The shining grate was heaped with glowing anthracite, the lamps burned pleasantly — a rich cheerfulness pervaded the apartment, contrasting with the gloom she had left behind.

Little Parke was waiting to see his mother, and receive her good-night kiss before he went to his crib. A servant brought in tea and set it beside her; she drank it with but little appetite, and when it was carried away, Parke climbed into her lap. She gave him a great many good-night kisses, yet could not let him go; her fingers lingered in his sunny curls, turning them back from his brow, while her eyes dwelt upon his fairness and beauty. A noble-looking boy he was, with his father's handsome features, and the promise of his talent. The sunny landscape of the future into which she had yesterday glanced with so hopeful an eye, seemed sadly changed; dark clouds were drifting over it; gloom and terror were usurping the place of beauty. It was but a phantom landscape though, conjured up by the weird words of a wronged mother's passion; and with a smile and sigh, she strove to call her mind away from it.

Still she hardly felt willing to let the boy go away to his crib; when he teased to sleep with her she gladly consented, and all night she held him closely in her arms, as if screening him from some invisible danger. Notwithstanding her fatigue she slept but little. Thought was busy with a new subject. There had not been in those days all this stir about temperance, which has led people since to think so much about the 'worm of the still,' and devise such good means for its death. She had no idea in what manner an attack might be made upon the evil thing. Little Annie's ghost hovered about her pillow, calling, with feeble cries of pain, for an atonement to be made, and refusing to be quieted with anything less than an earnest promise to cherish henceforth an unsparing enmity against the lawless robber who had deprived her of her wearisome life.

Lovely in spirit as in person, capable of profound thought as well as quick feeling, Mrs. Madison did not dismiss the subject from her mind, until she had come to the conclusion that it was her individual duty to wield one blow, however slight it might be, directed by the arm of a delicate woman, against the torturing worm that was eating into the heart of almost every family in the land. Its fiery fangs were not clinging to any of her beloved ones in the immediate circle of home; but friends she had, and friends of friends who suffered;— the world suffered, and something ought to be done for its relief. She did not dream, proud and happy wife that she was, she did not dream that her husband was like a fair and ruddy fruit, promising to the eye, but which was already a little ashen at the core, and doomed to swift decay.

"It was through the temptation of one who controls himself well, that poor Burns fell," she said to herself, "and my husband was the tempter. Never — never will I, remotely or in any manner, be the agent of another's destruction. Rather let my feeble light burn as a signal to warn all from the danger that is nigh."

Calmed by this good resolution, she fell asleep.

CHAPTER II.

THE first notable opportunity which occurred for Mrs. Madison to 'burn her signal light,' was upon New Year's Day. In the great city where she resided it was the universal custom of the ladies to receive their friends among the gentlemen, upon that day.

It was an honor, eagerly sought by the most aspiring, to enter the parlors of this beautiful woman, and receive her graceful welcome. Her distinguished position, as the fair descendant of an ancient, honorable, and wealthy family, the gentle patron of literature and the arts, and the wife of their talented senator, made every movement of her's, in society, conspicuous. It was with a little secret trembling of the heart, therefore, that she ordered the arrangements of her table upon that morning; for she had resolved to banish wine from it altogether. This was then an almost unprecedented movement. By the time she had finished dressing, she had recovered her composure; conscious that her dignity of position would enable her to carry out her ideas of right.

She descended to receive her guests in all the regal beauty of her womanly power. She had a well-chosen word for all — statesmen, poets, artists, beaux, and dandies. She fascinated all alike, by her sweet self-possession, her sprightly wit, her fine tact.

Sipping the fragrant coffee from cups of costly porcelain, anxious for every word and look of their hostess, her guests appeared both satisfied and delighted. Whatever they may have thought of the important omission from the table, of course none spoke of it, until the day began to wear to a close; and among the later callers the effects of previous hospitality began to make themselves unpleasantly apparent. Intemperance then, with a thousand-fold more fatality than the cholera now, raged among the brave, the noble, the gifted of the land. The brightest stars went wheeling and tottering down the firmament of society and disappeared in perpetual darkness. It is not strange that more than a majority of those who, in the latter part of the afternoon, presented themselves before Mrs. Madison, were more fitted to be presented to the kind care of their servants and beds, than to the presence of a refined woman. She had ample opportunity of studying the different kinds of madness which the same fiery tooth had infused into the temperaments of her friends. Some, it is true, seemed to glow with more intense brilliancy, to be only more extremely courteous; in others, their broad, good-humor provoked her smile; or their senseless flatteries her frown; again, their stupid inanities excited a disgust which courtesy could hardly conceal.

"I thank you, Mrs. Madison," said a gentleman, speaking rather thickly, who, when he had the control of his senses, was remarkable for his delicate devotion of demeanor in the presence of ladies, "but I would prefer a glass of wine."

"I have not given my guests any wine to-day," she replied with a pleasant smile.

"Mr. Madison's famous cellars are not growing empty, are they?" "Oh, no!" with another persuasive smile. "But I regard wine as a most specious, false friend — an enemy in disguise — whom I have had the courage to banish from my presence."

"Well!" with a polite, classic oath, "I fear you will banish me too; for I must confess its sinning outrageously against hospitality."

"If you find nothing to attract you to our house, Mr. Sinclair, but our wine-cellars, I am sorry," she replied with gravity.

"Oh — oh — oh!" I know you are very charming! but I like wine as well as women, and so does Madison; I ——"

"Good evening, Mr. Sinclair," interrupted his hostess, with a jesture of dismissal, while the roses crowned her indignant brow.

"Ah!— oh — I beg your par—" but his friends who had some faint sense of propriety remaining, took him by the arm, and departed.

It was with a deeper sense than ever of the magnitude of the cloud overshadowing the land, that the senator's wife dismissed that evening the last of her guests, and sat down to think over the events of the day.

Mrs. Madison's little light attracted a great many eyes. Mothers, wives, and daughters, with hearts bleeding over the secret or open excesses of those dearest to them, desired to set their lights a-burning too; but these were mostly extinguished by the command of those who stood greatest in need of being warned. Her own was not an exception. Upon her husband's return, in the spring, he laughed good-humoredly at what he called her silly excess of philanthropy.

"You are too peerless a woman to ride such a hobby as that," he said, kissing the cheeks that were glowing with feeling. "Let every body take care of himself. It is not our fault if some of our friends take a glass too much — we are only responsible for ourselves."

"All people cannot take care of themselves — they have lost the power — their friends must control them."

"Well, we will not assume these duties yet," and by his positive command, the shining worm came back to its accustomed place in the social circle.

And, while talking with him upon the subject, she ventured to relate the sad story of little Annie's murder. She did not wish to pain her husband, but to impress upon him the wrong and danger of leading others into temptation to which we are not ourselves particularly exposed. He was much shocked, and walked the floor a long time, pale and thoughtful.

"It *was* wrong!" he said with emphasis, "selfish, careless, wicked! But who would have thought of such a thing? everybody does the same. I promise you, dear Alice, it is the last time I will do such a deed."

He enquired after Burns, and she told him that for a month or six weeks he had remained sober, but that he wasted away to a skeleton, was deprived of natural sleep, and was at last driven back to his cups, by the gnawing agony of remorse.

"Mrs. Madison," he said to me once while I remonstrated with him, "Its no use for me to try ever to be a good man, unless I drive it away by liquor, the face of that child is forever before me — I hear her cry out — I see her dead and cold — I hear her telling her mother in piteous tones that I murdered her. Night and day — night and day — I've no rest except when the madness of the drink is upon me. Oh! if it wasn't for that, I would try."

"The tears rolled down his face while he spoke. Oh, my husband! his wretchedness is a dreadful thing to think upon. His wife, by my advice, has taken her children and gone back to her father's, where they will be safe from his drunken fury. But there ought to be a place for him, where he could be *safe from himself*. Why is there not an insane asylum, a prison, a something, where such lost creatures can be healed like the sick,— for they are sick,— and restored to hope, to life, and to God? Why do people furnish such victims with the means of accomplishing their own death? Better give an infant the blaze that it cries for! Why is there no law to protect and take care of such? Oh! Mr. Madison, I wish — I fervently wish that there was not a drop of ardent spirits in the land."

"Why should you trouble your pretty head about such perplexing questions, my Alice? Its a great deal you know about the policy of such things. You would banish health and comfort from many a poor man's hearth when you banished ardent spirits from the land. Your heart is too tender, pretty mother; I'm afraid you'll make a girl of our Parke, if you bring him up in the hearing of such nonsense."

"Oh! no, my heart's not too tender; its not half capacious enough for the claims of humanity upon it," she replied with a sigh; "and you shan't shut my eyes with your kisses, neither. They can see almost as far into the right, as yours, my honored statesman!"

And so he kissed away and laughed away her appeals.

Mr. Madison had made himself a favorite, and won an honorable position during his first session. He was one of the youngest members, but he represented an important district; and he was a man eminently calculated to attract attention and to please, though not perhaps to make a profound and lasting impression. In speaking, he was brilliant and effective; his rhetoric was sparkling, his satire was keen, his gestures graceful; he excited the passions of men rather than appealed to their judgments. Even his enemies conceded that he was a man of honorable sentiments, and generous to a fault.

Upon his return to Washington, he took with him his little family. He found his position more enviable than ever. His resources extended with the demands made upon them; and whatever of political distinction he won, was reflected in softer lustre from his beautiful wife, as she moved in the circles of society, adorning and adorned. She who, the previous winter, had read her husband's speeches in the solitude of her apartment, and silently admired and loved, now listened to them as they fell glowing from his lips, and saw their eloquence reflected in the varying faces of those by whom she was surrounded.

Who shall weigh the influence of a pure and lovely woman? Fashionable excess retired ashamed from the sweet glance of Mrs. Madison's rebuking eye. It may be that it lived and flourished as well as ever, but it kept itself more concealed from the public gaze.

At length she began to be troubled for her own happiness. She began to suspect an unwelcome presence by her own hearth-stone.

She knew, if others did not, that Mr. Madison could speak well only when under the influence of wine, and that his gay and fascinating spirits at an evening assembly were proportioned to the amount of a false and dangerous stimulus. But it was true of a greater portion of society. What of that? He was neither a mental or physical Titan; and such excitement, long continued, must soon begin to wear upon his powers. In the zenith of his prosperity, and the first fullness of his talents and beauty, his faithful wife discovered the first indications of premature decay.

She kept her fears to herself, and sought to withhold him, by the thousand invisible chains of a woman's power, from his dazzling but dangerous course. Perhaps, had she been constantly at his side, she would have saved her treasure from the hands of the mocker.

But the succeeding year she remained at home. A little daughter was added to their store of good gifts; who, as she developed from the formlessness of baby-blankets and rosy excess of plumptitude, was of course pronounced the tiny type of her beautiful mother. Wee Alice was indeed a fairy child; with her mother's dark-brown eyes, fringed with long black lashes, and crowned by delicate-arched brows — with her silken, shining hair — with her cunningly cleft lips, closing in the crimson semblance of a bow, from which was ineffectively winged the silver arrows of her lisping speech.

With two such claimants upon her time and love, Mrs. Madison had no desire to return to the gay Capital. Another and another year passed, and found her at home, devoting herself chiefly to her children. It was with a sad and anxious heart that she saw her husband depart — each time sadder and more anxious; until she would gladly have abandoned her peaceful life at home, and accompanied him wherever he went. But her health, which had been delicate since Alice's birth, would not permit it, and she could only follow him with prayers.

This fear for his welfare was the only cloud upon her happiness; when this was banished from her sky, she had only sunshine and delight.

It was in the fifth year of Mr. Madison's senatorial term that, one beautiful day in early spring, his wife sat in her favorite apartment — the sunset-room little Parke called it, because he could always see the sun set from its west window. She sat in her easy-chair, the light sewing she held fallen into her lap, regarding with a mother's heart-worn gaze the amusements of her children. Parke, a handsome aristocratic-looking boy of nine, was endeavoring to initiate his little sister into the mysteries of a game of marbles. She tried hard enough to acquire the necessary wisdom, but succeeded no farther than in rolling them far and wide over the carpet, in lawless confusion.

"I declare, sis," he cried, with a good-natured laugh, for he never got out of patience with the dearly-loved little creature, "I believe your head was never made to hold anything but doll-babies. I don't think girls are as smart as boys anyhow, do you, mother?"

The self-sufficient tone in which this question was asked called up a smile to the eye of his mother; but the young master was impervious to its roguish sarcasm, as she replied quietly —

"You must remember that Alice is not quite four years

old yet. How much of an adept were you in marbles, at that age?"

"Well, papa didn't bring me any until I was five. But if he had, I guess I could have found out what use to make of them."

"You *guess!* Wouldn't it sound better if you should say, 'you think?'"

"Guess is proper enough, and its a good Yankee word, if you please, mother. Here, Allie, bring me that alley which you have rolled away under the table."

"Allie, bring the alley," laughed the little girl as she crept under the table after the striped and tattooed ball.

"Yes, Allie bring the alley. Isn't that funny now? You're a pretty smart little girl, after all, if you do take to doll-babies so."

"She's a perfect little witch! isn't she, mother?" he continued, unable to resist the cunning way in which Alice held out the marble to him, and just as he was about to take it, gave it a toss behind her, which sent it into their mamma's cap. "Now you've got to give me a kiss to pay for that."

The soft little arms were about his neck, and the pretty lips held up to his face, when, with the wilfulness of boys in general, he concluded to refuse the offering, and over they both went, tumbling upon the floor in a burst of merriment.

"You play too rudely for little sister — you will hurt her" — interposed the matron, looking on with pleased eye, which still preserved its watchfulness. "Besides, you learn her to be boisterous. Papa would not like to find his pretty daughter grown noisy as you."

Parke instantly subsided into the most subdued tenderness towards his fairy play-mate, stroking her fair curls and pinching her rosy cheeks very softly.

"When is my father coming home?" he asked.

"I shall expect him next week—just a week from to-day."

"Hurrah for Jackson! that's good news. Did you hear that, Allie? Father's coming home in a week. I should like to dance, I feel so glad. Mother, won't you please to open the piano and play a waltz?—Allie and I want to dance."

"I think it is pleasanter in here than in the parlor," was the reply.

"Just one waltz, if you please, mother," urged Parke.

And "please, mamma," pleaded wee Alice.

So Mrs. Madison went into the parlor, where, inspired by the glee of the children, who were only too happy, she played with more spirit than she had done for months.

Parke, who had been taught by a master, was really a beautiful dancer; and even baby Alice, who already showed a genius for music, flew around like a sprite to the time of the brilliant notes. It was a lovely picture. The mother so youthful-looking and beautiful—the children so bright and joyful.

With glowing cheeks, flashing eyes, and hair tossed

back, the handsome boy whirled round to the measured melody, holding his sister carefully, who, with toes just touching the carpet, ringlets waving, and blue dress floating, went across and across the room with an etherial lightness that explained her pet appellative of "fairy Alice."

They were soon wearied with dancing; and their mother sent them away to ask their nurse for the supper of bread and milk, for the sun was throwing his setting radiance into the west room. When they had left the apartment, Mrs. Madison still played on. Spirits arose at the bidding of sweet sounds — spirits of the olden time, when she was a careless girl — a happy bride — a thoughtful mother. The past, the present, and the future swept around in a magic circle. The gay airs which had set her children's feet in motion no longer suited her mood; plaintive melodies, sad vagaries of music, floated up from the piano and filled the shadowy apartment with solemn sweetness. The door was open into the sunset-room, and in the mirror before her was reflected the dying flush of the fair spring day, while all around brooded the mystic wings of twilight. She did not make the effort to sing; but her hands kept on like a piece of exquisite mechanism, doing the bidding of her dreamy will.

Mrs. Madison thought of her husband's brilliant career, and she played a kind of triumphal march loud and grand; she thought of the swift change which had come over him in the last three or four years — startling rumors which she had heard of his excesses when away from home — how, forgetting his most admirable wife and lovely children, he had delighted himself with ignoble pleasures, and had once or twice nearly dishonored himself by ill conduct in the house — and, thinking of this, the notes sank down into the pleading pathos of a prayer.

She thought of his decreasing tenderness towards her — that her delicate health did not receive from him that affectionate kindness which the mother of his children was entitled to — of his frequent irritation, and even harshness when last in his family.

Trying to solve in her soul the perplexing enigma of the fall of so gentle, generous, and noble a nature, she was ready to set her foot upon the enchanting wine-cup and crush it into the earth. She knew that many of her husband's finest qualities had been the very ones which had made him a prey to temptation. His social disposition, his great generosity, his desire to please others and to be pleased, the very traits which had made him so generally beloved, were working to his ruin. What influence was there which could be set over against that to which he was yielding himself, since that exerted by his home, herself, their gifted boy, their sweet Alice, had failed? Oh, what was there now to be done? She felt the utter fallibility of earthly aid; and while her tears fell down like rain upon the keys, she taught them the voice of her entreaties to God.

There is mighty strength in prayer for all who are fainting or oppressed. Mrs. Madison grew composed; a quiet joy crept into her heart at the thought of meeting her husband so soon.

"After another year," she said, "I shall have him to myself; for I hope that no entreaties of his party will tempt him into public life again. Once out of the dangerous excitements of the arena, he will be won back to his old purposes again."

The last music which stole from the instrument was a subdued but joyous strain of "Home, sweet home." Then the mother arose and went, as she always did, to see her children safe in their nice little cots, to hear them repeat their evening petition, and to give them the good-night kiss.

"I don't think I shall half sleep to-night, thinking about papa's coming home next week," said Parke, with a bright smile, as his mother kissed him.

"You must sleep all the better for that, dear, so as to be wide awake when he comes. Good night, my darlings."

"Good night! — good night! dear mamma."

The pleasant sound of their voices — Parke's clear and boyish, Alice's soft and lisping — brought back the cheerfulness to their mother's fair face. It was with a smile of expectant pleasure that she enquired of Thomas, as she met him in the hall, if he had been to the post-office?

"Just returned, madam, with a letter, was bringing it to you," replied the servant, giving her one which she saw by the lamp-light was post-marked Washington.

Like a young girl with her first love-letter, Mrs. Madison retreated to the privacy of her beloved sun-set room, before she broke the seal of the precious missive.

Drawing her rocking chair close up to the table and arranging the lamp, she prepared to enjoy the greatest pleasure of the week — the reading of the closely-written, four-page letter.

Like one who is prolonging a bit of happiness, she held it a moment in her hands, kissed it, and turned for the first time to dwell upon the superscription, before breaking the seal.

It was not her husband's handwriting: the seal — the seal — was black! She arose from her chair in a sudden terror.

Pause a moment, loving and beautiful wife, before you break the warning wax which keeps from you the knowledge that you are a widow! She did not pause, but with trembling fingers tore open the envelop and read the first few lines. Then with a sharp cry she fell down, like one dead, upon the floor.

It was hours before the friends, suddenly summoned, brought back consciousness — the consciousness of her awful bereavement.

"Why did they not let me die?" she asked; "why did they lift me out of that black whirl of agony in which I had gone down to the verge of the grave? Better be there, beside my husband, than to live, and know that he is lost."

Some one ventured to whisper the names of her children.

"They are miserable orphans," she cried, and sank again into insensibility. For two or three days they feared for her life or reason. She did not rave, but laid in tearless, voiceless quiet, with closed eyes, and only the faint pulse, and an occasional trembling of the eye-lids to tell that she existed. People thought that in this stupor of her physical powers her mental powers found rest. But not for one instant did she lose the acute sense of her wretchedness. Her nerves were strained to such a tension that they could not even vibrate. Her thoughts rushed through her brain like a river of fire, bearing ever the same vision upon their burning waves — the vision of her husband, cold and dead, stricken down by the knife of the assassin,— her husband dead — murdered! What was it to her now that, of late years, he had sometimes been to her cold or unkind? The first fiery touch of sorrow had burnt up every such recollection; only the pure gold of their mutual love remained. She saw him, in the pride of manhood — beautiful, eloquent, beloved — suddenly cut down, with no time to send a message of dying love, or perhaps to breath a dying prayer. All to her was darkness — no hope — no ray of light. She lay there waiting her own doom; there did not seem a thread of mercy left, by which she could climb back to life.

Mr. Madison had got into a dispute with a southern member while they were both upon the floor, which threatened a personal *rencontre.* Heated by wine, he said things which he did not mean — uttered taunts more dishonorable to himself than to the one at whom they were hurled. Mr. Madison was a gentleman; but who can answer for the propriety of an insane man? and he was mad with intoxication at the time of his abusive attack. The two disputants were called to order; but unfortunately they met immediately after leaving the senate-chamber.

One had received a deadly insult; the other, still reckless, would make no apologies, but with an air of bravado followed up his empty assertions until silenced by the steel of his opponent at his heart. Alas! for the irretrievable moment of passion! A man sent unprepared to the presence of his Maker; another to be tormented through life with a vain remorse for having taken the life of a brother — the life, too, of one who, however gross the injuries he inflicted, was scarcely in a condition to be responsible for them. A career begun so brilliantly, closed in tumult and dishonor — a fine mind thrown from its proper balance — a noble heart perverted from its best impulses! Others, besides his unhappy family, might weep over the disastrous results, and turning from the fair temptation, swear eternal enmity to the wine-cup.

The corpse was brought home for burial. Hundreds, forgetting his late career, bowed their heads in lamentation over the dust of the statesman, citizen, and friend. Hundreds mourned in sympathy with the desolate wife, and women wept when they heard of the agony of bereavement which had prostrated her. Their tears, their sympathy, availed her nothing. Separated by her unconsciousness from human communion, she was alone with her grief and her God.

CHAPTER III.

THE mother's prayer for death was stayed by the thought of her orphaned children. She arose from a sick-bed to find relief, and at last consolation, in her care for them. Years rolled quietly along. Retiring almost entirely from the society she had once so brilliantly adorned, she devoted her shining talents to the development of these two young minds, and to moulding their plastic passions and feelings. The loss of the gay world was the gain of the poor and afflicted; for the time and wealth of Mrs. Madison were freely bestowed upon the suffering and destitute classes of a great city. In her frequent missions of mercy she was often cognizant of cases similar to that of Mrs. Burns; where all the wo, the want, the wretchedness of families, lay at the doors of grog-shops. She pondered these things in her heart, and asked herself again and again if there was no way for the salvation of those who had given themselves over to temptation and were beyond the reach of their own consciences and self-control.

"If it were feasible to erect a Hospital in this city, where such poor creatures could be kept from self-destruction until cured, I would gladly give half of my possessions. But a Hospital from here to the Battery would not hold them all; and, as soon as released, the fiery temptation would be forced upon them. Its a horrible thing — this traffic in liquor! These rum-shops might as well keep each of them a mad dog behind the counter and allow people to be bitten for sixpence a bite; and the law might as well allow it. Hydrophobia or delirium-tremens! if I were to choose between them, I would take that which was at least the less disgraceful."

Thus spoke Mrs. Madison to herself as she hurried away, with pale face and trembling limbs, from a house where she had been a witness to the horrors of the drunkard's direct earthly enemy — and the victim this time was a woman! — a woman who had little children cowering in the cheerless corner, gazing at their mother with affrighted eyes, as bound to her bed she glared at them with terrible looks of madness and fear.

Mrs. Madison knew something of the history of this poor creature. She was a drunkard's child, and had been born into the world with feeble health and a miserable, nervous constitution. She had a morbid appetite for slate-stone, chalk, and opium, and grew up sickly, afraid of the dark, of ghosts, of serpents, and with a mind so affected by her impaired nerves as to be in some measure insane. Nevertheless she married; and after the birth of her first baby, the physician recommended a little stimulus every day to support her failing strength. She soon became unable to drag through the day without her bitters; and before her husband suspected the extent of her indulgence, her strength, the poor strength bequeathed to her by an intemperate parent, gave way to a singular sickness, which the doctors told the alarmed man was nothing more nor less than delirium tremens. Ashamed and astonished, the respectable and honest laborer nursed her carefully through this first attack; but positively denied her the stimulus which she so passionately begged. He told her the nature of her fearful disease; and, with tears in his eyes, reminded her of her children, of his love for her, and of the terrors of her situation. She, too, was alarmed at the dangers past and impending; she thanked her husband for denying her appeals: but the passion was acquired; the shattered powers were not calculated for steady resistance to a burning appetite; and the very first day in which she was well enough to creep out alone into the street, she left her best shawl at the pawn-broker's, and readily obtained the liquid-fire for her funeral-pyre at the first corner.

With such feeble powers of resistance she could not struggle long. Her good husband struggled for her. Whenever he found any liquor in the house he destroyed it; he forbad the shops, far and wide, around that part of the town, from selling their poison to his wife; he entreated, commanded, and even punished. But where a wife's and mother's love is devoured by a raging passion, be sure that fear will have no control — not even the fear of those unutterable agonies which frequently assailed her. One after another of those little comforts which blessed their home went to the pawn-broker's. It was worse than useless to redeem them, for they only traveled back over the old road again. Another child was born; a poor, imbecile, helpless little thing, who would have been much better unborn than growing up to disgrace and suffering, nourished on the poison of its mother's milk.

Now the last struggle of the enemy was over; he was triumphant; and Mrs. Madison, who had yielded to the entreaties of the unhappy husband, had been present at that most terrible death-bed.

With those dying screams ringing in her ears, that dying face in all its contortions of anguish before her eyes, she hurried home to escape, in the cheerfulness of her own fireside, from the haunting memories of the scene.

It was a bleak day in the latter part of December. The snow lay on the housetops and in corners, but had been trampled from sight in the busy streets. As she entered her own house and came into the parlor shivering, Alice, now grown a young girl of thirteen, sprang forward to take her bonnet and cloak.

" How tired and pale you look, mother."

" I've witnessed enough to make any one look pale," she replied, with a shudder, as she drew her chair up and put out her feet towards the sparkling old-fashioned grate, so much more cheerful than anything else in the wintertime, unless it be the broad fire-place in the kitchen of some ancient farm-house.

"What have you seen, dear mother?" enquired Alice, as she rolled an ottoman beside her parent and leaned her head in her lap.

"I have seen a woman die of delirium-tremens."

"Oh! mother!"

Alice held up her pretty hands, while her large hazel eyes dilated with dread.

"What's that you've been frightening our sister with?" asked Parke, as he came out of the library. "But up with that chess-board, Alf., and let's hear this woful story."

Two boys, or rather young gentlemen, came out of the library. The first was Parke, a youth of seventeen, and as he came forward, and flinging himself down on the rug, pulled Alice on to his lap, we may see that the promise of his baby-hood is thus far liberally fulfilled. The thick brown ringlets waving and fluttering about his fine forehead, with just that careless beauty which had distinguished his father's before him; the deep-blue eye, fiery and soft; the straight, beautiful nose, the handsome mouth — all his features were both perfect in form and beaming with intellect and intelligence. His face had the pure, womanly expression, which a life at home in the society of such a mother and sister, might leave upon it, even after two years at college, finely blended with the pride and carelessness of his age. He had the patrician air, marking his descent from families of wealth and cultivation, and through even that, a more delicate and distinguished manner, revealing refinement of thought and poetical beauty of spirit. There did not seem the semblance of guile in the frank glance of his glowing eye; the only fault of his countenance was that the womanly sweetness of his mouth betokened a want of energy, which was not made up for by the bold eye and proudly-arched brow. There was spirit in the thin nostril, but want of purpose in the softly-rounded chin.

"Just help yourself to that royal throne of an easy-chair, Alf., and we'll listen to the story of wo."

His companion dropped comfortably into the huge velvet chair, that did seem a little like a chair of state. He was Parke's chum at college, and being too far removed from his own home, had accepted his invitation to spend the holidays at his mother's.

In good contrast with his friend, were his black eyes, black hair, dark complexion, and strong though not inelegant frame. When he first came there, Mrs. Madison rather wondered at her son's having chosen him for his intimate companion. He was a year or two the oldest, although no farther advanced in his studies; his talents were of a different order from Parke's brilliant and variable genius; he did not talk half as much, but what he said was usually full of character.

"You must not laugh, Parke," said Alice, sedately; "for mamma has been with a woman that had the delirium-tremens."

"A woman!" ejaculated Parke, as if it had never

entered into his head that a woman was capable of such a thing.

"Yes!" said Mrs. Madison, gravely, "and the mother of two little children. It is better for them that she is dead; but such a death! I shall never forget it; and as for sleeping to-night, I fear there will be anything but pleasant dreams for me."

"I never thought you were nervous, dear mother, the way you go gliding like a sunbeam into all the dark corners of this many-cornered city. I don't believe you can catch contagion any more than a beam of pure sunlight, or you would have had the measles, delirium-tremens, whooping-cough, small-pox, and all kinds of cutaneous and miscellaneous sufferings long ago, so I guess you will sleep well enough this night."

The youth looked up at his still beautiful mother as he made this speech, as if she were a being as faultless, and as much to be adored as the sun was by the orientals. Alice laughed to think of her mamma having the measles and said, "Oh, what a saucy brother!" but gave him a kiss at the same moment.

"But this has been to me the horror of horrors," resumed Mrs. Madison. "To die in so shocking a manner, and to be so little prepared for death. Ah! those who have supplied her so plentifully with the maddening poison have destroyed both her body and soul. There ought to be some punishment for them," she continued, while the color mounted into her cheeks. "Against the warnings of her husband, and the knowledge of her situation, they still furnished her with the means of death, and they should be as responsible as though they had sold prussic acid to an insane person."

"I don't think my mother has a fault in the world; but if she has one, its her idea about temperance," soliloquized Parke, aloud, for the benefit of the company. "Here she has banished wine from her table, while all her neighbors see proper to pay it the customary respect; and, what is worse, she takes her stand with those impudent reformers that are starting up all over the land. And now she wants the law to take it in hand. For my part," with an air of wisdom, "I do not think any one to blame but the wretch herself. Selling liquor is an honest business like any other, and it is not for those who get their living in that way to enquire of people whether they are capable of restraining their appetites within proper bounds. Every one should control himself or herself. If they cannot do it, let them take the consequences."

"You talk like a thoughtless boy, and one who had never been taught the golden rules of christian principle. Selling liquor is *not* an honest business, if some honest men do engage in it. Because what they sell *never* does people any real good, and *always* does them harm. Money spent for liquor is much worse than money thrown away. The person who trafficks in ardent spirits takes money, friends, house, home, character, health, life, and soul; in exchange he gives madness, disease, murder, riot, blasphemy, ruin, and the momentary pleasure of delirium. Is that an honest business? Does it not call for the interference of the law as much as gambling, counterfeiting, smuggling, conspiracy, treason, or any other unlawful thing? Is it kind, benevolent, brotherly, or christian to leave a fellow-creature, afflicted with the *disease of the love of strong drink*, to abandon himself to his fatal passion? Is it right to lead into temptation? If a man loses control of his appetite, are we to take advantage of his misfortune, his sin, even, to his destruction and our pecuniary benefit? Heaven forbid we should so outrage all the divine precepts that were left for our direction in cases like this."

"Oh, mother, you take a dreadfully serious view of the matter; I dare not argue with you in that style. The truth is you are quite too good. We can't expect all laws of business, and the nation, to be founded in the spirit of Christ."

"Why, certainly, in a christian nation they should be. What is there to prevent? If a nation consulted only its material and worldly welfare, it would increase in prosperity in proportion as its government corresponds with the government of Christ. How heavily does the curse of intemperance at this moment lie upon this beloved land. Supposing the law took the matter in hand and made this general traffick in ardent spirits dishonest and illegal; would not the people rise up with one voice and call their rulers blest?"

"No, I hope not. Their liberty would be injured; such a law would be arbitrary."

"All laws are arbitrary. They are not made for those who can govern themselves. Laws against theft are not made for the honest man — against treason, for him whose love of country burns purely in his heart — against murder, for the man of peace and good will; and a law to do away with intoxication would not fall upon the temperate and those who did not need it. It would not press very heavily upon me, for instance — *I* should not feel it arbitrary; and any one who would must stand in want of it. As long as men must be governed, let them have as many laws as are necessary and just. If this was the millenium reign of love, when the lion and the lamb are to lie down together, we should not need these restrictions. Now they are wholesome, necessary, and wise. The murderer, pulling against the fear of hanging, calls it an arbitrary check — the drunkard, if compelled to pull against the refusal to gratify his dangerous craving, would call it an arbitrary check. It is well for those who have no self-control to be judiciously controlled in the spirit of kindness. As for alcohol, and all its Protean diversities, I wish that the salt sea held every drop."

"Pshaw now, mother, do not wish that! I don't! for me, I *love wine!*— I always intend to drink a little; and I am not afraid but that I can control myself, either, without the aid of the law."

Mrs. Madison cast a sad look at her beautiful boy. She thought of his father's pride and self-confidence, and she did not like the ominous words — "I love wine! I always intend to drink a little." Alfred Clyde, silently listening to this conversation from the depths of his velvet chair, now turned upon Parke a keen gaze from his black eyes, which called the warm blood into his expressive face, for they reminded him with something of the force of a cool satire, of half-a-dozen college-revels in which he had proved that he could *not* control himself.

"Those were mere boyish freaks," he said to himself; "I only drank to show them that I was not afraid of the champagne, or their taunts either. What does he want to remind me of that for?"

"Come, Alice," he added aloud, "tea is not ready yet; let us see what we can do with our music to disperse these bad spirits that have gathered around our mother."

Alice was delighted. Passionately fond of music, singing sweetly, and already a fairy mistress of the piano, she never enjoyed herself so highly as when Parke would join her with voice and flute. She flew like a bird and perched upon the piano-stool. Looking around at him as he came forward and took up his flute, she laughed her fairy laugh.

"You need not boast so greatly of your self-management," she said; "I have heard mamma tell of your stealing to the table after a dinner-party, and getting a little out of your head over the wine-glasses, when you were only four years old; and of your coming into the room, glorying in the idea that Washington was your papa, and falling over an ottoman, and disgracing yourself before them all."

"Of course I was not more than four years old, or I

should not have made such a fool of myself," he replied, pulling at one of her floating curls just hard enough to make her cry "oh!" Alfred Clyde came up to the group and leaned his elbows upon the piano and his head upon his hands, while the brother and sister played a gay duet and sang. Then Parke accompanied with his flute, and finally Alice sang alone, a sweet and mournful melody, aiding herself with the piano. It was an almost angelic pleasure to hear her sing. Alfred, leaning his chin into his hand, never removed his dark eyes from her radiant face, as the notes with bird-like clearness, united to human expression, rose from her lips upon the air, seeming to hover around her little, slender figure a moment, and then to soar high, high through the ceiling, and die away in remote sweetness through the sky. Mrs. Madison turned from studying the grotesque figures glowing in the grate and listened with closed eyes to the delightful melody. Then young Clyde surprised and pleased them all by sitting down to the piano and playing one or two airs in a fine, bold style, so different from Alice's exquisite touch; and singing in a rich, sweet tenor.

The tinkle of the tea-bell, less musical, but probably as welcome, asserted its claims to attention, and the party betook themselves to the supper-room with cheerful faces. Young gentlemen when they are still growing rapidly have, of course, a great respect for a well-filled table, and Mrs. Madison, who was much fatigued with her afternoon's visit, also felt the need of a cup of tea.

"By the way, little one, have you grown to be too large

a young lady to think of hanging up your stocking; remember this is Christmas Eve."

"Santa Claus has not been down our chimney for two or three years, I believe. Not since Mary Ellis revealed to me the mystery of his invisible visits. Since the wonderful flowers which made him so enchanting a character have fled, I am content to find my gifts on the library table," replied Alice.

"I have a presentiment that he will renew his calls this night," continued her brother, helping himself to a slice of Christmas cake. "And if you sit up until ten o'clock perhaps you will see him. I don't believe any of this nonsense about there being no such personage at the present day; there certainly was such a fine old fellow when I was a boy. Alf. and I are going out about the city this evening, and if I catch a glimpse of him on the top of some tall chimney, I shall just signify to him that he had better call here."

"Well, do—do;" cried the young girl laughing, "and I will hang up my stocking. Which room do you think he will make a descent into? because I should like to get a peep at him, though you know he never comes until midnight."

"Pshaw! he can't visit every body at once, and if he comes here it will be earlier than that. How is it, mother, is there no other authorized way for him to enter a dwelling except through the chimney?"

"I never heard of any other way, but I suppose that he would be welcome if he came in most any manner."

"Well, Alf., its nearly seven o'clock, and I promised you a walk about the city to-night."

The young gentlemen arose from the table and put on their caps and cloaks.

"Oh! now, please to stay at home with mamma and me," pleaded Alice; "just think, you have only a week to stay, and I have hardly visited with you at all yet."

"I should like too, Alice; it looks gloriously pleasant in the parlors, but you see," laughing at her from under the shadow of his cap, "my friend Alfred is an outside barbarian, fresh from the wilds of the west, and I must do my duty to him, and show him the lions."

"I do not see how Parke can resist you," said Alfred, throwing off his cloak, "for my part, I do not believe I should find anything out of doors to compensate for what I leave."

He looked as if he could not be induced to leave the company he was in, for all the lions out of Numidea. Alice was quite flattered by this preference for her society, and looked with favorable eyes upon her brother's friend.

"Nonsense, Alf., come along," said Parke.

"Are you not a little selfish, Alice, in keeping the boys at home so much?" interposed the mother. "Go if you wish, but keep out of mischief, and be at home by ten o'clock, for I shall set up for you, and I feel like retiring in good season."

Parke kissed his mother's hand with an air of affection and respect in answer to her kind smile; Alfred ventured to kiss his *at* Miss Alice, and the two youths went out in high spirits.

"Don't forget the stocking, Alice," were Parke's last words, as they went out of the hall door.

"I wonder if he is in earnest," remarked the young girl as she came back to her mother, after escorting her beloved brother almost to the pavement. "I've a mind to put up that nice new stocking which I have just finished."

So saying she fastened it duly near the mantel-piece, in the library, while the indulgent parent regarded her movements with a quiet smile. Then both returned to the parlor, where the child beguiled the time with music until the clock struck nine. She had just taken the large bible to read a few chapters to her mother, when a sound in the library attracted her attention.

"I declare, I believe it is Santa Claus himself," she said, laying down the book, with eyes wide open, and stealing on tiptoe to the door of the adjacent room, she peeped in. A slight scream drew Mrs. Madison in the same direction, just in time to see a marvelous figure march boldly out through the hall, instead of vanishing up the chimney. It had a very wrinkled, black face, a bent back, which had grown into its present large proportions probably from long bearing of the basket and other burdens which adorned it; a long white beard, a short pipe, and a very queer little conical cap. Without deigning a glance at the intruders, whom he seemed to think ought to be a-bed, he marched out the door. When Alice had recovered sufficiently from the alarm caused by this unexpected apparition, she ventured to glance at her stocking, and behold! it was stuffed to its utmost capacity. Her mother would not permit her to inspect its contents that evening, however, saying that it was hardly fair, since they had caught the good Saint in the very fulfilment of his kind mission to endeavor to find out the amount of his presents until the intended hour. Alice returned her mother's smile with one of equal intelligence, and went to bed thinking, what indeed she thought all the time, that there never was so good, handsome, and mischievous a brother as her own.

In the meantime, Santa Claus, as he left the house, was joined by an ally, also bearing a basket; and laughing and chatting like very good-natured saints, they turned down the first alley they came to, and were soon trudging along a street which seemed mostly filled by the habitations of the poor.

"There's Smith's, and Ellise's, and McCurdy's, all have young ones, lots of them — I am afraid some of the good parents have gone to bed," said Santa Claus, as they paused before a door.

"Very well, we'll make 'em get up then," rejoined his companion, shaking a string of bells merily before the keyhole.

A head in a night-cap soon appeared through the cautiously unclosed door, and was immediately besieged with a small shower of paper parcels, and one great cannon-ball in the shape of a fine dressed turkey.

"Santa Claus to the children," cried that personage in an unearthly voice, and betook himself down the way, followed by his aid-de-camp, leaving the lucky recipient to pick up the package of candy, nuts, and toys, which lay before her astonished vision.

At least half a dozen houses received a similar visitation; and then the frightful-looking imps made their way back to the toy-shop where they had received their outfit, and having deposited their empty baskets, they came out of their disguises, two exceedingly merry and good-looking youths.

"Since we have made a score of miserable juveniles inconceivably happy for all day to-morrow, I presume we are at liberty now to delight ourselves with whatever we can find that promises the most fun," said Alfred.

"Its too late, I'm afraid, to go anywhere to-night. Mother expects us home at ten o'clock, and its nearly that now."

"Then I must say we've fooled away the time ridiculously so far; wasted it on those dirty little rascals."

"I've enjoyed it very much," replied Parke, laughing as he glanced at the mask he had thrown aside; "and I shall enjoy it to-morrow, thinking of the pleasure we have given."

"Well, you're a fine, philanthropic youth, mother's own darling," said the other, a little scornfully.

"I should be proud if I thought I was half as good as my mother," said Parke, his blue eyes kindling.

"Oh, of course, so would I; I did not mean anything else. But pshaw, your mother will not wait for us, and we might as well see what is to be seen. It is not often that there is as much to attract us as now."

"Come on, then, I will be your chaperon," said Parke, and taking his friend's arm, they walked slowly up the brilliant and fashionable thorough-fare. New York had on her holiday attire. The shop windows blazed with light, displaying their costly treasures.

Crowds of gay and happy-looking people were yet moving along the pavement. There chanced to be very respectable sleighing too, and the wide street was a bewildering chaos of innumerable vehicles of all kinds that could be fastened upon runners, winding swiftly through apparently impenetrable ways; of tinkling bells, merry laughter, shouts, prancing horses gayly caparisoned, and ambitious drivers.

The churches were brilliantly illuminated, and those who had thronged them to do reverence to the solemnity of the Eve, now poured out of their doors and mingled with the crowd.

Enjoying all these sights and sounds with the intensity belonging to the minds of students during the holidays, they sauntered along until arrested upon a crossing by a shout from a passing sleigh.

"Halloo! Parke Madison! we did not know you were home from school. You're the very fellow we want; jump in, we are going out to Cross' to have a time."

There were a dozen or more young gentlemen already

in the sleigh, all looking the picture of fun. They had four spirited horses and countless strings of bells. The temptation was strong; but Parke thought of his mother, and hesitated.

"What kind of a time?" he asked.

"Nothing that will injure your spotless good name," was the reply." "Only a supper, and home again."

"For mercy's sake, go," whispered Alfred, impatiently; "you are the greatest baby out of its nurse's arms."

"Of course my friend is included in the invitation," said Parke, as he climbed into the sleigh: "Mr. Clyde, gentlemen, a classmate of mine, and the best fellow ever punished with a Greek grammar."

"The more the merrier!" cried all; and Alfred Clyde made a very courteous bow and a very pretty speech, as they noisily made room for him.

"Drive on!" shouted they, the next moment; and away they went up the brilliant street, out into the more gloomy suburbs and on into the country, where the only lights were stars. Gaslight or starlight, it was all one to them; they abated not jollity and noise until in about an hour and a quarter they drew up at Cross', twelve miles from town.

This was not the first party which had arrived at that hotel during the evening, sleighing being so brief a luxury as to be well enjoyed while it lasted. As these gentlemen had no ladies with them, and were bent upon having 'a time,' the affable host gave them a fine, large room to themselves, with the injunction only not to disturb other guests in their frolics.

Such a supper as they caused to be served was worthy of the occasion. Wild turkey and canvass-back ducks, with art-compounded salads, oysters, and champagne, were but a few of the items of their costly feast. The great fireplace blazing with hickory, the luxurious table, and the choice wines, promised a glorious night.

Unfortunately for Parke, his friends were not as pure-minded and innocent of bad habits as himself; young aristocrats though they were, they did not disdain the chance of 'plucking' a wealthy 'pigeon' like him, and at supper they rallied him into drinking more wine than was prudent. He knew it all the time; he knew that a little affected him, and that after tasting it he could not always control his indulgence in it; but he could not endure to be thought a simpleton or a puritan by the rest, and so, when he had most need to think of them, he forgot all about his gentle-faced mother and his darling young sister. He was much the most intoxicated of any who left the table. At first he had only been witty and amusing, but he grew more boisterous than agreeable, and his remarks were more stupid than pointed. They were received with the same unmeaning eclat; wit or silliness are either in favor with a party of fools.

One would hardly have known the fair, spiritual face leaning up against his mother's lap that afternoon, with its clear, pure eyes and shining curls, as the flushed countenance, now debased from its look of intelligence, with glassy eyes and a smile of unmeaning good-nature.

Alfred Clyde had toyed with his glasses in a more careful manner. Not making himself conspicuous, except by an occasional brilliant sally, independent but courteous in his bearing, and showing that he knew how to take care of himself, with a perfect at-homeness in scenes like these, he won golden opinions from the society into which he considered himself very fortunate to have been introduced.

He did not warn Parke, as he might have done, against his perils; but when cards were brought out, and he saw intelligent looks among those who were inducing his friend to play with them, he spoke up in a calm tone, that carried with it a firm conviction of his courage.

"Gentlemen, I must claim my friend as *my* partner this evening. He knows but little about a game, neither do I, so we will be well matched."

There was no demurring to his polite manner; the party thought it a very disinterested act of kindness to keep the game out of their hands, but submitted with tolerable grace, and Parke played only with him. Notwithstanding his declaration that he was an indifferent player, he won all of Parke's money, and, lastly, a beautiful and expensive watch which he wore.

The sun was streaking the east with the first glow of Christmas morning, when the revellers found themselves in town again. Mrs. Madison had remained up until after midnight, and then retired with some uneasy feelings. She heard the boys come in at day-break and go to their room, and after that she had a long sleep. It was late when breakfast was placed on the table, but it had to wait some time for the young gentlemen; and Alice had abundance of time to admire the good gifts of Santa Claus. Parke could not help blushing vividly when he entered his mother's presence, and met her anxious, searching look; Alfred was polite and self-possessed as usual. It was not until the blush had died away that Mrs. Madison discovered her son's pale and weary looks.

"You were out all night," she said, in a tone which seemed to require an explanation, as she handed him his coffee.

"Why the truth is, dear mother," he began in a confused voice, "that we met a party of my best friends going out to Cross' for a sleigh-ride, and we were tempted to go along. There we stayed for supper, and it made us rather late. I hope that you did not wait for us."

"Only until twelve o'clock. It seems to me you look ill this morning — is anything the matter?"

"Well!" with another blush, "I believe I took a confounded cold, for my head aches horribly. I wasn't very well wrapped up you know, as we only went out for a walk."

Parke glanced at Alf. as he made this explanation, and saw him very demurely breaking an egg into his glass.

"Poor Parke, I pity you," said Alice, bending her large eyes tenderly upon his pale countenance; "shall I tell

Bridget to make you a cup of strong tea? — it is good for headache.

"I don't care if you do,— that's a good sister."

"I think, myself, it will be a fine thing for him," added young Clyde, raising his keen glance from the egg-dish.

The child sped to the kitchen on her mission of kindness; then returning to her plate and the engrossing subject of her thoughts, she cried, with an arch look —

"Santa Claus *did* pay me a visit last night!"

"Ah!" said the brother innocently, "did he find a stocking — and what did he bring you?"

"He must have guessed what I wanted most, for these were the very things he brought me. A beautiful little gold-bound prayer-book, just the right size — a pair of ear-rings to match with my necklace, and a silver paper-folder, besides enough confectionary to last till New Year's, and the drollest little man laughing at me from the top of the stocking."

"A bountiful saint," said Parke.

"May I be allowed to inquire whether you had a glimpse of his saintship?" asked Alfred.

"Yes, I did — I did!" cried Alice, laughing at the remembrance.

"You were not frightened I suppose?"

She looked at him quickly, and colored a little, to think of her screaming out the previous night.

"I *was* rather astonished at the first peep I took of him. Such a horrid-looking saint may I never see again!

But he was as good as he was ugly," and her eye rested affectionately upon her adored brother.

"I saw a strange-looking being, which might have been him, paying visits to all those little wretches that you were telling us about yesterday, that wouldn't have any Christmas, because they were so poor. Had he a pipe in his mouth?"

"Yes."

"And was he very bent in the back, and with a long, white beard?"

"Yes."

"And did he walk a little lame, and have a very queer, black face, and wear a funny cap, and look like — Old Nick?"

"Yes, sir, that was Santa Claus without doubt. What was he doing, I should like to know?"

"Ah! he was making a Christmas for the little children you have condescended to notice with new pairs of shoes. Such papers of raisins and almonds — such chickens and turkeys — such little bundles of sugar and tea, proved him to be a most worthy and liberal old fellow."

"Did you indeed do all that?" asked Alice, when Alfred had finished his story, coming around to her brother, and laying her arms softly about his neck. "What a good boy you are!"

"Me!" he replied in affected surprise; "Am I then such a fright of a fellow as all that comes to."

His sister's kiss, the cup of green tea, and the recollection of his innocent frolic in the early part of the preceding evening, made Parke a little more reconciled to himself, though a sense of guilt still made him feel uneasy under the eye of his mother. It was a feeling of relief with which he flung himself upon the sofa after she and Alice went out to attend morning service in their church, his headache excusing him from that duty, and Clyde staying at home to keep him company.

"I am heartily ashamed of myself and perfectly miserable," he said, with tears of contrition, as Alfred seated himself before his sofa, and mockingly felt the pulse in his wrist. "To think of boasting about self-control, and making a sot of myself the very same night. Oh! if mother should hear of it."

"I've always told you it wouldn't do for you to take wine," replied his companion coolly; "you like it too well. Now *I* can play with the fire and not get burned, but I'd advise you to be a little more prudent, my dear Parke."

"Why didn't you advise me last night? — you sat beside me."

"Oh, I wanted to witness your ability for self-protection, you know; it would have been arbitrary for me to have interfered."

"Now don't be sarcastic, if you please, for my head aches so that I can't stand it. By the way," after a pause, "do you know who I lost my watch to, last night? I must have that back if I have to redeem it with a thousand dollars. That was my father's watch, Alf."

"You need not fret about that," said his friend with a smile, "it was I who won it, and I have it safe for you in the dressing-case up stairs. I only took it to show you what would have been your fate if you had played with any one else. The fact is you know nothing about a game, as I've often told you, and those older scamps knew it, and meant to make you their victim. You are young and rich. I would not allow you to play with any one but myself."

"Then you won my money too?"

"Yes, and here it is," producing a roll of bills from his pocket. "Its against my principles to gamble, and so I return it to you with a little advice to be more wise in future."

"Fie! you know that I would not be guilty of accepting it," said Parke, putting back the money with his hand. "I'm a thousand times obliged to you about the watch; and I *will* be more careful hereafter."

"Very well. It ought to be some consolation to you to know that it will be made good use of. It could not have fallen to any one who needed it as much," and with a satisfied look, young Clyde put the bills back into his own pocket. "If you are in need of anything before you receive another supply, just borrow of me," he continued; "and now that I am so rich, I must think of something that will please sweet Alice. She's a heavenly little creature, that sister of yours, Parke, both in beauty and disposition."

"She is indeed," replied the brother, getting up from his pillow and looking quite restored to health. "You havn't any sister have you, Alf. ? then you cannot imagine how I love that child. I would not have her hear anything to make her love me less for the world. I shall always be a good man for her sake — that is, after I've got over these confounded college scrapes. I hope when she is grown a little older that you will both fall in love with each other, and be married. That's a glorious idea, isn't it?"

"Too bright — too beautiful to last! But," with sudden earnestness, "I hope you'll remember that, Parke, and that my consent is already gained. The lady, I am afraid, will not look upon the matter with such favorable eyes."

"Any one that I love will have a claim upon her affections, said the brother; "my pretty, pretty Alice!"

"Sister's hearts take stubborn fancies sometimes," responded Alfred, and then he fell into a reverie. A sudden fire glowed in his black eyes, deep down, as if he were forging some future purpose in the furnace of thought. Parke subsided into a light slumber, leaving him free to work out his ideas; and he sat silently musing until the return of the ladies from church.

And now, while he is lost in thought, it will be a good time for us to inquire a little into his character and history.

His parents died when he was about fourteen, leaving him a poor inheritance. From his father, who was a speculator, and living magnificently died in poverty, he inherited a love of luxury, a scheming, crafty mind, a hard heart, much physical courage, an empty purse, and beautiful, slender hands and feet, of which he was secretly vain. From his mother he inherited a portion of her dark, southern beauty, of her impressable fancy, of her pride, her indolence, and her love of loveliness as revealed in the human form, in works of art or scenes of nature. This latter passion tinged his otherwise hard character with a glow of poetry, and enabled him to show a fine enthusiasm on many occasions, which concealed the cold depths of his heart, as sunlight playing over the ocean conceals its darkness and chilliness. He was always older than his years in cautious reserve and prudent calculations; and when at fifteen he found himself thrown upon his own resources, he came to a set determination that he would not labor for a living. His pride, indolence, and love of splendor all cried out against it. "Better not live at all than to drudge through life with the common herd," was his conclusion; and turning over in his mind all feasible projects for establishing himself as a drone in the bee-hive of society, his plans reverted to an old bachelor uncle, living in an eastern State, who was only as wealthy as he was penurious.

"I always wondered what that old miser was hoarding up his money for, and now I know that it was for my particular benefit," was his mental soliloquy.

Having settled this matter to his own satisfaction, he left his birth-place in a western city and managed to introduce himself to his uncle. He was looked upon with suspicious eyes by Mr. Benjamin Clyde, who regarded all his relations as vultures waiting to prey upon his dead body. But the boy had a winning way with him, and as he carefully concealed his expectations of aid, and only asked his advice as to what pursuit he could engage in to procure him an honest living, his uncle promised to make some efforts in his behalf.

"The truth is, uncle," said Alfred, with a very grave face, "that it will be pretty hard for a boy of my age, without parents, friends or money, to work his way up to the station a Clyde should occupy. But I am going to do my best, Sir; and as I know you better capable of giving advice than any one else, and as a child naturally feels a yearning after some kind of kindred," with something like a tear, "I have come to you, to ask for your counsel. I've a pretty good pair of hands to work with, and I shall use them, Sir."

"A little too delicate! not quite the right color," said the old gentleman with a short glance at the white, taper fingers.

"I can soon alter their color, uncle, if that's all."

"Well, I have a friend, owner of a large store, wants an under clerk. Now you can get that situation, and if you please your employers can work your way up, and probably sometime be a partner in the concern. If it suits you, I will see that he accepts you."

"You are very kind, and I shall always remember the interest you have taken in your poor nephew. But I am ambitious—proud as the rest of the Clydes, Sir; and if you can propose anything at which I can support myself, and at the same time acquire an education that would fit me for *your* profession, Sir, I should indeed like it. I have a bent, I believe, for the law, uncle, and perhaps might not become an unworthy member of the bar which you have distinguished. It has proved a harvest, from which you have reaped golden sheaves, too, has it not?"

In short, Benjamin Clyde was induced to consider his nephew in the light of a youth who was very anxious to do something for himself, with commendable ambition, energy, and pride. The spirit of family glory which had nearly been smothered in bags of gold was aroused, and he resolved that so fine a young Clyde must have an education which would qualify him to do well for himself in the world. He was secretly pleased, too, at the thought of his nephew stepping into his shoes when he should retire from practice, which he designed soon to do; and it may be that into his desolate old heart there stole some warmth of affection for this orphaned relative.

Alfred's first grand manœuvre for himself was successful. In a few weeks he was in college, for which he was prepared before the death of his parents. It is true that he was kept upon an extremely moderate allowance of pocket-money, much smaller than his love of display could be contented with; but this only induced him to find out ways and means for increasing it. It was his purpose to be the envy and pride of his associates, to pass through school with tolerable credit, and then to settle down at his ease in his uncle's office. As for studying severely or becoming profoundly versed in the law, he did not think of it. He hoped that, by the time he had trifled away a few years in pretended industry, the old gentleman would drop off, and leave him in exulting possession of his close-hoarded wealth.

In the meantime, being, like many city boys, old in vice, and already an expert gamester, many of his fellow-students became his victims in a small way, and he kept his purse so well replenished as to keep up with the most extravagant. He had so much tact, and affected so much generosity, that his comrades thought his success a matter of indifference to him. He passed for the heir to a large estate, beside being the *protegé* of an immensely wealthy old uncle; so that whatever he chose to do was winked at, and he was toadyed to an unlimited extent, which was just what most pleased his selfish vanity.

He had been in College but a short time when Parke Madison arrived. As the son of a late distinguished senator, the descendant of an old aristocratic family, and the heir of wealth and station, he more than rivaled the dark Cincinnatian in his claims to attention. By his beauty, gentleness, and goodness, he won universal love, and by his talents universal admiration. He was the pet of the learned professors as well as of the students. Alfred was no longer the lion of the academic groves. He submitted with excellent grace, making advances towards the warmest friendship with the stranger. They were classmates, and together they buffeted their way through the junior, senior, and sophomore degrees. Parke returned Clyde's friendship with ardent affection, about which there was not a shadow of falsehood. Honest and warm-hearted himself, he thought the same of every one else. Alfred was so confidential with him as to reveal to him that he was a poor boy, dependent upon the charity of a niggardly uncle for an education; and often complained bitterly of his privations. He knew that in the frank soul of a noble fellow like young Madison, it would awaken sympathy, and strengthen the bonds of their attachment; and he was often able to turn it to the best account. If he wished to borrow a small amount, it was heartily given, without a thought of asking for it again. The sin and shame of this intimacy was, that Alfred, instead of protecting his younger companion from the temptations which surrounded him to secret dissipation, craftily led him on, and while he seemed to be keeping him from the hands of others, always let him fall into his own. He had great skill in concealing all infringements of college rules of his own or Parke's from the eyes and ears of the professors; laying his friend under tearful obligations to him for preserving his character, and keeping his occasional frolics from the knowledge of his mother.

It was in the third year of their college life that Parke had permission from Mrs. Madison to bring his friend home with him. More skilled in reading the characters of others than her son, she was disappointed in the impression Alfred made upon her mind. She liked his manners, wit, and apparent modesty; yet he did not gain her confidence. Something in his eye betrayed guile, and the lines of his mouth told of craftiness. Thinking him a young man of excellent habits and character, she said nothing to Parke, but that she was entirely pleased with him.

"How is your headache, Parke?" was his sister's first question, as she came in with her mother from church.

"Oh, its quite gone, I thank you. I have had the nicest sleep; and now I'm ready for any quantity of Christmas pie, pudding, and fun. Look here, Allie, I've been making Alf. a holiday present: guess what it was?"

"Oh, I cannot — you had better tell me."

"Its altogether the most precious thing that I possess."

"Perhaps its your watch and chain?"

"No, indeed. I think enough of those; but its worthy twenty watches."

Her brother regarded her puzzled face with a very merry look. She turned from him to Alfred, and perhaps she read the secret in his eyes, for the color began to deepen in her cheeks.

"You haven't given *me* away?" she asked, gravely.

"Yes, I have. I have given my only sister to my adopted brother. Isn't that generous? You must remember it when you get to be a young lady, Allie, and not smile with those bright eyes upon any one else. Give him your hand in token of consent, and we'll consider the affair settled."

Alice put her little hand into the white hand held out to her.

"I shall not give my consent," she said, smiling seriously; but I will promise to think about it. I have no doubt I shall see some one I love better."

"Nay, little Alice, you must not do that," said Alfred, kissing her fingers with a respectful, gallant air.

"But if I cannot help it?" she asked.

"Then you will have broken my heart; for from this moment I shall have no lady-love save you. You have become the star of my destiny — the 'bright, particular star' — the arbitress of my fate — the saint of the shrine at which I kneel. Your presence will be the Eden-land towards which I shall journey, — the light of your eyes, the beacon-fire leading me on to happiness, — the sound of your voice, the music for which I pine, — the hope of your love, the crowning glory of my existence:

"'Like a shrine 'mid rocks forsaken
Whence the oracle hath fled,—
Like a harp which none might waken
But a mighty master dead,—
Like a vase of perfume scattered,
Such would my spirit be;
So mute, so void, so shattered,
Bereft of thee!'"

"Bravo! Alf., you are eloquent beyond your years," cried Parke, laughing at his friend's affected air of tragic sentiment. "You woo with the grace of an Apollo instead of the becoming timidity of a sophomore."

"It is well enough to practice a little even now," was

the reply. "Despite my eloquence, you see that I am not very successful, for the frightened fairy has flown to the piano to take refuge from my pathetic invocation of Mrs. Heman's muse, deigning me only a saucy shake of her pretty head. Come back, lady Alice, and play backgammon with me, and by my faith, as a knight, I will no further declare my love for you until I can kneel at your feet, and offer there, not golden spurs, or glittering stars, but the pride of a college-youth — my diploma."

Alice came shyly back at his bidding, and they played a little while, until summoned to the sumptuous dinner which graced the Christmas board.

After dinner the young gentlemen went down town, and stopping at a jeweler's, Alfred purchased a beautiful ring for his little betrothed, as he called her. Parke wished very much to buy something elegant for his mother — but, alas! the very profuse supply which had been allowed him for the holidays was already gone, and he had not the wherewithal to get for her the smallest gift. He said nothing to Alfred, who was making a great display of his money. He was secretly a little displeased with his friend's manner, and still was angry with himself for his last night's folly.

The ensuing week flew rapidly by, bringing New Year's the happiest holiday of all. The sleighing was still good, for a wonder; and New York was alive with gayety and merriment. Many of the poor and suffering were made glad by the thoughtful kindness of the benevolent — but oh! how few compared with those who might have shared in the common rejoicing, had the majority of the rich and happy taken note of them.

Alice had a children's party in the evening. Mrs. Madison knew well how to make little people enjoy themselves; and Parke, who had faithfully avoided temptation, was the delight of the whole flock of young people. Alfred, too, exerted himself to be agreeable. He with the piano, and Parke with the flute, made good music for them to dance to; and Alfred was quite successful in introducing amusing games. There were some at the party who were as old as the two boys, and all the way down to little Rose Parish, who was but four, and danced like a sprite. Alice was as happy as she well could be; she took an opportunity after supper to thank the boys for their important help in entertaining her company. Mrs. Madison, with her sweet, grave face, and gentle manner, was constantly surrounded with groups of children; and her little daughter was delighted to see the love and pleasure with which she was regarded.

The brightest days must come to a close; and even this long evening had to do the same. The visitors were sent home weary, but still in high spirits. The young gentlemen went to bed with a sigh of regret that their holiday was over, and to-morrow they must hie back to their musty books.

Early the next morning they were gone, leaving Alice crying heartily by the window, and kissing her hands to them as long as they could look back, as they trudged on foot down to the rail-road depot, while John followed on with their carpet-bags.

CHAPTER IV.

A VERY young girl of exquisite beauty sat by an open window, looking off upon a garden, blooming with roses and the thousand fragrant flowers that unclose in the month of June. Fifteen such glowing Junes might have passed over her bright brow. Her form was round and slender, with an etherial grace in all its movements; her classic head was set daintily upon her beautiful neck, giving a spirited, proud look to a countenance which was otherwise all sweetness. Her forehead was fair as an infant's, and her eyes — liquid, dark, beaming hazel eyes — were softened by rich, black lashes; her hair, in youthful fashion, swept her crimson cheeks and snowy shoulders in smooth and heavy curls, dark-brown, with a golden tinge. As she wove the roses she had gathered in the skirt of her white dress into a wreath, and fastened back the muslin drapery from the window with it, she sang to herself in a low voice, whose lighted cadence was silvery sweet; while a smile, betokening her pleasant thoughts, hovered around her roseate mouth.

This lovely young creature was the carefully-reared Alice Madison; she was sitting in the sun-set room, idling away a summer hour, while her thoughts flew forwards a few weeks to the time when her darling brother would be at home to stay.

It was but a month until he would graduate, and that doubtless with honor and applause. The old family servants were already talking over the affair and making preparations for his reception. Bridget had made some fruit-cake, good enough for a wedding she declared, and iced it with his name in the centre, to adorn the table when he should come. His room daily received some addition to its comforts, and John was paying particular attention to the horses, and persuading Mrs. Madison to have new cushions to the carriage.

The young girl was thinking of all these things, and how delightful it would be to have him at home through the long evenings of the next winter, and how good and how gifted, and how altogether incomparable her dear brother was — her singing ended in a smile, her smile in a reverie, out of which she came with a low murmur —

"Dear — dear Parke!"

And looking up she saw him standing before her. At first she did not stop to think why he should be home so soon, but flinging down her roses to the floor, with a cry of joy, she sprang forward and clasped his neck.

"Oh! Parke, how glad I am to see you! what brought you back so soon?" He pressed her a moment tightly to his heart, and then pushing her away stood gloomily before her. She saw that he was pale and agitated; alarmed at she knew not what, she pulled him down beside her on the lounge and kissed him many times.

"Do tell me what is the matter?" she said.

"Nothing, Alice, only I am expelled from school."

She looked up in astonishment.

"Why, Parke, what will mother say to that?"

"Oh, that's the worst of it," he cried; "I should not care for anything else, but it will grieve mother so," and bowing his face into her lap he sobbed like a child.

"Well, dear, dear Parke, don't think of it, I know that you are not to blame — you cannot be — some one has been doing you a great injury."

"No one has injured me but myself. Its all my own folly, Allie, and I shall never, never get over it. I got *drunk*," he continued, bitterly raising up his flushed face, "and acted worse than a fool!"

"Why, Parke Madison!"

"Yes, its the truth, and everybody will know it now, and I can never hold up my head again among respectable people. I don't know why I did it; but the students, some of the wildest, were having a supper in the room of one of them, and they got me in and almost forced me to drink, and when I have once a taste of wine, I always make a fool of myself."

"But you have always been so well-behaved, and it was so near commencement, I should have thought that your teachers would have pardoned you. Its a shame for them to have expelled you; and in a month you would have made them proud of you."

Ah, Allie, I cannot blame the professors. For — for, the fact is, hiding his face in his hand, "this was the second time within a week, and I behaved so outrageously. Yes, they did excuse me the first offence, but my last was so conspicuous. Oh, dear! I wish I hated and abhorred wine instead of loving it. I will tell you what I know, Allie, and then perhaps you will pity me if you cannot forgive. My class were all jealous of me because I had surpassed them all, and they knew that I would have the prizes. Even Alf., who was second best, grew to be envious, and they laid a plot to get me drunk, and then to induce me to act disgracefully. I had not resolution enough to resist the first glass, and after that they did whatever they had a mind to with me. I shall never forgive them," he exclaimed, getting up and walking backwards and forwards across the floor. "I shall never forgive Alf. — he acted like a coward."

"It was cruel — wicked — shameful," cried the young girl, in an indignant tone, "and Alfred, too, I can hardly believe it of him — I should hate him for being such a traitor, if it was not wrong to hate anybody. Oh! Parke, if you had only remembered your mother's counsel, and read your bible, and prayed daily for strength, I do not believe you would have fallen."

"I have, Allie, the most of the time," he replied earnestly. "I do not know how it is, but sometimes after the most solemn resolutions, and asking God to give me grace to keep them, I have been drawn away into temptation so easily; I believe I have no energy, no self-reliance, or independence. Even companions whom I despise have an influence over me — I do that which I dislike, and then have only to be sorry and ashamed. If I could always be in such society as your'sand mother's —— where is mother, Allie ?"

"She is lying down in her room. She is not as strong even as she used to be; and she cannot keep about this oppressive weather without a long siesta. Poor mother! how will she feel!"

"Don't say a word, or I shall go crazy, I do not see how I can ever meet her; I had a notion to just go to Niagara Falls and throw myself over instead of coming home."

"Now please do not talk in that manner," said Allie, affectionately linking her arm in his, and walking to and fro with him. "Go to your room and lie down and get rested — you look pale and tired. *I* will break the news to our mother, and secure her pardon before you see her at all."

"You are a good sister," he said, kissing her, and with something like a sigh of relief, he turned away and went up stairs. Alice called John and sent him to the depot for Parke's baggage. She blushed at his surprised inquiry of "why he was home just at that time of all others, and if he was sick ?"

"The students laid a plot to get him expelled," she answered, the tears starting to her eyes; and not waiting to hear his observations she went to her mother's room thinking how hard it would be to have everybody hear of her brother's disgrace.

Mrs. Madison was awake, and got up when her daughter entered.

"You have come just in time to arrange my hair," she remarked. Now it was Allice's especial pleasure to dress her mother's soft hair, as yet but slightly streaked with grey, and she was particularly glad at that time to have something to do to conceal her face, while making her unpleasant revelations. Disappointment and mortification were only passing emotions in the mind of the mother as she listened. She was conscious of the defects in her son's otherwise beautiful character, which made him peculiarly liable to temptation, and when she heard this sad story of his weakness and error, the memory of his father's faults and fate struck to her heart with a sudden thrill of dread. A sense of danger overwhelmed her in an icy sea of terror.

The young girl set her brother's case before her with an eloquence which would fain have exterminated all his fault. The mother was not disposed to be harsh; her judgment and inclination both said that the wiser way would not be to irritate his already deeply-wounded sensibility, but to heal the wound with tenderness, and to restrain him from future error by the strong bands of an unfailing love.

Wiping away a few tears, she went up stairs and knocked

at his door. A choked voice bade her come in; she entered and found Parke sitting gloomily upon the side of the bed, his eyes cast down and his lip quivering.

"I do not believe you will ever punish yourself with your own folly again," she said, sitting beside him, after kissing him with all or more of her usual affection. "But cheer up, dear boy, and do not look so completely heart-broken. Its a bad commencement in life, but you have plenty of time to live down a mistake like this, if you only do right hereafter."

"Oh, mother, I am so ashamed and miserable."

"You ought to be a little ashamed," she said with a smile.

"If you would only scold me, mother, and treat me as I deserve, I think I could bear it better, but you are so kind, and Allie, too; I can't stand it!"

"A mother's love will outlast more than one fault," was the gentle reply. Think no more about it now; nor ever, only when you are tempted to the same again — *then* you may think of it as much as you like. By the time you have rested awhile, bathed and dressed, tea will be ready, we shall be glad to have you with us to tea again."

Pressing his hand, she left him to himself — no very pleasant company in his present frame of mind.

Bridget, when she heard of her boy, as she called him, being at home, and had inquired out the reason, was very angry for an hour or two. She had the good name of the family she served more at heart than any other thing; and to think that Parke, its pride and promise, should of all others bring this blot upon it, was too much for her equanimity. She vented her ill-humor upon luckless John, the cook-stove, the coal, and a strawberry girl; and gave Alice, who happened into the kitchen, a fine scolding on her brother's account.

Looking up from her ironing, and finding the young girl in tears, her anger suddenly subsided into a dismal fit of weeping, during which all her old affection for her darling boy returned, and she concluded that she would treat him as well as if he had come home loaded with prizes.

The cake bearing his name should grace the tea-table; and they should have strawberries and cream if they *were* enormously dear. When tea was ready, and she made an errand into the room with an urn of hot water, and beheld Parke leaning his elbow on the table with a very dejected look, quite unmindful of the luxuries of which he used to be so fond, eyeing with a melancholy look the cake which seemed to mock him with a name which he had disgraced, her kind, old heart was overcome. She sat down the urn hastily, and, marching round to him, clasped him about the neck, and said, with a little tremble in her voice, that "she was mighty glad to see him, no matter what he was sent home about"—and hastened back to the kitchen with her apron to her eyes.

The mortification, excitement, and grief of the young student were too much for his delicately organized frame. His sensitive soul could not bear so severe a shock. He fretted himself into a fever, and for a few weeks was seriously ill. Alice was constantly with him, and no one seemed to retain even a memory of his fault. The most censorious were disposed to pardon a youthful excess for which so much sorrow and contrition were shown. It got about, too, in what manner he had been beguiled into it, and for what purpose. His mother's friends and his own thronged the hall with inquiries, condolences, early fruit, and boquets. His good name was restored to its pristine brightness, and his apprehensions of having always to struggle against society's bad opinion were done away with. As soon as he was well enough to go with them, Mrs. Madison and Alice went into the country to remain through the hottest weather; and here he quite recovered his spirits, romping with his sister, wandering through cool, green woods with her, fishing, gathering wild-flowers, talking classic poetry *at* the trees and rocks and streams.

In September, the family returned to the city. Parke, resolved to atone for past misconduct, went immediately into the law-office of his guardian; a gentleman of high talent and character, who was admirably fitted to influence him for better things. Here he studied perseveringly for several months; but in the first part of the winter, Alfred Clyde returned to New York. He had fallen out with his uncle, through some lack of his usual caution. The old man had been displeased with him several times; and on this occasion his displeasure was so severe that the crafty youth could not turn it aside. Thrown for the present from this track upon which he was riding with rail-road ease to fortune, he bethought him of the plan he had already studied for reaching the same point by another way. From his first acquaintance with young Madison, he had resolved to make him serviceable in case of necessity. Like many bad men, he was jealous of those purer than himself, and he had no scruples about dragging his friend down to his own level.

When Parke first encountered him in the city, he declined any farther acquaintance with him, believing, what was really so, that he had joined with others in effecting his disgrace at college. Alfred soon made it appear that such a suspicion was doing wrong to his best friend, who had only joined with the rest in order to have a chance to warn and protect him. Why he did not do it was never made very plain; but he succeeded in restoring Parke's confidence, and they were better friends than ever.

He was invited to the house a great deal by Parke, and kindly received by the family, who accepted the son's excuses in his behalf. Despite of his pleasing address, Mrs. Madison was suspicious of his good qualities. When Parke began to study less and to stay away from home more and more, — to be out late evenings, and be unwilling to give an account of how they were spent — to come down late to breakfast, with pale cheeks and heavy eyes — to ask his guardian frequently for money, — the old deadly fear returned to her heart. She warned him tenderly and often, and finally exerted all her authority as a parent to break up the intimacy between the two young men; but Parke only became more infatuated, and resented his mother's interference in a manner very different from his usual affectionate and reverential behavior.

Alfred knew that he was no longer a welcome guest; but he continued to come often and stay long. Mrs. Madison saw the reason. He was deeply enamored of her lovely daughter. He would sit silent a whole evening to have her sing, leaning against the piano and gazing down into her face. Her singing was like the Lady Geraldine's:

> "Oh, to see or hear her singing! scarce I know which is divinest—
> For her looks sing too: she modulates her gestures on the tune;
> And her mouth stirs with the song, like song; and when the notes are finest,
> 'Tis the eyes that shoot out vocal light, and seem to swell them on."

That innocent countenance, unconscious of his passionate admiration, radiant with its own beauty, and giving a divine expression to her music, would fix the glow of his black eyes, until startled by the thought of the mother's grave observation, he would withdraw them hastily, and perhaps join Alice in her song.

The young girl was unsuspicious of any other than a brotherly attachment, and that by degrees grew unwelcome to her, as she attributed her brother's present mode of living more or less to his influence. She did not dream of half, and could hardly have realized it had it been told to her, but she suspected enough to make her feel some bitterness towards him.

"Where is the ring you was to wear until I received my diploma?" he inquired one day, taking her fair hand in his own.

"I took it off when Parke came home from college," she replied.

"But why have you not restored it to its former enviable place? Is the giver put away with the ring into your casket of cast-off valuables, never to be restored to his old station in your regards?"

"I fear that he is not worthy of restoration!" she said, with a melancholy smile; and looking a little alarmed the next moment at her own frankness.

"You must not think so — you shall not!" he exclaimed, with a lowering of his dark eye. "I cannot hear it from you!"

He pressed her hand so hard that she shrank with the pain.

"I hope that I shall have no reason," she said gravely.

These winter evenings to which Alice had looked forward with so much delight became the darkest hours of her hitherto happy life. They were long, long hours, spent many of them in watching and weeping. Her mother, whose health daily declined, was unable to remain up after nine or ten o'clock, but nothing could induce the devoted sister to retire to rest until Parke came in. Often the alabaster clock on the library mantle would ring out twelve — one — two; while she sat by the smouldering grate with a pale face, trying to interest herself in a book, nervously listening to every sound in the nearly-silent street.

She always went out into the hall when he came in. Sometimes he would brush rudely by her, with an angry exclamation at her silliness in sitting up — sometimes he would kiss her hastily, looking guilty and unhappy — and sometimes she could persuade him to come into the library and sit down a little while, when she told him that he was breaking his mother's heart, and her own too, and ruining himself. He would confess with hot and bitter tears that he was doing wrong — that he was very unhappy — and that wine was the instigator of all his evil conduct. He would promise amendment, and for a few days would be the beloved, adored Parke of other days. Alice would go singing about the house with a step light as a fairy; and the youthful bloom upon her cheeks which belonged there. The promise would be forgotten, the watching renewed, the sad faces come back again. Even the servants had not the independent, contented look they used to wear when all was well with the family. Bridget petted and fretted about her mistress' sorrowful, fading countenance. John drove his carriage down the avenue with a shade less dashing air than the one which used to become him so well. Pete, the cunning-looking little negro waiter, who dusted the parlors, laid the plates, and attended the bell, was the only personage who seemed to preserve indifference to surrounding perplexities. *His* eyes were as bright, and his smile as sly as ever; with good reason, for he never troubled himself about the door after eight o'clock of the evening; his young mistress attended to that; and the young master threw him more dimes than usual, probably out of gratitude to the little imp for always grinning at him with imperturbable good nature, whether he was in a state to deserve it or not.

Mr. Crawford, Parke's guardian, came often to see Mrs. Madison, and consult what was best to be done with the young gentleman; telling her that he spent enough money to support five people in his station, and that he never liked it when his guardian refused to let him have such extravagant allowances; that his studying law was a mere pretence, for he made no regular application to the books; and that he was known to associate with some of the most reckless young men of the metropolis. The agony of the mother's heart was partly betrayed by her slow step and fading form; but who can measure the depth of a mother's love, or the anguish of her fear, when she sees a child like Parke breaking from the tears, the prayers, the ties of home, to madly follow his leaders to ruin, to death, and to the judgment. The secret misery corroding the peace of hundreds of thousands of families, brought by one husband, father, brother, or son who has gone astray, may speak to its victims of the despair which crowns with a ghastly death's-head the cup of glowing wine; but who else can think of it as it is, or hate it with deserved hatred?

In the spring, following her own judgment, as well as the advice of Mr. Crawford, Mrs. Madison rented her beautiful city residence and removed entirely to the farm where they had spent a portion of the last summer.

It was a lovely spot, removed far enough from New York to be out of the hearing of its witcheries. The house was large and old-fashioned, with one great parlor, and a nice room for a library opening off of it. The chambers were airy and pleasant — each member of the family had a room for him and herself; the mother had an apartment opposite the parlor, whose beauty of situation more than compensated for the loss of the sunset-room. A piazza run round three sides of the main building, whose columns were profusely draped with multi-flora and honey-suckle.

Alice's sleeping room looked off over the orchard, the clover field, the great barn, into a lovely grove of maples; Mrs. Madison's over a wide expanse of beautiful meadow-land, girdled with a silver stream, and crowned by distant hills; close under the window was a sloping green sward, shadowed here and there by elm and maple trees, breaking her view of the scenery into picturesque patches. Rose-bushes grew by the casement, and there was a little bed of carnations and gilly-flowers under it.

The family who managed the farm had removed into a smaller house which had been repaired for them; so that Mrs. Madison kept house for herself, and retained her old servants. The piano, the pictures, the books, the furniture, and the whole household were there.

For the first few weeks Parke was sullen and restless. He wandered about like some one tormented with thirst, and seeking the means to quench it. The quiet, the beauty of the place soon wrought a change in him. His character assimilated itself to the nature of things about him. The expansion of the green leaves, the budding of the flowers, the springing of the wheat, the swelling of the brook, became objects of interest to him; his mind and body grew healthy. He regarded his last winter's life as a fever, hateful to think about. Those things which had so attracted him, now appeared disgusting — his former pleasures degrading, his associates vile. By degrees all wish to return to the city left him.

Everything here was new. There were a thousand things to learn and to do. Alice bloomed more beautiful than ever. The early roses could not compare with her delicate grace. She had never been so happy before; the weight which had depressed her spirits for so many months was removed, and the rebounds left her on the summit of happiness.

Parke was once more the handsome, gay, hopeful, affectionate brother. The great old mansion was a perfect playhouse for them; from the cellar to the garret all was envious and delightful. The stone dairy-house built over the brook, the old log-house at the foot of the garden, built by the first settlers, and now gone into romantic decay, with a huge apple-tree growing in at the open window, and heaps of last year's nuts in the rickety loft — the grape-vine swing in the woods — and the little quiet place in the stream where the fishes most did congregate — all these received their frequent visits. Nothing was so sweet as the fragrance of apple-blossoms when the night-breeze wafted them into the windows, while Alice made the old mansion ring with the melody of her voice, in concert with the piano. But when the roses came, *they* were the sweetest; and when haying-time came, there was nothing, positively nothing, so refreshing as the fragrance of the new-mown hay, nor so delightful as tossing it about and following the loaded wagons to the barns.

Parke was very efficient aid in time of hurry, and Alice learned all the mysteries of butter-making from the farmer's wife. Old Brindle sometimes came home, to the great astonishment of that good woman, with her head, neck, and horns strangely bedecked with wreaths of leaves and flowers which Alice had coaxed her into standing quiet to be adorned with. The lambs when they could be caught were similarly decked, and even the fat, nice, little pigs did not always escape some marks of her favor. Parke learned her to ride on horseback. He had been taught in a riding-school, but she took her first lessons from him.

That was a happy summer. It had one shadow, however, in the ill-health of Mrs. Madison. Not even the country air could restore her to her old animation; and as the hot days of August came on, she drooped more and more. She was confined a great deal to her room and her sofa. The family physician came frequently from the city to see her. He seemed to think her present abode as favorable to her health as any could be; and she was glad to hear it, for the children were doing so well, and she herself felt such quiet and peace, that she dreaded the thought of change.

Of visitors from town they had a great many during the hot weather, whom they duly feasted with country luxuries, and gave a glimpse of country pleasures.

After haying and harvesting came the fruit-season. This was indeed a glorious portion of the year. Even Mrs. Madison rallied a little through September and October. How beautiful were the golden autumn days; the purple valleys, the misty hills, the fragrant air, the gorgeous maple grove. How delightful to wander with rustling feet through the wood, gathering up the various-hued leaves, listening for the dropping nuts, and plucking the plentiful wild grapes.

Parke Madison thought that he could never do another sinful deed as long as he lived.

The Indian-summer came and went like a dream of Paradise. Then the young people had an opportunity of testing the pleasures of a winter in the country. The tongue of the babbling brook was frozen into stillness; the trees once beautiful with waving foliage were standing bare and dreary, or sparkling with a thousand rainbow pendants of ice, or muffled in heavy habiliments of snow. The distant hills stood grand and stately, like white-headed old men. The fields, beautifully clothed in snowy garments, were lying at rest after their summer labor, gathering strength for another season of toil. The dairy-house seemed to have grown short and bulky, with its heavy cap hanging over its brows. The portico, sometimes, after a litttle thaw would be hung about with glittering fringes, and the graceful stems of the multi-flora would flash and gleam like sprays of diamonds, while its red berries made a handsome contrast.

Within-doors there was comfort and plenty. The cellar was full of fine apples and the garret was stored with nuts As often as once a fortnight Mr. Crawford sent out new books, and they had a paper almost every day in the week But some of the apartments, which were so spacious and airy in warm weather, could not be made comfortable now; the great parlor was abandoned, and the little library became the favorite room. Here reading, music, and games of chess, knitting, painting in water-colors, and letter-writing, went smoothly on. Here was stationed Mrs. Madison's favorite sofa, and here the tea was made every evening. Here Parke began to be ambitious to become a sculptor, littering the hearth every day with chips until he had carved a strange-looking head out of a bit of wood, which, he flattered Alice, was meant for a copy of her own.

Sometime in January, Mrs. Madison took a severe cold, which confined her to her bed for a long time, and left her with an alarming cough. The rest of the winter her health was miserable. She grew more and more feeble, lying all day upon her lounge, and being almost carried to her bed at night. Alice slept with her, to be near her in case of a sudden increase of her illness, which sometimes occurred. Parke was devoted to her comfort. He read to her by the hour, in his rich, mellow voice; he carried her in his arms when she was well enough to go out in the sleigh for a short ride; he hung around her constantly, on the watch for some opportunity of serving her. In his deep and solicitous tenderness might be traced the workings of remorse. He knew that the many hours of anxiety and anguish he had caused her were partly the reasons of her present sufferings; and he strove to atone, by faultless conduct and filial attentions, for the past.

Never had an invalid two children who were more affectionate nurses. In quiet and happy occupations the winter wore away, the cheerful spirits of the young people checked only by an occasional fear of their mother's being taken away from them. The mother's own presentiments were more constant and powerful. She knew that she never should be well again. She looked death in the face every day, calmly, smilingly. Only when she thought of her boy! only when she thought of Parke! — with his generosity, impressibility, want of purpose, love of gayety — who had been so nearly swept away in the vortex of vice, and who could never play a moment upon its alluring shores without danger of losing his foothold and being drawn into the dizzy current, — *then*, in what an agony of prayer she laid her fears before her Maker, and implored of Him to be the Parent and the Savior of her child. Alice she was content to leave with her own holy and religious heart, her sweet temper, her gay disposition, and her habits of prayer; satisfied that the dear and beautiful child had the promise of happiness in her gifts of wealth, loveliness, grace, and talent, well guarded by the golden breast-plate of her piety. Still it was with yearning eyes that she followed the movements of that slender figure and gazed upon that blooming, child-like face. It is hard for a mother to leave her children, even when her destination is to the unspeakable beauty of the promised-land.

Ever since she was a young girl Mrs. Madison had been a disciple of Jesus Christ. In the palmiest days of her brilliant career, when flattered, courted, and boundlessly beloved, — the accomplished daughter of a superior family — the admirable wife of a distinguished man, — she had never been bewildered into forgetfulness of her professions of an humble faith. Would there were more professed followers of the 'meek and lowly Jesus,' who 'went about doing good,' to imitate the example of this lovely woman, who was as familiar with the homes of the destitute and the cry of orphans as with the glow of her own comfortable hearth and the singing of her own fair children. Her faith was serene, her hope cheerful, and her charity boundless. She always gave more than many who think that they have done their whole duty. To the golden droppings from her purse was added the sweet smile, the ready tear, the words of encouragement, consolation, or merited reproof. Now that the hand of sickness was laid heavily upon her, she had a useful and beautiful life to look back upon, and a glorious future to look forward to. All her old sweetness lingered about her, dying away like the sun at the close of a bright day in a halo of radiance. Her greatest earthly happiness was in listening to the almost seraphic melody of Alice's singing; it reminded her of the golden harps of heaven; but sometimes it moved the passion of her mother's heart, until she felt that she could hardly part from anything so dear. A few concealed tears, a silent prayer, or a holy and comforting psalm, would restore her mind to its usual serenity.

With the soft winds and flitting showers of April came the consciousness to the souls of the brother and sister that they were to lose their mother. Wasted and helpless she lay upon her couch, which she could leave only for the dark and narrow home. A few brief days and she would be no more. So placidly she spoke of it, as if she were going on a delightful journey, that in her presence they could hardly realize the great sorrow that was coming upon them. Eagerly they watched for every smile, growing now so rare and radiant, and so soon to beam on them no more. Day and night they lingered by her side, holding the thin, white hands, the pressure of whose slender fingers thrilled them with strange emotions of grief and love.

There was a house-full of friends and relatives attending upon the last days of the beloved invalid, but the children would yield their places to none. If they yielded to her solicitations and sought rest from watching, they only wept until they were back to her presence.

One day, early in May, she lay more at ease than usual. The window of the room was open, and the faint fragrance of the first lilacs was wafted around the bed. Her attendants thought that she slept; but while they gazed, a change came over her face that all recognized as the sign of the presence of the destroyer. Alice was afraid that she would never speak again, and leaning pale and breathless against her aunt, she looked upon the dying countenance; her brother buried his face in the bed. Presently the eyes unclosed, bright and large; they wandered around until they rested upon the head bowed down upon the counterpane.

"Parke," she said, in a clear whisper.

"Dear mother," and all in a tremble, he bent to hear her last words.

"Promise me that you will never again touch the wine-cup. It brings only sorrow and remorse."

"I promise — willingly. I never meant to any more, and with God's help I will keep this promise."

"Bring me that promise unbroken to heaven, Parke. Now, oh, Heavenly Father, I do die content, and blessing Thee." She fixed her eyes with a soft expression upon the western sky which seemed opening its golden gates to let her waiting spirit through. All sobs were hushed to silence, while the friends gazed in reverential love upon the saintly beauty of her face.

"Alice," she said again, speaking aloud, "you have been a good child — you will come to me I know — and Parke — love one another — be faithful — remember your Creator in the days ———," here the voice died away, the unearthly radiance faded out of her countenance, and as the sun sank suddenly below the horizon, she sighed and fell asleep in Jesus.

There was a great burst of lamentation from the group gathered around — the two oldest servants wept and groaned — Alice threw herself upon the bed, shivering like a leaf chilled by a winter wind.

"Come, Alice, this is too much for you, — come out into the open air with me," said Parke, mastering himself, and speaking in a changed, husky voice.

He put his arm around her waist and led her out to a grassy knoll under the favorite elm-tree, and there, when they sat down together alone, all composure forsook both. Clasped in each others arms they gave uncontrolled expression to their sorrow. It was long after dark before they retured to the house.

"Oh! Parke," said Alice, as they went slowly back, "we are all that is left to each other now."

"Let us remember our mother's dying injunction to be faithful — let us indeed love one another," replied the brother, speaking in an earnest and agitated tone.

"We will — we will," was the sobbing reply, as Alice carried her brother's hand to her trembling lips.

Mrs. Madison was buried beside her husband in a beautiful spot in Greenwood Cemetery. Countless friends followed the corpse of the honored and idolized woman to its resting-place. If compassion and sympathy could have alleviated the grief of the orphans they would have mourned no more. As they stood beside the grave, clasping each other close, struggling for strength to go away, leaving their mother behind forever, many tears were dropped for them. There was mourning, too, in many a lonely dwelling and lowly home where the remembrance of the kindness of the dead lingered, and grateful hearts, thinking of their own little ones clothed and nursed by the good departed, now prayed for the brother and sister who were left alone.

There were many families of relatives and friends who would have welcomed Alice Madison to their midst as a cherished member; not only for her gentleness, accomplishments, and beauty, but a little too, perhaps, because a youthful heiress has seldom any lack of attention. But to Mr. and Mrs. Crawford, who had been the best-beloved friends of their father and mother, both Parke and Alice decided to go. Having no children of their own, and having always envied Mrs. Madison her beautiful pair, they were received at once into the hearts of this lady and gentleman. Their weary spirits were soothed, and their desolate hearts comforted. A thousand acts of almost motherly kindness from Mrs. Crawford at last began to pierce the veil of grief in which the young girl had wrapped herself. The hopeless melancholy of her lovely face gave place to a less dejected look — she began to eat more than a bird or a kitten — and the roses resumed their seat upon her cheeks, though paler roses than those of old.

"If you would only *let* me love you more — if you would only accept my love," the lady would say, laying her hand upon Alice's drooping head, and looking yearningly into her sweet face.

Mrs. Crawford was a pretty little woman, still youthful-looking, with large, blue eyes, a delicate, transparent complexion, and a charming smile. Alice's heart would melt with gratitude at the touch of her light hand upon her head, as she would tearfully reply to those fond looks which seemed to beseech a daughter's love.

"I do let you love me — I am thankful for every bit of affection which you give me, I am so grateful for it — so glad of it — and you are so dear to me — dearer than any one else in the world but Parke — but your speaking so softly makes me cry, because it is so like my own mother. Oh! Mrs. Crawford, how can I live without my mother!"

The lady would take the fair head upon her bosom, and cheer away the flowing tears, while all the time her own heart, yearning for a mother's bliss and blessing, would be secretly jealous of that touching fidelity to a parent's memory.

"You shall have two mothers, darling," she would say, "one in heaven looking down upon you with the power of an angel to protect and guard — and an humble earthly mother who will never tire of taking care of you here."

Parke used a man's expedient for driving away grief.

He became very much immersed in study and business. He made fine proficiency in the law, and did a good many little affairs of the office for his guardian. He copied and transacted commissions of trust which it might be convenient for Mr. Crawford to transfer to him. His evenings he invariably spent with Alice. The older people said and felt that their house had never seemed so home-like as since these young folks had come to gild its gloomy corners with the sunshine of beauty and youth. Mr. Crawford was nervous, not naturally the most cheerful of men, and sometimes trifles would disconcert the harmony of his feelings Alice's eye was so quick, her foot so fleet, her hand so ready, and her voice so soft, that she pleased him more than any one he had ever had about him. She must read to him, sing to him, wait upon his morning meal, and attend upon his evening easy-chair and slippers.

Parke must play chess with him, and let him beat about three times out of four; so that with the acquisition of two such excellent children, his happiness was greatly increased, and his nerves kept comparatively comfortable.

CHAPTER V.

"PARKE MADISON has been playing saint since he got that weed on his hat. Deuce take him! he used to be one of us, and we can't afford to spare him."

"His acquaintance would be worth cultivating if he were not so uncomfortably good all at once. I wish I stood in his shoes. I tell you what it is Hal, to be coming into such a property as he is in less than three months, to be the adopted son of that rich old lord of a lawyer, to have the *entree* of the most unexceptionable circles, the most distant stars of the aristocracy, and to own such a glorious sister, is too much for one man, if he *is* pretty bright and good-looking. It makes me envious to think of it, while here I am hanging on to the narrow skirt of an old aunt that may live a thousand years to distress me with playing the dutiful. If there's anything I hate its hypocrisy, — I'd rather be known for what I am, a lover of good-living, and a patron of Fleming's, than the discreet darling of a maiden-aunt. As for Madison, I mean to bring him down."

"Pooh! let the fellow alone. I am glad he is doing better. There is nothing to prevent his being an honor to the town; and if he has a mind to be, I have no objections. It would be a pity — it would seriously — to see him throw himself away on a few years of dissipation. He's made of fine stuff, I can assure you, and will not stand much wear and tear."

"Those are fine sentiments for you, Henry Jenkins; but you must remember that our pockets are not as well lined as his, while our ambition is as great. He has more than he wants, and he might as well pay for our suppers, our horses, and our debts of honor as anybody else."

"That's a very sage remark of yours, my friend, but I guess you'll have to give young Madison up. I have heard that he promised his mother upon her death-bed to never taste of wine again, and you know a fellow that will not drink, is too cool-headed to be victimized."

"I'll lay you a wager of anything you please, that I will get him drunk within one week, despite of his promise."

"Pshaw! impossible! I'll stake my black horse, Otello, against that diamond on your little finger, that you do no such thing."

"Done. The living are more powerful than the dead, my dear boy, and you may prepare your mind to part from your favorite steed:

"'For he'll never bear his master more
Through the bright ranks of ——— Broadway.'"

The speakers were two young men, occupying a private room at Fleming's. A bottle of wine, another of brandy, a bowl of sugar, some iced water, a brilliant lamp, and a pack of cards occupied the table at which they sat. This table was drawn up to the coal-stove, whose ruddy glare threw a warm lustre over the handsomely-framed pictures, the costly curtains, and rich carpet which decorated the apartment. The polished boots of Henry Jenkins rested their elegant soles against the top of the stove; his stylish imperial, carefully arranged black hair, handsome but dissipated countenance, and bold, dark eyes, glimmered mistily through the blue clouds, floating in airy undulations around his head, and emanating, like the smoke from the crater of Vesuvius, from the corners of his mouth, where glowed a fairy spark, that was undoubtedly the nearly-consumed end of a fragrant cigar. Below this misty personification of a volcano, his shirt-bosom gleamed like a snowy plain. It was fringed with dainty ruffles of cambric; and sparkling in its centre, as a fountain might sparkle in the midst of a plain, was a diamond pin of great brilliancy.

A well-shaped hand, unsoiled by contact with things more useful and laborious than white-kid gloves, supple rattans, and dealing the cards, reposed gracefully in his bosom, and its mate was employed alternately in removing the mysterious fire from his lips, and in raising to the same place a glass of brandy-and-water. His companion, sitting opposite, leaned his elbows upon the table, and dipped lumps of sugar in brandy, displayed while nibbling at them a very fine set of teeth; but his features were not otherwise prepossessing. His hair and whiskers could not be coaxed into the elegant silkiness of his friend's; his cheeks and nose had a certain glow that does *not* indicate early rising and morning air, but evening staying-up and night air — which speaks more of the freshness of mint than of roses. A weak look in his light-grey eyes, which grey was originally designed for blue, but had faded out, indicated that the jeweled eye-glass which hung at his watch-chain might be designed for use as well as ornament. His dress was unexceptionable, and his manner might be agreeable when guarded in the society of ladies; but here it was reckless and almost vulgar.

"That ring was given me by my affectionate Aunt, on my last birth-day," he said, with a light laugh, "and she would be very inquisitive if she missed it from my finger; but I am willing to run the risks. I never met a young gentleman yet who could not call himself of age who could not be coaxed or fooled into a peep at the mysteries of Fleming's."

"But this one has cut his eye-teeth. He has been behind the scenes with the best of us, — the worst, I mean," — with a mocking smile; "so you'd better resign your Aunt's diamonds and let the baby alone."

With an expression of infinite contempt upon his face, that 'one of us' could have been so weak as to have reformed, Harry Jenkins finished his cigar, buttoned up his coat, rang the bell for the waiter, and, after paying for their evening's amusement, took his companion's arm and sallied out in search of their hotel, four hours after their intended victim was safely asleep under his guardian's roof.

A few evenings after this, as Parke was walking briskly home, with a new book in his hand, which he designed reading with Alice, one of his cast-off acquaintance, to whom he had hardly spoken since his return to the city, six months before, came up and put his arm in his.

"How do you do, Madison?" he said, familiarly.

"How do you do, St. Ormond?" was the cold response.

"Will you please to walk up here a moment?" continued the other, as they came opposite the rooms of the speaker; "I have something that I wish your judgment upon very much."

"I am in haste to-night; will it not do in the morning when I am going to the office?" replied Parke, hesitating; for he dreaded to even set foot in any of his old haunts.

"It is doubtful about my being out of bed at so unseasonable an hour," said St. Ormond, laughing; "I wish to show you a statue of Hebe, which has just arrived from Italy, to-day, by my especial order. They say it shows best by lamp-light."

Sculpture we know was one of Parke's passions, and he turned eagerly, and followed his companion up a flight of stairs, where a door from the landing led them into two large and handsome rooms. Young Madison drew back when he saw half-a-dozen or more of his old associates lounging about the apartments. He would fairly have ran away had he not felt too dignified; and a glimpse of the beautiful work of art which stood unveiled just within the folding-doors, glowing with life-like loveliness in the blaze of light arranged to fall over it, arrested him.

Every gentleman came forward and greeted him with marked earnestness and cordiality, expressing in looks or words their regret for his recent affliction, and making no boisterous display of their pleasure at seeing him among them. Thankful for their respectful sympathy, he went forward with a more comfortable feeling to admire the sculptured Hebe.

"Well, what do you think of it?" asked the owner, when the young amateur had stood several moments wholly lost in delight and admiration.

"Exquisite! wonderful!" replied he, in pleased tones, gazing upon the lovely, uplifted head, with its backward-streaming curls, its garland, and its face of smiling beauty; upon the matchless grace of the bended knee and foot, the delicate roundness of the arms, the perfect symmetry of the hands bearing the cup, and upon the youthful buoyancy of her kneeling posture.

"How naturally the drapery falls to her elegant limbs, as if it were the pliable silken fabric itself, instead of unyielding marble," he continued, after a long contemplation.

"And how lightly the fingers of the left hand lie upon the cup, as if all the duty of bearing it devolved upon the right," said St. Ormond. Harry thinks the fore-arm is shortened a little too much, and the upper-lip ditto. As for me, I think the mouth is lovely as a dream, and the exquisite upper lip is half the charm; but Jenkins is always critical. If I could find a pair of lips like these, belonging to a living, breathing woman, I swear I would kiss them if they beautified the face of a nun!"

Parke was just about to say that the mouth was precisely like his sister Alice's, but the latter part of the remark checked him, and he was glad that he had not breathed her name in that place.

"I see no fault in the work now," he said, as he turned to go, "but I am probably blinded by profound admiration; I congratulate you, St. Ormond, upon possessing such a gem."

"It is a costly gem, I assure you. It was rather extravagant in me to order it, but I have a passion for such things. What! you are not going?"

"Yes, I must go. I thank you for this peep at your glorious Hebe, and will come again with your permission to look at her."

"We are going to have a bit of supper by-and-by, Madison, and I shall take it as a positive affront if you leave us, for this is my birth-night, and my friends ought to take pleasure in celebrating it.

"I have a sufficient excuse for not joining any such party as this," said Parke, moving to the door. "If I do not visit any one, you cannot take it as a particular slight, and will pardon me." St. Ormond closed the door and turned the key as he said with a most fascinating and overpowering manner —

"We do all respect your grief for your great loss. But we hold that it is neither wise nor right for you to retire any longer from all suitable society of your age, and mope away your brightest years in the dust of a law-office. No one should desire that you should waste your health nor deny yourself reasonable enjoyment. Youth was made for happiness. Come, Parke, my dear fellow, be contented to remain. It is only a quiet supper; and we are going to break up early. If you consent to stay with us a little while, just long enough to eat an English oyster, or a prairie chicken, we will pledge ourselves to be perfectly decorous while you remain."

Parke looked around. The fire of youth glowed warmly in his heart, and emotions long slumbering in quiet thrilled his frame. The youthful Hebe holding out the wine-cup with that impassioned smile, as if she were a living, blooming woman, the fragrance of some costly flowers upon the mantel, the bewitching odor of some purposely-spilled wine, the glow of lamps, the sound of enchanting music played softly in an adjoining room, the sight of cordial faces, were all overcoming the placid purpose of his mind in a sense of pleasure.

"If I should stay, I would not touch wine, and would only remain a half-hour at the table," he said to himself. He looked at his watch. It was nine o'clock, and Alice had been waiting for him an hour. At that moment, folding doors opened into a third apartment, from whence proceeded the invisible music. A table, bountifully decorated with living flowers, and flooded with light, upon which a faultless supper was delicately displayed, occupied this room.

"You see that I sup three hours earlier than I used to. You can be at home, if you wish, by ten o'clock."

Up between the gorgeous apartment, with its music, lamps and flowers, its pleasurable atmosphere and impure faces, arose to the spiritual sight of Parke, a room flooded with sunset radiance, sweetened with the faint breath of lilacs, and his mother tranced in her dying visions.

"I thank you, but I cannot stay. Good evening, gentlemen." He turned to open the door. It was fastened, and the guests all came towards him in a body; laughing, and laying hold of him, they would have carried him into the supper-room.

"Gentlemen!" he said, shaking them off, and standing erect with flashing eyes. "This is unpardonable rudeness. If any one lays a finger upon me, it will be at his peril. St. Ormond, unlock that door!"

His first anger and icy, untouchable look, caused his detainer to open the door and forbear further effort.

Following Parke outside, he begged pardon for the thoughtlessness of his guests, saying that they desired him to remain so much that they had forgotten his claims to their consideration.

"Come to-morrow at twelve and visit with Hebe as long as you like," were his parting words, and Parke, somewhat abating his resentment, wended his way home.

"You have lost your bet," cried the delighted set as

soon as their host re-appeared. Henry Jenkins wears the ring!"

"Be quiet, my friends, if you please, and come to supper. It will be cold, I am thinking, before we set down to it; and, as it is rather early for our fashionable appetites, there will be two drawbacks to its perfection."

"The man who cannot find an appetite for one of St. Ormond's suppers, even at nine o'clock, is to be pitied," said one; and all gathered around the board enjoyed the discomfited looks of their host.

"Gentlemen!" he said, after he had himself carved a rare bird, which the waiters set before him, and gave a bit of it to all who desired, "there remain two days yet before this bet is decided. I do not doubt but that I shall ride Henry's princely Otello yet. You have all of you an invitation to be my guests to-morrow night; at what hour, and in what rooms, I will let you know in the morning."

This speech, made with recovered composure and seeming confidence, was received with great applause. No one seemed to think that there was anything more important at stake than a fine horse and a diamond ring. The promise given to a dying mother, the ruin of a noble soul, and the unhappiness of a family of friends, were not taken at all into account. Some of the guests glanced over the costly exotics, the marble Hebe, the rare wine, and the celebrated musicians, and wondered what greater temptations money could purchase. The pleasure of anticipation added a new charm to the present hour.

In the meantime Parke hurried home as if the tempter still pursued him. It was not until he was fairly in the presence of Alice that he felt safe. The beaming smile with which she met him, the soft pressure of her arms about his neck, and her lips upon his cheek, were never more welcome. And when he sat down beside her upon the sofa, and she nestled her head in his bosom and looked up into his face with a happier smile than she had worn since their mother's death, his breast swelled with thanks to God for saving him from imminent peril, and he secretly renewed his vow, as he held his fair sister closely in his arms.

"What if I had been tempted to remain — then tempted to drink — and returned to her with the fumes of wine upon my lips?" he asked himself, with a shudder. "Would she not have paled and shrunk away from me? — would she not have reproached and despised me, and tortured me with the memory of my pledge? instead of clinging to me with such love, such confidence, such innocent sweetness."

It was too late to cut the pages of the new book. The rest of the family had retired, and after an hour of happy conversation, the young Madisons followed the example, leaving their volume for the next evening's entertainment.

But when the evening came, Parke bethought him of its being the night of the weekly lectures upon law, the science of government, and such other subjects, which he lately attended. So Alice was fain to content herself with her music, and a new number of the Mirror, as they were resolved to enjoy the reading of the book together.

It was ten o'clock when the lecture closed, and Parke was walking briskly home through the sleet and rain of a dreary November night, picturing to himself the fine warmth of the grate in the back parlor, with Alice waiting for him alone before the fire, perhaps ensconced in Mr. Crawford's great chair, or perhaps leaning pensively with her forehead against the mantel, as she sometimes did. He had reached the square in which the house was situated. It was so quiet and aristocratic a part of the city that the police were not very watchful; and as he turned the corner he heard a slight scream, and beheld, by the dim light of the street-lamp, a female struggling in the arms of a man.

"Scoundrel!" shouted the young man, with a powerful blow in the face of the villain. Anger had given him strength, and the reeling man, thinking such an opponent not to be despised, took to his heels, leaving the object of his pursuit fainting in the arms of her protector. Parke feeling her slender figure sinking heavily upon his arm, bore her closer to the light, and lifted the wet hood from her face. It was a youthful face and beautiful, though now the eyes were closed in terror.

"For heaven's sake, child, where do you belong?" said the young man; "and why are you out unprotected this dreary night?" "Oh, Sir," she sobbed, unclosing her large dark eyes, "if you will only take me home; my mother is very sick — I was afraid she would die, and went out for the doctor and got lost; oh, Sir, please to take me home!"

"Poor young creature!" said Parke, "where is your home — where shall I take you to?"

She named a number in a miserable street of the suburbs. It was some distance, but the young man would have walked miles in a colder storm than that, rather than leave the shivering, frightened girl to find her way alone.

"I can take you there," he said, supporting her upon his arm, and walking as fast as she seemed able to go.

"How Alice would pity her!" he thought, as he felt her clinging tightly to his arm. She spoke only once as they hurried along the pavement, and then she uttered, sadly — "Alas! my mother!"

They came to the No., and he was about to leave her at the foot of the wretched-looking stairs, when she asked him in a soft voice if he would not go up with her and see her parent? "She may be dead," she cried wildly, and fled up the narrow way.

He followed almost as fleetly, and they entered a desolate-looking chamber, through which they passed into an inner room. Parke stood amazed and bewildered when he found himself in a large apartment, in which the defects of age were so concealed by furniture that it looked quite comfortable, and surrounded by a party of gentlemen instead of in the presence of poverty and sickness.

"Gentlemen," said his conductress, "I have brought you a guest;" and shutting the door on him, she disappeared.

He was greeted with shouts of merriment.

"Well done, Mr. Madison!" cried St. Ormond, "to decline our company so stoutly last night, as if it would harm your youthful innocence. And now you stumble upon us in *that* society. Well, we forgive you the past; you are as welcome as unexpected."

Blushing with shame and confusion, he would again have made good his retreat; but the door was barricaded by the laughing group, and he could not now fall back upon his dignity, appearances being so much against him.

"I beg of you to hear me," he cried earnestly.

"Oh, yes, it must be an excellent story," interrupted another; "we are all anxious to hear it. But first take a comfortable seat, and tell the tale at your ease."

They seized him by the arms and sat him down in a chair.

"Take a sip of something to give spirit to your narrative," said St. Ormond, approaching him with a glass of wine on a server. The laughter and jeers of the company maddened the sensitive young man into forgetfulness of everything but his present situation. Humiliated, angry, thrown entirely off his guard, he thought of nothing but of being equal with them.

"I am neither a fool or a coward!" he said, seizing the glass and tossing it off with an air of affected carelessness.

Yet the moment he had drank it, he felt that he was both, and worse — oh, a thousand times worse!

"What have I done?" he cried inwardly, with agony.

"That will make a man of you, I am sure," said Harry

Jenkins, tauntingly. "Now let us have the interesting history of your adventures, and how you happened into this out-of-the-way spot."

The wine, which was mingled with a goodly portion of brandy, flew to Parke's already excited brain. He gave them a grotesque account of his rescue of the young girl, drinking, while he talked, all the liquor that was offered him; and ridiculing his own tender-heartedness in coming up to see her sick mother. St. Ormond soon had the pleasure of seeing him drunk as he well could be, and of being congratulated as the owner of the splendid Otello.

"It has cost me five times as much as the horse is worth," he said to himself. "But I can make it pay well, with that simpleton in my power;" and he glanced coolly towards the unfortunate victim of their heartless wager.

He would hardly have thought the *éclat* of the thing amongst his own set, nor the future spoils out of Parke Madison's fortune, would *pay*, if he had thought of the account set down against him in the Book of the just Judge of the Universe, which must sometime be accurately settled. But he did not think of that, or if he did he dismissed the unpleasant reflection, as he said in high good-humor, —

"Good friends and fellows! you will now do me the honor to sup with me at Fleming's. Mr. Madison, I dare say you have no objections to accompanying us. Allow me to offer you an arm — I see that your nerves are agitated by the undue trial to which they were subjected a short time ago; you do not walk with the boldness becoming a man who has knocked down another and rescued a poor child from being carried off."

The whole company fastened on their cloaks and made their way to Fleming's with just little enough noise to escape from the embarrassment of being locked up for the night. Here Parke, lost to all sense of propriety, caroused as long and as high as the wildest of his gay associates. His 'promise to pay when he should become of age,' to the amount of three hundred dollars, was in the hands of Harry Jenkins when he left, and five hundred with St. Ormond.

One of the company, whom liquor did not affect in so woful a manner, escorted him to the door of Mr. Crawford's residence, and there bade him good night, though it was nearly morning.

Alice, who had waited through the long and dreary hours, a cold weight of dread sinking heavier every moment upon her heart, sprang to the door, as she heard him endeavoring to open it. Letting him in, she clasped his hand and led him to the light.

"I was afraid you had been murdered," she murmured, looking up into his face.

The next moment she sprang from him as if she had been stung by an adder.

"Parke Madison! you are *drunk!*" she said in a stern voice, while her face grew as pale as ashes.

"Oh no, my dear, you are mistaken," he said, smiling upon her with an air of good nature. "I know most people would think so, but *you* ought to know me better," he continued, with drunken gravity.

"You have broken your promise to our mother — you have degraded yourself — have sinned beyond repentance — are lost!" she cried, walking hastily to and fro, wringing her hands. "Oh, my brother, do you know what you have done?"

She paused before him, with the tears streaming down her white face — her hands were involuntarily lifted as if deprecating the divine anger which might visit so dark a perjury.

"I — I suppose I've been taking supper at Fleming's, from my feelings," was the stammering reply to her solemn inquiry. "What are you crying about, Allie? I've — I've not been drinking, though you may have some reason to suppose so. Cheer up, sis, and if you hear anything about the affair at Fleming's, you need not believe it."

She sank down in a chair in a stupor of indignation and grief, which settled down into despair.

"Oh, Parke! Parke!" she cried in a low voice, "my happiness is gone forever. You have made me indeed miserable."

He took up a small lamp and ascended the hall-stairs.

"Do not make any more noise than you can avoid — walk lightly," pleaded his sister coming after, for she did not know but that this night's ruinous work might be kept from their kind protectors.

She followed him to the door of his room and then hastened to her own. She lay down upon her bed with a far bitterer sorrow than had shaken her the night of her mother's death. *That* was chastened, holy, and in a measure hopeful — this was burning, sudden, and dark, mingled with shame, fear, and anguish. The brief remainder of the night passed sleeplessly away. She arose at seven to breakfast with Mr. Crawford, as was her custom, the rest of the family not breakfasting until nine, during the cold weather. He noticed her pale cheeks and spiritless expression — said he guessed she got up too early to make his coffee, and she must not do it if she didn't like — kissed her as he went out — and then she laid down on the library sofa, waiting for and dreading, she hardly dared to think of what.

The two hours passed by, and neither Mrs. Crawford or Parke came down to breakfast. The former was quite indisposed and had taken her coffee in her room. Alice went in to see her a moment, and then stole to her brother's door. She did not hear him dressing, and so opened it and entered. He was not there. Stricken by guilt and remorse he had risen an hour before, and crept out into the open air, where he might endeavor to fly from the faces of friends and the reproaches of his own conscience. The first breath of pure, morning breezes dispelled the illusions of the past evening; he felt that he had been duped by a silly artifice, and then betrayed by his own passions. He dared not go to the office, and, disgusted with himself and the world, he called at a saloon and took a glass of wine to banish his horrible feelings. Was a man in his situation capable of self-control? had he the full use of his own judgment? and would it have been arbitrary to have refused him what he called for? Or was the piece of silver which he laid upon the table a fair equivalent for this new sorrow in his sister's heart, and this new link in the chain that was forging to drag him down?

The air of his room was foul with the fumes of his feverish breath and the odor of cigar-smoke which filled his clothes.

Alice opened a window, lest the servant coming to regulate the apartment should suspect more than was pleasant. His bible, which she had given him when he first went away to college, lay upon his dressing-table; and the slippers which their mother had embroidered the last winter of her life, set by the bed-side. She sat down and leaned her forehead upon the treasured book. Thoughts of his old errors, and the old unhappiness — days of sorrow and doubt gone by — came over her; the times when she used to watch and weep, and her mother to go about with a smileless face: then of the bright year rolling by in a golden round of hopes and pleasures, and ended by that heavy mourning for one that went with it to return no more with other years; then of this worst grief of any.

"If he has broken from the vow that he made a dying mother, and in so short a time, there is nothing that can restrain him now. My love will come to nought; it will be powerless. Why should I love him? he is not worthy any longer even of my forgiveness," she mused bitterly.

But the stern resolution was followed swiftly by a memory —

"Parke — Alice — love one another — be faithful."

"Oh, my mother, I too promised, and I will fulfil. I will never forsake him for any degradation or crime that he may be guilty of. I will cling to him through all — forgive him — love him, and fulfil to the utmost the love and duty of a sister."

She fell upon her knees and prayed to Christ to intercede for her erring brother, and for strength to endure the day of trial. It was long before a gleam of consolation entered her soul, but when she arose from her prayer, patience and love sat upon her sweet features. She sat as long as she could with Mrs. Crawford; and when her anxiety grew too strong to be resisted, she went down and stood looking out the front parlor windows at the passers-by, until her guardian came into dinner.

He inquired for Parke, saying, that he had not been in the office during the morning. She tried to reply cheerfully that he went out quite early, and she did not know where he was, unless he had ridden out to the farm.

So he had; and he came back at dusk, tired and gloomy. The associations of the place had more than balanced the effects of the hard riding.

The ladies were sitting by the centre-table, knitting while they waited for tea.

"You have not been a very dutiful boy, to-day," remarked Mrs. Crawford, pleasantly, as he drew his chair up to the fire. "Here I have been kept in my chamber until about an hour ago, and you never came to inquire after my health, or to wish me better."

"I have been away all day to the farm," he replied, glancing swiftly towards Alice, and back to the fire again.

"Good evening, Parke," said she in a gentle voice.

He looked up and met the sad but affectionate gaze of her dear eyes, and his own fell moodily to the floor. She drew her chair beside of his, and laid her hand upon his shoulder. Once the look and the touch would have melted away the barriers of pride, and he would have wept his contrition upon her bosom. But he had grown into a man now, and the impressibility of his nature was hardening into less yielding stuff. In his present irritated humor he felt her affection as the most humiliating reproach. He saw that she had guarded his secret from the family, and the very gratitude which he was obliged to yield was more now than he wanted to give. He was more discontented than ever, because he could be discontented with no one but himself. He gazed gloomily into the fire while Alice gazed tenderly into his face. She knew that it was the sullenness of remorse which lowered upon the fine brow and drooped in the dark fringes of those usually sunny eyes. She longed to lighten his burden of guilt, and to make him feel the greatness of her affection. The little hand pressed harder upon his shoulder, constraining him to look again into those pure and pitying eyes.

Mr. Crawford came in, shivering with the cold of the

first snow-storm. He cast a keen glance at his ward as he saw him sitting moodily in the corner; but hearing that he had been at the farm, he, as well as his wife, concluded that old recollections had something to do with his taciturnity.

Tea was served; and after that Alice beckoned her brother to a seat beside her, and the new book was produced.

"I have kept it unopened to share with you," she said, as she severed the first few pages with her silver paper-folder.

The work was one of absorbing interest, but they did not get along very well. Each was heedless of when the other turned a leaf, and both felt it a great relief when the elder couple left them to themselves.

The book fell from Parke's hand as they went out, and he sat gazing fixedly upon the carpet. Alice kissed him.

"Can you caress me, then, Alice?" he cried, turning towards her; "me, a perjured wretch?"

"You are my brother still — and ever will be —" was the grave reply, as the tears at last overflowed her eyes. "Oh, Parke, I know there must have been great temptation. Tell me of something that will take away from the sinfulness of your act — not that I cannot and have not forgiven you — but that I may think of you with some consolation."

He received her hand and grasped it tightly in his own, as he went on to tell of the plot that had been laid for him, and how, carried away by sudden excitement, he had weakly and miserably fell a victim to it.

"Oh, my poor brother! their crime is greater than yours! but if you had only resisted—if you had burst from them in scorn as you should have done! Yet do not be utterly discouraged. God will forgive even this, and he asks only repentance. Let us put our trust in him."

"But I have lost all trust in myself," groaned the young man. "My self-respect, my confidence is gone!"

"Oh, no! oh, no! there is time and chance to redeem yourself. Your truest friends, save me, know nothing of this, why should they ever? God and your mother wait only your asking to forgive. Let us pray for it now, and then you can renew your promise."

"I dare not renew it, I have no more trust in myself. But pray for me, my sister; never neglect to do that; however low I may fall beneath your love."

CHAPTER VI.

PARKE was banished from Mr. Crawford's house.

For several weeks after his first excess, he had, by his sister's aid, concealed his conduct from the family; although he had at three different times been out the most of the night. In that time he had lost two thousand dollars at the gaming-table. When his guardian discovered these facts, his indignation was overwhelming. Strict in the performance of his own duty, he was the sternest judge of the faults of others. Of that calm, strong, unsusceptible temperament which is but little exposed to temptation, he could tolerate in others of more yielding minds no dereliction from the right. Had Parke been his own son he would have turned him out with still less regret. He considered it inexcusable for any young man to form bad habits — but that a person educated as Parke had been by a christian mother, and surrounded by every inducement to virtue and goodnes, that *he* should pursue such a course was equally as-

astonishing and awful — and that, with the first summer's flowers withering over her grave, in the very days of mourning, that he should be faithless to the assurances required by that dying mother, was to him a proof of the utter depravity of human nature. A person so lost to all remains of goodness should not be allowed to approach the family-circle gathered around any hearth, and with the full weight of his anger he crushed the young man in the presence of his sister and Mrs. Crawford. His words fell scorching upon the bare soul of poor Parke, and the glances of his eyes seemed to wound like blades of steel. Pale and quivering, the brother cast a look upon his sister, who stood weeping in the room; and strode without a word into the hall. Heedless of her guardian's reproof, she followed him, laying her hand upon his arm just as he opened the outer door.

"Parke!" she said, in a stifled voice, "for my sake, for heaven's sake, do nothing rash. Remember that *I* am the same as ever."

He wrung her hand and darted away. She returned to the parlor. Her heart was bursting to plead her brother's case; but Mr. Crawford was tramping through the room with a tread as if his heel was ground down every time into the brain of a wild young man; and his wife, although she took the weeping girl to her bosom, did not dare to let her open her lips in remonstrance.

Several days went slowly by. Alice pined in silent sorrow; for as her guardian gave no signs of relenting, she could not approach him upon the subject which lay nearest her thoughts. Redoubled kindness was shown to her, but she could hardly receive it when the part that should have been another's was refused him. Her usually busy fingers laid idly in her lap, the piano was closed, and she sat hour after hour at the window, her sad eyes following the people who passed by, in the hope of obtaining a glimpse of the banished one. But he never walked on that street. Pride and resentment both kept him from the most distant advances, even to an interview with his sister.

One afternoon there was a ring at the door-bell. Every time that it rang of late, Alice's heart had given a great bound at the thought that perhaps it was Parke who had returned, and several times she had opened the door herself. She hastened to do so now; and was greeted by Alfred Hyde. He gave her a note from her brother; and she invited him in.

"There may be an answer expected," he replied, and accepted her invitation.

She introduced him to Mrs. Crawford, and withdrew to a distant part of the room to read her letter. Her hands were all in a tremble as she broke the seal. As she read the hastily-penned page, the tears gathered on her eyelashes and rolled down her cheeks. She was unconscious of the earnest glances fixed from time to time upon her face by the old acquaintance who sat conversing cosily with the elder lady. The note ran thus:—

"My guardian did not know what he was about when

he sent me away, Alice. It may be that I would have been ruined anyhow, but now I certainly shall. Why should I be good, when I am thrust out as fit only to associate with the worst?—denied even a word of encouragement from you. The moment it became known that I was discarded by my guardian, the whole pack of my former companions were after me like cats after a mouse. They know that I am rich, and that in a week or two I will be of age, and they do not want any better fellow than Parke Madison to pay for their champagne, or for a partner in a little game, I am such a confounded fool as to gratify them at my own expense. I have taken rooms at ——— Hotel, and if I am frowned upon by nice people like Mr. Crawford, I am flattered and praised by a very dashing set of fellows, I assure you, who can overlook a small indiscretion, drink my wine, pocket my money, and eat my suppers with as good a grace as if I were better than the Bishop. Do you wonder that I seek to consol myself for the loss of my good name? A young man who has been publicly disgraced, and the door shut upon him by his *best friends,* must needs go where the door stands wide open, and a hundred smiling lips are calling upon him to enter and make himself at home. So I have been drunk three days out of the eight since I left you—I have lost another thousand at billiards, and paid for two champagne suppers."

"Alice! Alice! can you forgive me this reckless talk? Yet it is all too true. When I make a giant-effort to overcome all, and make a better man of myself, despite of discouragement and bad reputation, the solitude to which I flee for strength is peopled with such frightful shapes of doubt, remorse, shame, and self-distrust, that I rush back to temptation to get away from them. If I did not love wine — if one taste of it did not awake such a fatal thirst, I might save myself from these lesser evils. But with this innate passion, what am I to do? There is no safeguard, for I have already destroyed the most powerful; and I am in despair. Oh, my sister, I am ready to cry out as my mother once did — 'would that every drop of alcohol in all its Protean shapes was banished from the land.' My noble father fell its victim — I shall be a still more hopeless one. Fatal inheritance! my father has bequeathed me his inclination for the bowl, and I am coming into full possession of the dread bequest. You see I am trying to work my way into your compassion, by laying a part of my faults upon the shoulders of others. You, too, may have cast me off by this time. If not, send me some little word by Alfred. Do not be suspicious of him; he is sorry for me, and trying to serve me. Tell me where I can see you, and talk with you a little while. PARKE."

Alice took a small sheet of paper from between the leaves of a book, and wrote with her pencil —

"DEAREST PARKE: — You must not, and shall not, stay any longer where you now are. I shall talk with Mr. Crawford to-night, and if he sends you permission to come home to-morrow, you must come — because I ask it of you. If he will not consent, or if you will not accept, then I shall have to follow you to your rooms, for *I am determined* that I will not give you up. Of course you will not compel me to leave a safe home to track your wandering steps; so only return with good resolutions, and we will all be happy again."

Folding it and giving it to Mr. Clyde, she bethought herself of how her absorbing care for her brother had caused her to neglect to pay him the attention he was entitled to, and which she felt more disposed to give since she read what Parke said of him.

Alfred was now three-and-twenty, and appeared two years older. He was elaborately dressed in the height of the fashion, and still not showily; a rich diamond stud, glowing in the centre of the dainty frill of his shirt-bosom, was the only article of jewelry he wore. He had lost a little of his former reserve, and talked agreeably, though something in the deep glance of his eye, and the low fullness of his tones, seemed always hiding itself from the observer.

He informed Alice that his uncle, Mr. Benjamin Clyde, was dead; that he had forgiven him the little quarrel that had parted them the year before, and had died, regarding him as a son. Of course his listener understood that he was heir to the large fortune which the old gentleman had accumulated. His splendid dress and haughty bearing were becoming to him; and Alice would have felt a friendly joy that he was at last in circumstances to do justice to his tastes, had not the old suspicion of his sincerity returned to her with every sentence which he uttered.

The very pure and good seem often to be possessed of a

sympathy which repels them from falsehood, however speciously disguised. And the more she looked at that dark face, with its restless lip and cautious, searching eyes, the more distrustful she felt towards it.

He remained an hour, and went away with an invitation from Mrs. Crawford to visit them again. She had heard so much of him from her young friends that she knew his station and claims to their acquaintance; and as she admired him very much, she at once concluded that it would be pleasant to have him for a visitor through the winter evenings. She was sure that society would enliven her sweet child's drooping spirits. Pretty little Mrs. Crawford! she had scarcely a fault; but she had one! She aspired to be a match-maker. Having had no children to occupy her leisure, she had taken great notice of the young people belonging to other folks. As many as half-a-dozen excellent marriages she was sure had been brought about through her important management. Though Alice was but just seventeen, and so child-like, and so saint-like in her innocent ways and looks, that she should have been regarded only as a white rose-bud growing upon consecrated ground, too holy and too fragile to be gathered and worn; yet her new mother, looking smilingly at her, as she sat pensively by the table, had already arranged how charming it would be to fasten the bridal veil upon that beautiful head.

She had not failed to observe the earnest looks which Alfred could not refrain from fixing upon the young girl after an absence of more than a year. That a young gentleman so rich, elegant, refined, and of good family, should at once fall in love with her pretty Alice, was delightful. Her mind ran gaily on to the future, and she cast glances up and down her parlors to imagine how they would appear, illuminated for a wedding-party. Yes! they should stand there, just between those two large windows, to be married! and there should be no lack of camelias for adornment! and it might be that Mr. Crawford could be coaxed into the purchase of new curtains! All this while the unconscious performer of the chief part in this drama of the future sat with her head upon her hands, thinking of how she should most successfully approach her guardian on the sore subject of recalling Parke. She replied at random to her companion's praises of their visitor, and was oblivious to all the little wiles that were used to discover the state of her feelings towards him.

"I think Mr. Clyde was a little agitated when he first came in. What expressive eyes he has! at least, when he is looking at my little daughter!"

Alice blushed; but it was with emotion at hearing Mr. Crawford in the hall. Her heart first gave a bound, and then sank down — down! for his sternness was terrible to her, who had been reared in an atmosphere of gentleness; and if he should utterly refuse to listen to her plea! Then —— ah! she was resolved what she would do then; and her cheeks became so crimson at the thought, that her guardian, entering, patted them cheerfully, and said that he was rejoiced to see her looking so much better.

Tea was over. Mr. Crawford was established for the evening in the cushions of his huge chair. Alice had arranged the lamp, brought him his slippers, paper, and spectacles, and before he made use of the two latter, she had perched upon his knee. She laid her little white hands upon his shoulders. He looked fondly at her, thinking this young thing, with her shining curls and fairy form, the fairest child he had ever seen; but when the dew began to gather on her eye-lids, and her lips to tremble with what she wanted to say, he pushed her farther back upon his knee, and his countenance settled down into unpromising severity.

Alice was frightened, but love made her bold.

"Father!" (it was not hard for her to call Mr. Crawford father, as she had but slight remembrance of her own) "I have had a letter from Parke to-day, and I want you to read it."

She held it out, but he would not take it.

"Does not Miss Madison remember that I have *forbidden* any intercession for that person?"

Miss Madison! when had he ever called her by so dignified a title before? But she could bear his cold tones as well as her poor brother; and if other people were to be harsh and unrelenting, why should she not take part against them? She felt some of the real old family blood, which she inherited from her mother's father, thrilling her breast. A firmness of will which distinguished them, and which it would have been well for Parke to possess, she now felt for the first time springing into energy, called to life by the dreadful anxiety she felt for one dearer to her than her own life.

"You had better read the letter," she said, getting off of the extreme edge of his lap to which he had pushed her, and standing before him.

"Why so?" he inquired a little curiously; for, despite of his gravity, he could scarcely forbear a surprised smile at her commanding attitude and the firm tones of her voice.

"Because you *ought* to read it, father. Certainly it can do you no harm to read it; and, if you refuse, you may sometime regret it. 'Blessed are the merciful, for they shall obtain mercy.'"

"And you think I may sometime need it — is that it?" he asked, smiling at what might seem like disrespect from her.

"I don't think anything about it! I only wish to know whether you will read this yourself; for if you will not, then I shall read it to you."

He looked a little angry at this, and made no reply, except to call her a "saucy little girl."

So after waiting a moment she began. It would have been weak for him to have got up and ran out of the room, and as she read in a clear, distinct voice, he was obliged to hear every word. His brow darkened ominously at the beginning of the epistle; and where it came to the reckless confession of his new sins, he stamped his foot as if he would command silence. The young girl continued to the end, with a slight falter towards the last; then turning her bright, dark eyes upon her guardian, she seemed to be asking him with that steady look, if it would not have been better to have shown more mercy.

The look of a righteous judge had given way upon his face to a more troubled expression, as his eye fell before hers, and he repeated to himself her silent question. It had never occurred to him before that his casting his ward back upon his own inclinations was making him worse, for he had flattered himself that there was no worse to such conduct. Now he did not like the responsibility of four days of intoxication, two suppers, and a large gambling debt, thrust thus unceremoniously upon *him*.

"Are you going to send for my brother to come back home?" asked Alice, watching the changes of his brow.

Mr. Crawford was nervous at the thought of his having been too hasty with the son of his dead friends; and when he was nervous he was always irritable. If he answered yes, after hearing the letter, it would be a tacit acknowledgment that he had done wrong; so he threw himself upon his temper, and thundered — "No!"

"Very well! then," said Alice, folding up the letter, "I consider it my duty to go to him."

Both her friends regarded her with amazement, as she stood before them, her slight figure erect, her lips pressed together, her cheeks burning, and only the tears softening her eyes to show that she was their timid young ward.

"Go to him!" cried her guardian, "where? — to ——— Hotel?"

"Yes, Sir! if you drive me to that. You may think it your duty to be very severe with poor Parke, — I *know* it is mine to be faithful to him to the last: oh, Sir," here her voice trembled, "you heard my mother's last words, that we should 'love one another' — 'be faithful' — and now that he is left to the mercy of his own strong inclinations, and beset by temptation on every side, is *now* the time for him to be without his friends — his sister! What would friends be worth if they deserted us in our fall? Oh, my mother," she continued with upraised eyes, "*you* would not thus easily have cast off your child."

The tears were now running down her cheeks, but she walked with a proud step towards the hall.

"Mr. Crawford," she said, turning at the door, "can I have John to protect me through the street, or must I go alone?"

"Are you going to-night, Alice," asked Mrs. Crawford, in terror.

"Yes, madam! I *must*, — I must be where my poor brother is, to watch over him, and, if possible, save him. Who can tell what a night may bring forth of danger to him."

"You will do no such wild, foolish thing," said her guardian, rising. "Have you fogotten, Alice, that I have the control of your actions?"

"It is the last command of my mother which controls me now," she answered repsectfully. "It is stronger than the law — stronger than any love for you," and she passed out into the hall.

Mr. Crawford followed her. She was already tying on her hood, when he laid his hand on her arm.

"You are a stubborn girl, Alice; but if you will have it your own way, you must take the consequences. Take off that rigging and come back to the fire."

"You will send for Parke, then?" she asked eagerly.

"Of course, if I must to keep you out of such mad mischief."

"But to-night? to-night? shall John go right away."

"As well now as any time," he replied; and she flew to write a note for the messenger.

In a moment it was ready, and John was dispatched.

"Its a mighty blustering night to be running about in, but I would go to the bottom of the city to serve you, and to search out Mr. Parke," he said, as he went out the door, hurried by Alice. This was their own old household servant, and who had been almost half as anxious as his young mistress since Parke was sent away.

"Oh, Mr. Crawford, my father, you are so good — so good," said Alice, coming back to her old place on his knee. "And now I know you will receive poor Parke kindly — he will be so distressed and ashamed — "

"Deserves to be," was the gruff response.

"I know it — he ought to be — oh dear, I don't know what punishment he doesn't deserve except to be turned away from *home* — his only place of refuge, you see! — But still, you will speak to him — try to forgive him, dear, dear father."

" Don't tease me any more to-night, or I shall be sorry I didn't let you go where you wanted to," he said; but it was with a smile, and something like a sparkle of water in his eyes.

So the young girl was content, and kissing him, she went to the window to listen. The roar of the storm without prevented her hearing much; but after three quarters of an hour passed in suspense, the stamping of feet was heard in the hall. Alice glanced towards her friends, and then flew out to see if any one had returned with John. There was Parke taking off his cloak, and lingering as if loth to enter.

The same instant she lay sobbing in his arms. His tears fell hot and large upon her face.

" I should not have come had not *you* written the note," he whispered.

" Oh, hush, Parke, do not say anything of the kind. We will love you as well as you deserve."

Radiant with tears and smiles she led the way in. Her tact and her emotion covered half the embarrassment of the meeting. If Parke and his guardian did not shake hands very cordially, she embraced both with such affection that they might have mistaken her joy for each others. Mrs. Crawford kissed his cheek and appeared really glad; and then when all set down, and an awkward silence threatened the group, Alice opened the piano and played such delightful melodies, and sung with such touching sweetness, that all hearts were united, at least in love and admiration of the singer.

When she came back, they talked about the storm, wondered if there were any vessels endangered along the coast, spoke of a new play which they all wished to attend the next evening, and so gradually recovered their ease of feeling.

When the others had retired to their room, Alice rested her head upon her brother's bosom, and they sat silent for a long time; at length he spoke.

"I did not think a short time ago that I should ever be as happy again as I am at this moment."

"There is a life-time of such happiness for you, if you will only take it," she replied. "But there is no true enjoyment except in doing right, our mother always taught us."

"And I feel it as you cannot feel it, who know not the misery of shame and remorse. Oh, Alice, when I wake in the morning, sick in body and soul, disgusted with the feverish excitement of the preceding night, — when memories of rude revels, wild intoxication, of gas-light glaring upon a chaos of wine and broken goblets, cigar-smoke, and billiard-tables, of profane jests and reckless merriment, stand out deformed in the pure beams of the morning sun, — I loathe myself and wish I had never been born. The thought of the hours we spent together at the farm steal upon me like glimpses of a lost heaven. Alice, I wish I was like you. You are too good for earth. But *you* are exposed to no temptation — allurements do not rise up before you every step that you take out of doors. The saloon and the gaming-table do not expect you nor invite you."

"If they did it would not lessen my abhorrence for them. The scriptures say, that we are tempted with no temptation greater than we are able to bear."

"They say, too, what is truth of me; I find there a law that when I would do good, evil is present with me. For I delight in the law of God after the inward man. But I see another law in my members warring against the law of my mind, and bringing me into captivity to the law of sin which is in my members. 'O, wretched man that I am! who shall deliver me from the body of this death?'"

"Jesus Christ will become your deliverer, even from such straits as these. Dear brother, to-morrow, let us go to our mother's grave. It is long since we have been there; and even the snow that now covers it is precious to me."

"It is *not* long since I was there," said Parke, in a sad voice. "Last night, I lay upon that grave more than half the night, groaning in bitterness of spirit."

"Is it possible? Why! my poor, poor brother, turned from your home, did you take refuge in that solemn spot from your unhappiness."

She shuddered and wept; then both knelt and prayed. Their sleep that night was sweet; and the next day a kind of chastened happiness sat upon each face. The day was calm and bright, and they rode out in the carriage to the cemetery. In the evening Alfred Clyde called early, and went with the rest of the family to the theatre to see the "Lady of Lyons."

At every impassioned word from Claude Melnotte, Clyde would turn his dark eyes to the face of Alice. And when he described the palace-home, with its beautiful environs, to the delighted Pauline, Alfred turned and whispered in the ear of Alice —

"Such a home shall be yours if you will be true to the promise which the little girl made to the school-boy."

The maiden shrank back, with a slight blush, saying gravely — "It was not I that promised, Mr. Clyde."

The young man laughed, and affected to have spoken only for the purpose of reminding her of their old frolics.

After this he became an almost daily visitor at the Crawfords. He was quite devoted enough to Alice to justify the little lady of the house in dreaming of a wedding at some future day; but the heroine herself preserved a most perplexing indifference, and seemed more annoyed than flattered by those distant allusions to the subject which the match-maker ventured to indulge in. The house was divided in its opinions of Alfred Clyde. Parke still cherished an enthusiastic friendship for him; and Mrs. Crawford admired him more than any young gentleman who called at the house. Her husband, on the contrary, had taken a decided aversion to him — not for any reason that he could make satisfactory to others — but the first evening which Alfred spent at the house he had taken a dislike to something haughty and repelling in his manner. He had met him frequently in Parke's company in former years, but not to form any acquaintance with him. His prejudices did not prevent him from treating their visitor with politeness, or lead to his objecting to Parke's intimacy with him. Alice, although she said nothing about it, and always received him with friendliness, still cherished a distrust of him. She never heard of anything against his character or habits; he had the respect of a highly honorable circle, and was generally admired for the ease of his address, the tasteful splendor of his attire, and his good judgment upon men and things. But she could not feel attracted towards him by that powerful sympathy that draws together kindred natures. It was in vain that she tried to conceal from herself that he loved her. The hints of her adopted mother, the raillery of Parke, and the manner of Alfred, all made it impossible for her to shut her eyes upon the unwelcome fact. She appeared to do so, and always received any warm avowal from him as if it meant no more than the old play of brother and sister. She sang and played for him when he asked, was social and kind; but she could take but little pleasure in his society, because she wished to give him no encouragement.

"It is absurd for him to think of a child like me," she thought. "He will soon forget it when he meets ladies older and more beautiful, and who take more care to please him."

He met such ladies every day, saving the beauty, for few could be more fair than Alice, although there was no stateliness or magnificence in her looks. Slight and elegant, pure and etherial, graceful as a spirit of air, she needed to make no effort in order to please. Albert met agreeable ladies; but his dreams were all of that youthful figure attired in sorrowful black — that sweet, bright smile, and those beaming hazel eyes, and the voice both sweet and low. Ardently as he had loved her for years, he dreamed not of the volcano of passion in his breast until he saw her the object of admiration to another.

St. Ormond, the brilliant, extravagant, and heartless man of pleasure, who induced young Madison to break his vow made to a dying mother, and gloried in the triumph, called one evening to see Parke, upon some affair of little importance. The object of his visit was to get a glimpse of the beautiful sister of whom he had heard. Parke had himself boasted of her angelic qualities once over his wine, when the subject of beauty was introduced. St. Ormond, for a man who lived as fast, preserved a very good appearance before the world, being obliged to use great caution to keep the good opinion of a maiden-aunt, from whom he expected a fortune.

Presuming that his true character was not known in the family, he ventured to call on that evening to tell the young gentleman something about a picture or an opera. Parke was anything but pleased to see him there, saying suave things to Mrs. Crawford, and fixing burning glances upon his sister. Alfred was also present, and his quick jealousy detected the intense admiration which the young girl excited. When she looked up with her innocent, bright smile, and appeared pleased and interested in something the stranger was saying about music, he was ready to bite his lip through with chagrin. St. Ormond, too, as Parke had previously done, remarked the likeness of Alice's mouth to his Hebe's. He remembered vowing to kiss the first woman whom he should meet with such a mouth; but now he felt the vanity and emptiness of the boastful assertion. He could no more have approached that bright young girl with such a thought, than as though the air that seemed to encircle her with a different atmosphere was alive with living lightnings. He soon arose to go, and bade her good evening with profound respect. His fellows would have had food for ridicule if they had guessed his thoughts for the rest of that night. Visions of becoming a reformed and useful member of society — of abandoning brandy, cigars, and billiards, for tea, books, and a game of chess at home — of a quiet and elegant home, with a wife — a wife, lovely, young, pure as the morning, flitted through his brain. For twenty-four hours he was thoroughly disgusted with his manner of living, and serious resolutions of becoming a better man agitated his reflections, as he denied himself to callers, and sat musing in his arm-chair, lost in his dreams and his dressing-gown.

For several days he went about with a dejected air. The sight of so much innocence and goodness had reminded him of the immense gulf lying between him and it. Conscience was awake, which for so long a period had lain dormant through the winter of guilt, and now stung the bosom where it lay. Ghosts of old sins — a long array of broken hearts, broken oaths, broken promises to pay, and broken goblets gathered around him and tormented him with their unwelcome company.

Unable longer to resist the desire to gaze upon that spiritual face again, and see if the charmer who had conjured up this burden of feeling could not remove the load, he made another call at Mr. Crawford's. But Parke, indignant at his former visit, and suspecting its object, had informed Alice that St. Ormond was the person who had taken so much trouble to get him intoxicated, the particulars of the bet having afterwards become known to him. If she could have cherished a sentiment of hate it would have been bestowed upon the cruel and heartless destroyer of their happiness. Parke was still occasionally drawn away into dissipation, and when she thought of this, and what imminent peril their safety was in, her heart struggled with bitter feelings. It was some small return for the anguish he had caused, when St. Ormond retired in haste and confusion from his second call. Alice had not deigned him a word or look — the ineffable scorn she felt for him curled her lip and flashed in her averted eye. Mrs. Crawford had merely bowed, and Parke was the only one who had addressed him. He found it convenient to speedily withdraw; and as he went down the steps, with burning cheeks and contracted brow, the late desire for amendment was thrust from his breast. No such vision of purity ever again returned.

His fleeting passion, however, had alarmed Alfred Clyde with the fear that some more acceptable devotion might be offered at the feet of Alice before he himself had besought her favor. He resolved to seek the first opportunity of declaring his preference. He had but faint hopes of her returning his love — he had never been given cause to think that she loved him. But he had not the slightest idea of living without her. He had settled it with himself that no other woman would ever be so pleasing to him as Alice Madison, and he was determined to win her. At present he thought only of persuasion and perseverance. He looked upon her as his future wife with as much complacency as though she had already promised him as much.

One day they were out riding together. It was a clear, cold afternoon in January. The earth was covered with frozen snow, beat down into a smooth track along the road. The fences had a comfortable, muffled look, and the trees glittered with icy pendants. The air was still and keen — it was just such weather as Alice delighted in — she enjoyed her ride very much; Alfred had not seen her in such good spirits since their acquaintance was renewed.

As they sped rapidly along towards the city, he resolved to take advantage of her happy frame of mind to induce a favorable reception of what he wished to say.

"The day is so beautiful — the earth looks so fair, the

very sense of living is so pleasant, and you, dear Alice, seem so glad and bright, that I am full of happiness,—so happy, that I can no longer repress the hopes that are rising in my heart. I wish to be always as happy as I am now, and I shall be if you will only say that you will always be my companion. Dear Alice, promise it now! think how long a time I have waited for you—ever since you were a little girl."

His tones were musical and tender; she cast a brief look into his face to read—it was involuntary—whether the usual concealed something was there. It was glowing with feeling—the dark eyes were fixed upon her with an intensity that made her tremble.

She was embarrassed, of course, and her timid heart fluttered as if caught in silken meshes; but they were whirling swiftly along, and she turned her attention to the flitting trees and fences, while she replied—

"I cannot promise you, Alfred. I am too young to make any such promises, and if I were not, I do not think—that I———"

"Could give yourself to me? Do not say that, Alice, after I have passed years in dreaming of *our* future—after all my hopes and wishes have become unchangeably fixed upon you. You know all about me—my character, my tastes, and disposition. If these are not displeasing to you, why can you not say *now* whether you will be my wife or not?"

"I can say now. I cannot be your wife, because I am sure that I do not love you. Besides, I do not think that I 'know all about you.' I have always felt as if we were not perfectly acquainted — as if each had traits of character which the other did not understand — and with such feelings, we could not be very happy."

"I think that I appreciate all the traits of your character. Your loveliness and goodness have made too deep an impression not to have been understood. That you *can*, if you will, love truly and well, I know by your temperament, and by your noble devotion to Parke. Only love me half as much as you do him, and for the present I will be content."

"I shall never love you, I am certain," replied the young girl with a sigh, but still earnestly.

She felt that she should not, and she did not wish to deceive him by kindness now at the expense of future disappointment.

"But I shall wish to have you for my friend and Parke's," she continued gently.

"Friend! you know that I cannot be anything so lukewarm — I must be more or less! oh, Alice, the sunshine has gone out of the sky, the fairness has fled from the earth!"

They were now in the city and nearly home. After a pause he said again, in less disconsolate tones —

"Do not think that I have given you up, Alice. I cannot relinquish the hope of five years so easily. I shall wait and wait, and love and aspire, until you are married or dead, or gone to the Hebrides — or until you consent to be my wife."

They were at the door. He pressed her little hand tightly as he lifted her from the carriage; and she went in, wondering why love was not mutual always, and thinking what a pity and sorrow it was for affection to be unrequited. Still she could not school her heart to love where it was not inclined. Love has dreams and ideals of his own which he will pursue, nor turn aside to worship at other shrines, though the gods upon the altars beckon with imploring hands.

True to his purpose, Alfred made no difference in his habit of seeking the society of Alice. He came and went every day, and it was generally believed among their acquaintance, that when she laid aside her mourning they would be married. Mrs. Crawford finally asked her about it, and said she hoped it was so. Alice said she hoped not, and that it never would be; but kept to herself that she had refused the young gentleman. Parke knew it, however, for Alfred told him; and he was very much grieved and surprised, and ventured to remonstrate a little with his sister. The strong influence which the subtler mind of Clyde first gained over his companion seemed to increase instead of decline.

Parke thought that to have Alice married to Alfred, and keeping house, and he, living with them, in a nice, quiet kind of a way, was a "consummation most devoutly to be wished." And *why* she was not willing to make the rest happy in so easy a way, was what he could not understand!

CHAPTER VII.

The sunshine of a spring morning gilded the little parlor of Mrs. Van Duyn. The light curtains were drawn back, letting in a full sweep of fragrance through the windows, where the May roses were peeping curiously in. The sunshine and fragrance seemed to hover most around the form of a fair girl who was giving a child of twelve a lesson in German. A guitar in the corner was almost the only article of luxury in the room. A neat chintz-covered lounge, a little sewing-chair; a round table, on which was a boquet of flowers, a few books, a beautiful porcelain basket, and a piece of muslin embroidery which was in progress; an ottoman or two, likewise covered with chintz, constituted the principle furniture. On the mantel were some old-fashioned and expensive ornaments, which seemed to have been brought from the Father-land; and a painting in oil, of a lovely German scene, hung upon the wall.

Mrs. Van Duyn was a widow of middle age, and had three or four children. Her father had come to America when she was a baby. He had been a man of wealth and education among the middle-classes of Germany; and when he settled near New York he had a competence. But he had, too, a large family. The boys were sent to school and received thorough educations; the girls were also well instructed and accomplished in embroidery, singing, music, French, and German. This daughter married a prosperous young emigrant from her own country, and received as a marriage portion only the pictures and ornaments mentioned above, and a tolerable set-out of clothes and furniture. She was a happy, blooming, intelligent woman, lady-like and accomplished; and besides being a fair wife, she was the beloved mother of several children — when her happiness was suddenly cut short by the death of her husband. One of the children, a sweet little girl, died soon after; and for a long time the widow strove with a great sorrow. But the voices of her little flock called her back to do her duty to them. With noble resignation she put aside the outward expressions of mourning, and turned to the task of bringing up a family of children alone, and in comparative poverty. For the strong hand that had brought plenty and comfort was mouldering in dust; and although there was their pretty cottage-home and little lot of ground a few miles from the city, and money in the bank, yet the income from all was insufficient. The cottage made a charming home; the brothers one or two of them came forward with cheerfully-offered assistance; so that poverty never did really pass Mrs. Van Duyn's threshold. It had stood there some hard winters and peeped in, but some kind relative would step up and drive it away. The eldest of her children was a girl, Lucy, the one now grown into a maiden of eighteen, who sat by the window giving a lesson to her younger sister. She was a lovely and spirited-looking girl. Her face would not have been so charming, but for its expression of intellect and refinement. She had the brown eye peculiar to a class of Germans — large, soft, and expressive; a noble forehead, a profusion of dark hair, neatly arranged, and a mouth that would have been too large for beauty, were it not so perfectly lovable, frank, and sweet, and adorned with such an enviable set of teeth. The smooth German accents fell from her lips with delicious richness, and the sympathizing smile with which she encouraged her scholar to attempt them was doubtless a greater aid than some teachers may imagine.

Katy, the youngest, was peeping in to see if sister Lucy could not come and do up her sun-bonnet, for she wanted to run down to the meadow below the garden and look at the tiny fishes in the water, and mother would not let her go out in the sun without her bonnet. It may be that the whole family were a little too careful of the fair complexion of little Katy, so becoming to her blue eyes and golden hair. Lucy promised to attend to the matter within five minutes; and was proceeding with her lesson, when the quick clatter of hoofs down the road caused her to look out the rose-laden window. She had only time to note a fiery steed and a youthful rider looking bravely in the spring sunshine;

when the spirited animal, frightened at the sudden apparition of little Willy Van Duyn swinging on the gate, with a flaming soldier-cap on his head, and a piece of Katy's red dress for a banner, sprang with a bound so unexpected, that the careless rider, wondering who was concealed by the rose-curtains of that pretty cottage, came with terrible force to the ground. The horse galloped madly away; and little Willy, throwing down his mischievous flag, rushed into the house.

"The man is killed, I'm certain, sister Lucy, for he lies so still!"

She had raised from her chair with a cry when she saw him fall; now trembling with alarm, she called her mother, and they ran out to see what was to be done. Surely, the unfortunate rider did appear to be killed. His head had struck a large stone by the side of the road, and he lay dead or insensible were he fell.

Lucy burst into tears, not knowing what else to do. Her mother, more composed, but pale, tried to decide upon something that might avail him.

"He may be only senseless," she said; "but he will die, lying there. You and I can never get him into the house in the world; and there is'nt a man, that I know of, within a mile. Willy! Willy! run to the nearest house and ask them to come; or if you meet any one on the way, send them."

Willy ran off, and the mother continued—

"It is dreadful to see his head lying there bleeding in

the dust. Sit down upon the stone, Lucy, and lift it upon your lap, while I get a bandage and the camphor." Lucy sat down with a slight shudder, and raised the poor head tenderly. The pale and youthful features were stained with blood, and the rich masses of light-brown hair were clogged with the same.

"So young — so gay — so unprepared! Oh, I wonder who he is, and where his friends are. I wonder if there will never be any help — he will die."

Little help there was for some time, except that Mrs. Van Duyn bathed his face with camphor and washed the blood from his wounds. After a while, two gentlemen came along in a buggy, and stopping, carried him in and laid him upon the bed in a little room off the parlor. They were going on into the city, and after doing what they could, promised to send a physician immediately. As they were strangers, the lady gave them the name of an eminent Doctor, and they drove rapidly away. In about an hour, during which time the young man had uttered two or three feeble moans, the physician arrived.

"Is it possible!" he muttered; "why this is young Madison! I know him well — distinguished family — a little wild, but very superior young person, very — pity if he should die — break his sister's heart — do'nt think he will though. No — no," as he proceeded with his examination — "no danger of that — a fracture, but slight — slight."

Here the young gentleman began to recover a consciousness of his calamity, and to groan so as to drive the color from Lucy's face. But she was obliged to assist the Doctor, and did it so firmly and well that he praised her fortitude.

"Young lady of some nerve — good — most ladies have too many nerves but no control. How's this? arm broken — upon my word — *humerus* — that's what he's groaning about. We must attend to this, Madam, really."

It was a happy thing for Parke Madison, since he fell from his horse, that it should be before the door of Mrs. Van Duyn's cottage; that is, unless he could have been thrown especially before his own door. Mrs. Van Duyn was the best of nurses, and so convinced the physician of her skill, that he was content to leave his patient with her, while he rode back to the city to attend to other engagements.

"Be delirious — have fever for two or three days — be kept quiet — be here some time, I'm afraid, but fine fellow, and will know how to repay kindness. Upon my word! couldn't have dropped into a better bed!"

He glanced admiringly around the neat apartment — at the refined-looking widow and her young daughter — and out into the little parlor at the Father-Land painting.

"Shall bring Miss Madison with me this afternoon. She won't be kept from her brother, I know — lovely girl!"

Taking his hat and gold-headed cane, Doctor D——— returned to his carriage. In the meantime Parke's horse had galloped on until tired, and then drew up before a gate several miles distant, to which he was tied by the proprietor of the grounds until something should be heard from his owner.

About four o'clock in the afternoon Doctor D——— returned, and with him came Alice. The first she had heard of the accident was from him. He was Mr. Crawford's family-physician, and knew the young lady well. He told her that he should not permit the rest of Parke's friends to see him at present, but she might go along with him, if she would be a good girl, and not make any confusion. Assuring the anxious Mrs. Crawford that there was no danger of anything but a run of fever, and that her boy was in the best of hands, he took Alice into his carriage, and they soon arrived at the cottage. Despite of his assurances, she had her secret fears, and her strength so completely left her, that he was obliged to carry her into the house like a baby.

"This little girl is not as brave as you, Miss Van Duyn," said the good doctor, as he sat his burden down on the lounge.

"No wonder you are alarmed," said Lucy, gently untying the stranger's bonnet. "But there is nothing to fear —I am sure we may all have confidence in the assertion of Doctor D———." Here, having removed the bonnet, and seeing a beautiful, pale face, with a pair of trembling lips and beseeching eyes, with the impulse of her affectionate nature she kissed the agitated girl and said more kind words.

"Where is he?" was Alice's first inquiry.

"He is in this room. My mother is with him, and the doctor says we must be quiet. I am sure you will be stillness itself! Come, let me help you."

She passed her arm around Alice's waist and they went softly in. The latter could hardly repress a cry when she saw her brother so dreadfully white, his head bandaged up, and his arm splintered, lying with closed eyes upon the bed, seemingly nearly unconscious, except an occasional moan. Mrs. Van Duyn sat by the bed-side. Faint and trembling, Alice clung to her companion.

"My poor brother!" she whispered.

Lucy led her out to the dining-room, made her drink a glass of water and compose herself; then she gave her the particulars of the accident in the gentlest manner.

Parke was delirious for several days and his fever ran high. Alice remained with him constantly — the only sleep she took was upon the chintz sofa, in the adjoining parlor Mrs. Van Duyn nursed him as carefully as if he had not been a stranger, cast by accident upon her kindness.

At last he was slowly recovering. Never had an invalid so delightful a convalescence. Lucy and Alice had formed a friendship which was both natural and pleasing between two girls so nearly of an age, and of such excellent minds and accomplishments. Each considered the acquaintance of the other a new store-house of delight, and they regretted that the time must arrive for one to return to her own home, much as they rejoiced at the well-doing of their charge. When Parke got so that he could be moved to the sofa, and lie there nearly all day, listening to the conversation of the young girls, and plucking June roses to pieces with his attenuated fingers, scattering the bloomy showers over the carpet for Lucy to brush up, one might have thought that with an easy carriage and a few pillows he could get back to town. But neither he nor his sister had any inclination. They were enjoying themselves very much; and as Mrs. Van Duyn had given them a ready permission to stay as long as they liked, they were in no haste to depart.

Lucy touched the guitar with melodious fingers; and sang *almost* as sweetly as Alice. Her voice was of a different quality, and she could accompany her friend's singing with a deep, sweet alto. These two harmonious voices mingled with the tinkling of the guitar, and, heard in the long June twilight, seemed to Parke, whose senses were refined by sickness, a music more of heaven or of dreams than of earth.

He did not wish to get any better than he was — at least for two or three years. It was so pleasant to lie with his head in Alice's lap, her loving fingers thridding his curls, while Lucy sat near them busy with her embroidery, or flattered his poor appetite with strawberries, gathered by her own hands fresh from the garden, with real cream to make them more delicious. It may be that he sometimes fretted because it could not occur that Lucy should hold his head, while Alice gathered the berries; but was this so, he kept it to himself. There was such nobility in the expression of Miss Van Duyn, such dignity and grace in her gestures, that Parke reverenced while he admired. He wondered how such a regal flower could blossom in this cottage-home. But the child had only the same nobility as her mother, except that it now appeared in more youthful guise; perchance, too, the trials of the parent had strengthened and developed the attributes of her own and daughter's mind.

There was no longer any excuse for lingering in the country; and Mrs. Crawford was so impatient to get her children back again, that they were obliged to go.

The price paid for their board had made the stay of the brother and sister a pecuniary gain to the widow, and after the first discomfort of the illness was over, she had enjoyed their society very much. The young couple loved her for her motherly kindness as well as for her good sense and accomplishments. The children were desperately attached to Alice, and cried heartily when she went away. And Willy, whose red banner had caused such a serious accident, did not know who would any longer carve him ships to sail in the rain-barrel, or whistles to pierce the surrounding air, or puzzle-boxes which all his ingenuity could not open, but that when they did get open were sure to hold five-cent pieces. Thinking of these things, as he saw Parke helped into the carriage, he, too, was disconsolate, and lifted up his voice and wept.

However, these partings were not without hope. It was not a week before the Madisons were back to spend the day. That was a great day in the cottage history. All the children had presents, and were given a holiday from their lessons. Alice brought Mrs. Van Duyn a handsome black-silk dress pattern to persuade her to let Lucy go back with them and spend a week in the city.

Such a dinner the towns folks declared they never got at home! Coffee was made, because it was such a luxury with pure cream. The strawberries had vanished, but there was honey tempting to look upon as the crystal sweetness dripped from the delicate cells. The tender green-peas, the sweet-corn, and the chickens smothered in cream, were the better for being the earliest. After dinner they passed the afternoon out in the meadow, under the shadow of a huge oak, and by the border of the creek now dwindled to a brook that Willy could leap across. Here Parke contrived to make Katy fall into the water, and she had to be sent to the house for a dry frock. He atoned for the misfortune by completing her toilet when she returned with a string of corals, which he fastened about her pretty neck by their golden clasp. The long, bright hours rolled by; they stayed to tea; and a moonlight ride home, accompanied by Lucy, crowned the enjoyment of the day.

Lucy Van Duyn's week in the city was a happy one. It was not the season for gayety, but there were plenty of things to be seen and enjoyed. There was good music in the evening, and picture-galleries, and works of art for the day. She had seen and heard a great deal before; but in the enthusiastic company of her young companions, all was doubly appreciated.

Alfred Clyde took Alice into his own care, so that Parke could give his undivided attention to their guest.

Lucy, who had become acquainted with him at her own house, where he visited the invalid often, also suspected, with the rest of the world, that there was an engagement between him and her friend. His manner was decidedly that of an accepted lover, and Alice's demeanor was regarded as only timid. Lucy would have felt lonely when she returned home, had not the children been so crazy with joy to get her back, and her mother welcomed her so affectionately.

That she did have many lonely hours through the rest of the summer was true; for in a few weeks, the Crawfords went to Saratoga, then in the heighth of its glory, and took with them the Madisons and Mr. Clyde. The circle of her associates sprang back to its old dimensions, and though her own dear family were all there, how small it seemed, and how much brightness it had lost. She had a letter every week from Alice, with messages from the rest, and these were a great happiness.

Alfred Clyde would not have thought it consistent to permit Alice Madison to enter the splendid crowds at Saratoga, to be admired and coveted, unless he were present like her shadow, intimating to all others that his right to her favor was exclusive. She was too artless to think anything about this, and as she had rather have his attentions than those of strangers, she permitted him to linger by her side, without much care for the opinions of the throng, with whom she mingled but little, and that with no attempt at display. She still wore mourning for her ever-remembered mother, and would not and could not be made a belle of.

Parke, on the contrary, was a distinguished beaux; and Alfred would have been, if his devotion to one person would have permitted it. The young ladies were divided in their admiration of the pair of friends. Parke was the handsomest, and interesting from being something of an invalid; while Alfred had a Spanish look that was adorable.

One appeared consumptive, and the other had such eyes as ought to belong to a Spanish-bandit of the mountains who turns out to be a lord in disguise; so that both were perfectly fascinating. Their fortunes being nearly the same, there was still a balance of favor on account of the distinguished name of Madison which was set off by a report of the romantic southern origin of Clyde. Both dashed into the highest of the high-life of the Springs; kept their span of mettlesome horses each; and took the ladies to ride in their own elegant barouches. Both paid for exquisite serenades, and were lavish of fresh boquets. And when it became suspected how much they both expended for champagne, Mr. Crawford became uneasy about going home, and Alice was feverish to depart. Mrs. Crawford was ready to acquiesce in the wishes of the rest: the young gentlemen would not remain without them, and all suddenly vanished from Saratoga, leaving a dreary blank in their brilliant place.

One day in the latter part of August, Lucy Van Duyn sat in the old seat by the front window. The roses were all gone now, but the green leaves still made a grateful curtain, wooing every passing breath of air. Her hands were folded idly in her lap — her eyes looked dreamily out upon the dusty road — her whole attitude expressed utter unconsciousness to surrounding objects. She had been sketching, and her drawing-materials lay upon the round-table. The sultriness of the weather justified any amount of indolence even in the industrious Lucy, but it did not account for the shade of melancholy upon that usually serene brow. Perhaps it was the shadow of the vines, leaves trailing to and fro across her face as if in love with its fairness, which gave it so pensive an expression. So wholly was she absorbed in reverie that she did not see the carriage which crossed directly her angle of vision until it drew up at the little gate. Pit-a-pat! went her heart against her white boddice, and a glow rich with emotion shot into her clear cheeks. Gay laughter out of door and light feet running up the walk so confused her that she could only rise to her feet and stand waiting the expected entrance.

"Dear Lucy! we are all home again, and the first thing Parke and I have done, is to come and see you!"

Alice Madison stood in the room, looking bright and beautiful despite of six miles of suffocating dust. Behind her came her brother; but as Lucy had first to give the sister half-a-dozen kisses, and be clasped a full minute in her arms, she had time to send the foolish heart down to its proper place, before she held out her hand to him. It was a brilliant face, though, that she turned to him; brilliant, even with the eyes hidden beneath their long fringes; and when the next moment, she lifted them, their soft fire kindled a great glow in the bosom of the young man.

"We left Saratoga two weeks before we expected, and as I had no time to write you about it, we thought we would surprise you by a visit, before you should hear of our return," said Alice, taking off her hat and gloves.

"A delightful surprise!" replied Lucy, carrying away the mantilla and bonnet to the bed-room, where her visitors followed to brush off a portion of the dust accumulated upon them.

"Dear mother," cried Lucy, as Mrs. Van Duyn came in from the arbor, where she had been sitting with her sewing; "we have some guests — can you guess?" She had hardly time to exercise her skill in guessing, and not being a Yankee, except by adoption, she might not have made out very well; but a pair of arms about her neck, and a sweet kiss, answered for her. She returned Alice's embrace with the most affectionate earnestness.

"I think your sojourn at the springs has done you good — you look well for such warm weather — better than when you went away," she remarked with a motherly look at the young girl.

"It must be because I am so happy to get home, then; I assure you it is a tiresome place at Saratoga. I would not go again, if I wished to escape with life. I was drowned — I was suffocated — I was starved — I was persecuted by day and night; no rest, no peace. Melted by day and kept awake all night by serenades. It was amusing though to see the people! Oh, Lucy, if you could only go to Saratoga, and feast your eyes upon its fantastic multitude!"

"It has not done you any harm to go there, I know," replied Lucy, gazing admiringly upon her friend. "Despite of your persecutions, you have escaped with several pounds more of very rosy flesh, and a little gain of spirits too."

Here Parke entered from the bed-room, and was welcomed by Mrs. Van Duyn. His gratitude for her care during his illness, and his respect for her fine qualities, amounted to a goodly degree of affection, while she really loved him. Of course his health had to be discussed, as it was still delicate when he went away, and now did not appear much improved. The widow had some suspicion of the cause of his transparent complexion and the feverish brightness of his dark-blue eye. Rumors of dissipated habits had reached her, and she now looked from his dazzlingly handsome countenance, to the face of her own child, with anxiety. What she read in both caused a feeling of uneasiness.

"You are an artist are you?" said Alice, in pleased surprise, taking up a sketch from the table; for she had not been acquainted with her friend's talents in that way.

"Oh! I had forgotten!" cried Lucy, blushing with

more than the vividness of an artist's modesty, and springing for her drawings. They were already in the hands of Miss Madison.

"Look, Parke! here is a likeness of you—and perfect!"

"I do not think it as good as this one of *you!*" said Lucy, presenting the one she spoke of.

But all present declared the representation of the brother to be the best—although both were admirable.

"You must give me this sketch of my brother; it is so very natural; and with his 'happiest expression' too. That earnest soul looking out of an eye that smiles with its own beauty—that saucy curl floating over upon the temple—and that half-gay, half-proud curve of the lip, are all Parke's."

"You flatter me, Allie," laughed he.

"Since I can make another easily, you may have that," said the artist. "But what do you think of this?"

She took out of a little box upon the table a miniature, exquisitely painted upon ivory, of a female face.

"Did you really do it?" cried Alice; "why, you witch! to never tell me you could do such delightful things."

"Whose likeness is it?" asked Parke.

"I do not know the lady, except as a sitter. I sometimes paint these miniatures for the pecuniary reward they bring, as well as the pleasure of doing them. "Else," and she colored and smiled, "how should I have fit dresses in which to visit my city acquaintance?"

"This will be a fine excuse for me to stay a week and get my picture done for a locket," said Parke.

"And for me to stay three, and get mine," added Alice.

"I am sure we can make a satisfactory arrangement" was the smiling reply. Here the children trooped in to be welcomed and caressed, and the drawings were put away.

Lucy could have shown Parke another likeness of himself, already finished on ivory; but as it was something she kept for her own especial delight, she said nothing about it now.

When the visitors arose to depart, they perceived that a thunder-shower was coming rapidly up. So the horses were driven down the lane under shelter, and Mrs. Van Duyn had the pleasure of setting her tea-table for guests. The storm was a real August storm, brief and wild. The wind tore the clinging vines from the window, and laid the tall corn in the garden all aslant. Darkness swept forward on rushing wings, which seemed to pause just overhead; its garments were torn every moment by lightning, and its wings wounded by flaming swords. Every time the lightning smote, its voice was heard; first in far and solemn reverberations, then sharp and startling in the surrounding air. As long as Mrs. Van Duyn would permit them, the girls stood, their arms encircling each other, upon the little portico off the dining-room, watching with half-fearful delight the magnificence of the western sky. But when the storm came immediately overhead, and large drops of rain and hail dashed across the porch, she made them come in and close the door.

"They who put their trust in the Lord, need have no fear," she said. "Still it is not well to mock at danger."

So the girls went in and sat down near the centre of the room, with their pretty feet drawn up to the rungs of their chairs, looking upon each other gravely through the gloom, and listening with awe and pleasure to the close and deep rolling thunder.

"I can never think of anything but the words of the grand old Prophets during a storm like this," said Alice, in one of the pauses. "Their voices alone equal in sublimity the voice of Nature as she speaks through her thunders."

"Byron's famous description of a storm amid the Alps, always recurs to me," answered Lucy. "Its majestic lines seem to roll and reverberate with the very music he heard amid the mountains; and they shine in grandly with the roar of the elements. But above all, and in all, seems the prevailing Spirit of God."

"What do you think of, Parke? you love a scene like this, do you not?" asked Alice of her brother, who had retreated long ago to the lounge, and laid with his face buried in the pillows.

A sharper flash, a louder peal, a fresh sweep of winds, and a wilder rattle of hail, deafened all ears, and prevented the necessity of reply. Ah! Parke little cared to reply to that question! For guilt is always cowardly; and never, since he broke the vow he vowed to a dying mother, could the young man take pleasure in a thunder-storm. The lightning to him seemed a sword of vengeance, and the thunder a voice calling upon him in threatening accents for atonement. He would fain have flown from both; but as that was impossible, he could only lie pale and trembling, thinking of his mother's grave, of an offended God, and of judgment. Had he convinced himself of the sincerity of his repentance by the innocence of his life now, he might have heard tones of hope and mercy as well as reproach. But he was going farther and farther every day from good, and conscience in such moments asserted her mute power. The storm swept on towards the east, and again the doors were thrown open, and the little party gathered on the portico. What a delicious change its brief visit had wrought! The air was cool and fragrant — the unhealthy heat was gone — the fields sparkled with rain, and there was no fear of being smothered in dust during the ride home. But the west! the west! what a gorgeous sky was there! swimming and melting in a sea of azure, crimson and gold, the light clouds floated, like white swans in a silver sea, or birds of Paradise in Eden's amber air.

Parke could look now with composure; but his features still wore the marks of his secret struggle.

Tea was eaten with an appetite. When the carriage came round to the door, the sun was just sitting amid purple clouds, and a young moon lifted her silver brow timidly from the orient. With a promise to return soon and talk over the matter of the pictures, the Madisons drove away.

As the horses sped lightly along through the clear twilight, overcome by the beauty of the hour and the fervor of his late emotions, Parke dropped his head upon his sister's shoulder, while the tears ran swiftly down his cheeks. It was the first time in months that he had wept, though the tears used to gather on his eye-lids easily as on a girl's. Weakness was that? yes the weakness of a heart not hardened — a heart full of sympathy, laughing with the gay, weeping with mourners, as hearts were made to do. Since habits of dissipation had come upon him, and he had grown familiar with the words of contempt and ridicule hurled at goodness by reckless youth, tears had been less frequent visitors. Perhaps the vision of that noble and pure girl who stood at the gate with the sunset radiance illuminating her brown eyes and tinging her roseate cheeks — whose soft good-bye still lingered in his ear — had a good deal to do with this melting down of his heart.

Alice did not observe that he was weeping, but the touch of his head upon her shoulder called up the olden times when there was nothing but innocent, unquestioning pleasure in the bosoms of each, when in each other's society. Her love for him was still unchanged. Every wound he inflicted by his misconduct seemed to incite deeper love, as it awoke pity and forgiveness. The evening breezes blew the curls from his temples against her face — one of his hands she held in her's — her eyes were fixed upon Hesperus, who, large and bright, shone in the still faintly-glowing west.

"Parke! that star is so serene, so brilliant, so gentle, I can liken it to nothing but our mother's spirit. I can imagine that she is standing there in the sky, smiling upon us, holding one silver-white hand upward, and with the other beckoning to us."

"Smiling upon *you* Allie; but not upon me! I dare not raise my eyes to it," he replied, his glance following the wheel-marks along the road, instead of Alice's look. She heard him weeping, and hardly dared to comfort him; for his promises were so often made and so often broken, that she almost dreaded to hear him renew them. She kissed his hand and his forehead, and he felt her tears falling warm among his curls, but she said nothing.

Many and many times were scenes like these enacted; when it seemed as if a "broken and contrite spirit" was about to offer acceptable sacrifices upon the altar.

But darker clouds ever swept on over the glimpses of sunshine, until it seemed as if there never again would be a day of brightness and beauty.

The miniatures upon ivory were began and completed; but a shadow rested on the brows of the painter and her sitters — it hovered around the easel and flitted over the pallet — it was not always there, but often — none spoke of it, but all felt its weight. It affected the pictures too. Do all she could to give it the beaming smile of Alice, the artist could not do away with the melancholy in the eyes and at the corners of the mouth in her picture. As for Parke, Lucy gave up trying to satisfy herself with his present expressions either of excessive gayety or spiritless fatigue, and painted from her old sketch of him, taken when his physical powers, weakened by illness, were held in bonds by the soul.

There was a musical and golden vein of poetry flowing through Parke's nature, that leaped into light in his very darkest hours, and would show itself in an hundred sparkling shapes in as many moments. So that when dull after an excess, or just warmed enough with wine to be eloquent, or when in the full tide of a riot, he preserved always some glimpse of his original character.

In his palmy days, those days when the family dwelt upon the farm, and those passed during convalescence in the society of the Van Duyn's, he could make himself indescribably interesting in conversation, and agreeable as an associate. His father had been distinguished for wit; and the son transcended him; to wit he added sensibility, humor, and pathos, in a high degree.

His memory was stored with graceful anecdotes and bright snatches of poetry — with stray bits of sentiment and little tragedies in one act — with fanciful facts and happy illustrations — all of which came from his lips with a winning and genial grace. Now the spell came over him but seldom. His dark-blue eye, instead of being fixed upon your face with that clear and sparkling glance, had a downcast and uneasy expression, and the laugh, once so thrilling with its contagious mirth, was short and mocking. No wonder that the two girls lost some of their happiness in his society.

CHAPTER VIII.

"Good-bye, dear mother; I shall come home every week, if I can. Good-bye, Katy, darling. Good-bye, Willie," cried Lucy Van Duyn, with a kiss for them all, as muffled in hood and cloak she came forth from the cottage.

A trunk was already in the sleigh; John, the driver, and a goodly pile of lined buffalo-robes, took up nearly all the rest of the room; so that there was just a place left for the bundle of wrappings, with Lucy inside, which was lastly added to its contents. Ugh! how cold it was! too cold for Alice to venture out, who was not very well; so she had sent John with the pleasant commission to bring back Miss Van Duyn, who was to stay with her at least two months. This had long been arranged between them, provided Lucy could make up her mind to leave her mother so lonely; and as Alice had promised that she might spend a day at home every week, this was concluded very satisfactorily.

The cold made the spirited horses doubly fleet, and a

very short time after the good-byes were spoken, the bundle of wrappings and the trunk were set down in the hall of Mr. Crawford's mansion. Alice appeared from the parlor, looking very glad, and helped bring down the pyramid of cloaks until her entombed friend was brought to view, smiling and serene, not the least bit bitten by the frost — not even her pretty nose. She then led her in to Mrs. Crawford, who welcomed her warmly, and who was really very glad that her daughter was going to have a companion, who might do something towards calling back the roses to her face and the laughter to her lips. For Alice was growing sad — not the sacred sadness which mourned once for a newly-lost mother — but a restless, pining melancholy, that seemed fretting into her health. It did not disturb her temper, except to make her more patient and less gay; over that, which was too gentle to need much governing, she still had sweet control.

The young ladies had plenty with which to busy themselves. It was near the holidays; and Mrs. Crawford was bent upon giving a party on New Year's Eve. They interested themselves in her arrangements — there were some new dresses to be made — and Lucy painted Mr. and Mrs. Crawford's miniatures, by means of the liberal reward for which she was enabled to purchase a suitable evening toilet.

Besides all of this, Alice was composing some music, for which she had always shown genius, and was capable of doing more than passably well. They were not interrupted much, evenings, for Alfred Clyde did not visit them as often as formerly, and Parke seldom came in until after they had retired. Once or twice during the week he might remain at home with them; but his eye was heavy, his manner constrained.

Despite of all this business, they could not "drive dull care away." If Alice wore a dejected look, Lucy's was as spiritless; it was as often the latter whose heavy sigh first startled an unconscious response. Yet there was no confidence between the two on the subject of their grief, except the mute sympathy of looks.

New Year's Eve came, finding Mrs. Crawford's rooms a-blaze with light, and wearing a festive air in honor of expected guests. The girls were in their chambers, taking a last peep into the mirror before going down. Mrs. Crawford, who had finished dressing, was giving them that careful survey befitting her important responsibility in bringing out two such beautiful young ladies. She might well look satisfied and happy; there was but one fault to be found with her youthful friends, and that was that both wore a grave and anxious expression little befitting the gayety of the occasion. She begged of them to look a little more animated; and to please her they tried hard, but down would drop the corners of the mouth the next moment, and the delicate brows would settle into gravity. Both wore elegant dresses of white. Lucy's sleeves were looped and fastened with two old-fashioned jewels which were heir-looms in her family; her hair was braided in a rich coiffure by Mrs. Crawford's dressing-maid, and its dark beauty set off by one or two white flowers.

The back of Alice's hair was prettily knotted, and the rest fell in lovely curls down either cheek. As her friend, being taller and more queenly in her look, wore the camelias, she contented herself with a few rose-buds from a rare tree which blossomed in the conservatory.

The fans and delicate handkerchiefs were ready to be taken up, when there came a light knock at the door. Alice hastened to open it, and there stood Parke, looking more like himself than she had seen him for weeks, and in fine spirits. He brought two costly bouquets, which he handed to his sister, designating which one he had caused to be made up for Lucy. It was wonderful to see how both the ladies brightened up; the anxious expression fled, and they went down to the parlors as happy as they were fair. A dread lest Parke should appear in a condition to disgrace himself and others had been the secret of their sadness; and now to see him so well and bright was the removing of a weight which allowed their spirits to rebound with more than their usual buoyancy.

The evening was pleasant to all; to most of the guests delightful. Little Mrs. Crawford, as we have said before, had no children to occupy her mind, and as it was naturally inclined to such matters, she excelled the most of her five hundred friends in the arrangements of all kinds of parties from a ball to a pic-nic.

Alice was always urged for music — not that she had to be urged — but people were never satisfied when she had given them as much as she thought she had a right to. After singing several times, she declined to sing again; but she played an accompaniment while Lucy, who only had a knowledge of the guitar, sang these words:

Return! return! a voice is calling,
  I hear it down the stormy sky,
Distant and sweet the tones are falling
  Like silver dew distilled on high.
It is an angel-mother crying
  Unto a lost and wandering child —
"From heaven — from me, why art thou flying?
  Dash down — dash down the wine-cup wild!"

Return! return! I hear her praying,
  A sister on her bended knee.
"Where are thy poor feet darkly straying? —
  Return to happiness, and me."
Her tears and smiles so sweetly beaming
  Call thee from the alluring way;
False is the light before thee gleaming —
  Dash down! dash down the wine-cup gay!

Return! return! they faint and falter,
  Those accents with such sorrow breathe;
Dash down the wine on pleasure's altar,
  Tear from thy brow the glowing wreath!
It is a maiden pale who calls thee —
  "Come back, to love, to hope, to light!"

Break from the shining chain that thralls thee —
  Dash down! dash down the wine-cup bright!

Return! return! it is the pleading
  Of Jesus with a wandering lamb.
How darest thou still stray on, unheeding
  That voice rebuking, heavenly-calm?
Ah! soon will cease the loving warning —
  The sainted mother lose her child!
And thou be left to angel's scorning —
  Dash down! dash down the wine-cup wild!

Her voice quivered a little through the first verse, but after that she sang with thrilling sweetness and power. She dared to let her eyes rest on nothing but the sheet of music before her, but she seemed to be pleading with some one present; with such impassioned pathos did she sing. The words and music were both new; and while the listeners were expressing their pleasure and asking some questions about the song, Parke, who had leaned by the piano when it was commenced, quitted the apartment. The first words had fixed his eyes upon the singer; he had grown pale as she proceeded, but he listened till the last quiver died away, and then went out, and appeared no more during the stay of the guests.

If others had not noticed his emotion, it was because all were in a measure spell-bound by the earnestness of her manner. There were others besides Parke who might have felt the appeal — who did feel it for a moment, and then forgot it as they had done other appeals.

After the company had left, as the young girls stood by the library table, pulling the flowers from their hair, drawing off their gloves, and talking over the events of the evening, Parke came in, walking up to Miss Van Duyn, he seized her hands in so tight a grasp that she nearly cried out.

"Lucy, how *dared* you sing that song this evening? Did you do it only to mortify me? Every one must have known at whom it was sung with such effect; I shall never forgive you — never!"

And flinging away her hands, he went out again, leaving the offender in tears.

A fortnight from then, Mr. Crawford again banished Parke from his house, and with no hope of restoration to his favor. Of age, and at liberty to pursue his inclinations, the young man would have long ago left the home of his former guardian, whose strictness of principle was a continual reproach to him, had he not been restrained from love to his sister. She was still the star whose changeless ray beamed brightly over his fortunes; the farther he fell from self-respect the more deeply he reverenced and adored her. She seemed to him a creature without fault, yet who, amid all her own perfections, could love and cherish him. He was unhappy if denied her society, and he was unhappy when in it, as he felt the gentle sadness of her mannner the severest rebuke to his wild behavior. He mockingly thanked Mr. Crawford for dismissing him; and taking rooms in a gay part of the town, he furnished them with great splendor, and set up the establishment of a rich and reckless young bachelor.

Alice did not this time propose to follow him. She gave herself up for a while to dismay and despair; then struggling with her cares, she endeavored to throw them off and be free. She never failed in love, nor in making every effort which seemed worth the trial, to save her brother.

Lucy was called home by the illness of little Katy, so that the poor child had no real friend and comforter. Mrs. Crawford worshiped her, and could not bear to see her in any trouble; but she was not a woman capable of giving sound advice, or of bearing up a sinking spirit.

The most terrible hours of life are those passed alone in struggles with one's self. Whether it be a struggle for the mastery over temptation, over an evil fortune, over fate, over affliction, over remorse, we shudder at ourselves and the power of our own passions. Parke Madison was holding such a war with himself. Midnight had long rolled by, and the lamps in his chamber were burning dim. He did not think of sleep.

"Ruin! ruin!" he muttered, flinging himself into a chair, and the next moment starting up again. "It is all over with me now. My fortune is gone — my health, my good name — Alice's heart is broken, the family honor forever sullied — and I am a wretch, fated to pass the hours of a cursed life within the walls of a prison. Yes, a prison! Alice, can you bear that?" asking the question, with bitter emphasis, as if his sister stood before him. "But I will die and rot in the darkest cell before he shall have the reward which would purchase his silence. Alfred Clyde, you are a traitor — oh, you are a traitor, or you would not force upon me this bitter choice."

It had chanced to Parke, that having surrendered his judgment, prudence, and reason, for a glass of intoxicating beverage, while in that helpless situation where he had placed himself, he had committed a crime. His suppers, horses, cards, billiards, and bets, for the last eighteen months, had amounted to nearly the whole of his once fine fortune.

Added to the lavish expenditure upon his new rooms, he had of late been very unfortunate at the gaming-table, so that he found himself burdened with a 'debt of honor' which he could command no means to pay. He dared not ask Alice for the amount out of her fortune, for he knew that she could not procure it without the knowledge of Mr. Crawford. He applied to his friend Alfred; but he decidedly refused to loan him anything for such a purpose. Mortified and angry at this refusal from a friend, he went home and drank several glasses of brandy-and-water, and while in the excited mood induced by these, Alfred came in.

"I have been remembering our college-days," said he, "when I was indebted to you for aiding me out of many a tight place; and have repented, almost, my refusal; though I blame your folly, and tell you truly that you will be a beggar before the end of a year."

'If I could only free myself from this affair, and win

my money back again, I would be willing to forswear play," replied Parke.

"Well," said Alfred, sitting down at a table and writing, "I am going to write an order on my banker for five thousand dollars, and leave it here, but I shall give it no signature, so that it will be a mere piece of paper. Bring it to me one week from now, with the assertion that you have not been a drunken man for that length of time, and I will put my name to it, and you may take your time about returning it."

"That's a little more like it, Alf., my boy! but why not sign it now? That debt was to be paid to-morrow, and I'd rather have three thousand then, than the whole of it in seven days."

"You can put them off a week easily. I've a fancy to see if five thousand dollars will tempt you to keep sober a week. I do it for Alice's sake, my friend — you know that you are killing her. So be a good child for once," he added, laughing as he went out, "and don't be tempted to fill out that little piece of paper with my name until I see fit to do it myself."

"Alf. always concludes to be generous, whatever ugly freaks he may take," mused the young man when left alone. "Why in the mischief, though, does he want to keep me waiting? St. Ormond will suspect I am pretty hard up, and cut my acquaintance. Very well! I hate him anyhow; but he's such a sneering way with him, that I'd rather fail to meet any other debt than that. By the way, that was a timely hint of Alf.'s. If my hand was only steady enough, I might just as well add the signature to this and get the money for to-morrow. Of course I can keep my senses a week if I have a mind to try, and it will make no difference with him when the time is up."

A thousand times he had imitated Clyde's signature when they were at school together; he now sat down, and with a few flourishes of his pen, the paper was ready for use. The mouse had nibbled at the bait so temptingly laid, the trap was sprung and fastened upon its helpless victim.

Alfred Clyde hardly dared hope so easily to get poor, foolish Parke into his power. At the end of a week he called upon him.

"So you have been a little up in the clouds once or twice lately, despite of a weight of five thousand dollars to attach you to earth?" he asked, carelessly. "You can give me back that draft, Parke, for I am a man of my word."

"Pooh, Alf., I've been trudging along as soberly as any man — only two bottles of genuine old Madeira, 'Sheffield' on the wax, that some unknown friend sent me. Too late for you to repent now, at all events. Your order was presented six days ago, money received, and, what's better, spent."

"The deuce it was! without any signature?"

"I could always write more like you than you could yourself," said Parke, laughing; "and as it was inconvenient for me to await your further action, I tried my skill on your banker."

"Ah-h! are you aware that was forgery?"

"Why I suppose it would have been to have used any body else's name in that manner," was the easy reply; for if he had served Alice so, he would as soon have looked for its being taken up.

"And it is to have used *mine*," said Alfred, with icy coolness. "You shall learn, Mr. Madison, that I am not to be trifled with."

Parke looked up in astonishment. There was no appearance of affectation in the dark eye bent threateningly upon him.

"You promised to lend me the amount, Alfred. What difference can it possibly make with you? you are not in earnest?"

"Am I not? Well, perhaps I had better relinquish all claims to anything of my own, since a man, who is half the time less responsible than a fool, can at any moment help himself to a few thousands, without as much as saying 'by your leave.' No, Sir! You have done a pretty deed, and *not* with impunity."

"As you please," replied Parke, offended at such language. "I am very sorry that I ventured to 'trifle' with a brother. But since I have been guilty of such indiscretion, he shall be satisfied. By the sale of my black ponies, disposing of these rooms, and a few other sacrifices, I can have the money returned to you in a very few days."

"But that will not satisfy me. You have committed a forgery, and you are in my power."

"What would you have me do?" asked Parke, indignantly, the fire flashing from his eyes as he turned abruptly and faced his companion, whose countenance wore a look of unpleasant triumph.

"Nothing very difficult for you, but of vast importance to me. You can keep your ponies and your establishment. All I ask of you is to try and interest Alice in my favor. Parke!" continued he, with sudden earnestness, that was almost sadness, "I have loved her for years. You know it. So well, that I have never, like all other young men, had any passing fancy, any fleeting passion, that was not true to her. I have been a faithful and humble worshiper of her maiden beauty; and in return I have received nothing but the calmest friendship. I cannot live so any longer, and since you have such influence with your sister, I wish you to use it. It is not that I wish you harm — it is only that I cannot live without Alice."

"I have not the control of my sister's affections; if I had, they would have been yours long ago; you know that, Alfred. It seems to me that your course of proceeding is more worthy of her dislike than her love. This is more the act of a traitor than an honest man and a friend."

"Oh, it is a forger who talks about honesty. The devil in the pope's robes! I have wooed Alice long and modestly, and she would not be won. Now she shall take her choice between a brother disgraced and in prison, or a husband whose fault is that he has loved her so well as to stoop to falsehood towards a friend, rather than give her up."

"I would bear the severest penalty attached to my error — under the circumstances I will not call it crime — before I would even make known to her your disgraceful proposition," cried Parke, waving his hand towards the door.

"Oh, undoubtedly! the son of the late Hon. Everard Madison, convicted of forgery, sentenced to ten years in the penitentiary — beautifully arrayed in striped drawers — hair cropped — nobly employed in pegging shoes under the eye of an overseer!"

With this fascinating picture held up before the eyes of the dismayed young gentleman, he made a mocking bow, turned on his heel and departed; leaving his whilom friend to ponder upon his frightful dilemma.

It was the master-hand of art which painted his parting words. Had he referred to a lonely cell, where no ray of light was permitted to enter, where years must be worn away in solitary confinement, and untold pangs of anguish endured in silence, Parke would have brought romance, proud endurance, sublime fortitude to his aid, and taken a gloomy comfort in looking upon himself as the victim to a friend's perfidy, and of unparalleled devotion to a sister. Now he saw himself the beau, par-excellence, of Broadway, the elegant, the accomplished Parke Madison, whose horses were the finest, whose wines the oldest, whose dress the most fastidiously graceful of all the admired aristocrats of New York — he saw himself in a convict's dress! — he turned to a mirror and ran his long, fair fingers through his luxuriant locks, and shuddered. It was more than human nature could endure! There was no dignity — no gloomy grandeur in such a sacrifice. Would "The Prisoner of Chillon" be an object of noble symyathy if presented to view in striped drawers, head shaved, sitting on a bench, beating a lap stone? Parke was beautiful, was youthful, was fond of pleasure, was dainty in all his tastes. His fortitude gave way — he sank into an arm-chair with a groan of agony.

He had fretted the night away in contending with the passions of fear, sorrow, remorse, anger. The first gleam of morning found him exhausted, but with his mind still undecided. He threw himself upon his bed and slept heavily for three or four hours. When he awoke it was with that weight upon the breast which reminds us of the anguish under which we have sank to slumber. He rang for his servant, and dispatched a brief note to Alice, begging her to come to him at once and without any other person's knowledge. Before he had finished dressing she was awaiting him in the adjoining rooms. She scarcely noticed the air of voluptuous luxury which pervaded these bachelor's apartments. Sinking into an arm-chair, with her feet nervously patting the carpet, and her eyes fixed upon his bedroom door, she passed the five minutes of delay, impatient to learn what new calamity this wilful brother had brought upon himself. She could hardly repress a cry when he came into the apartment. Late nights, late mornings, brandy and cigars, the excitements of gambling and betting, with the anguish of the last sleepless hours, had nearly erased God's inscriptions from that once eloquently expressive countenance.

"Is this my brother?"

No wonder she asked the question in a tone of touching reproach; for the eye sunken and dim with lowering lid, the haggard brow, and colorless cheek, were these the ones her mother kissed and praised? the ones she regarded with a pride than was only less than the fondness which softened it? *And the trembling of his hands!* A fear deadly and dark rushed over her soul, staggering it beneath a weight of horror, so that she could not rise from her seat to welcome him, nor could her tongue frame a syllable in response to his agitated "Good morning, Alice." To see a young man of twenty-two so wrecked by excess, that he should come from his morning toilet, trembling as with the infirmities of four score years, what a frightful spectre of approaching insanity did it conjure up!

"Do not look at me so, Alice!" implored Parke in a faint voice, and, as if unable longer to stand, he sank into a chair.

"Parke Madison," said she at last, "I tell you truly," and she lifted up her right hand, "you are upon the very verge of a horrible madness and death! you totter upon the brink of delirium-tremens! be warned! be warned!"

"It is not the only brink upon which I stand," he replied, summoning up the last remains of his sinking courage, but shivering from head to foot; "I stand upon the precipice of disgrace, and when I fall it will be into a prison.

There is a chance of safety, but I will not avail myself of it. You can be my savior, Alice, but you shall not be."

"How? go on with your story, sir!"

"Alice! for Heaven's sake be more pitying! — you have no conception of what I suffer. It is mental agony, not physical weakness, that shakes me so."

"It is both," she said, leaning forward in her chair as if desirous to hear quickly what he might have to say.

He began in a faltering voice and explained the peril of his present situation. He made no vain attempt to extenuate the extravagance and excess which had led him into difficulty, but the manner of the forgery, and the advantage which was taken of it, he spoke of, as one speaks who feels himself wronged by a friend.

"I always knew that Alfred Clyde was rotten at heart," said Alice; "but what are those conditions to which you refer which shall ensure your safety?"

"You know he has always wished you to become his wife; — but I do not ask it," he added, as he saw her grow pale.

She arose and walked several times across the floor.

"Why do you not fly?" she asked.

"An outcast from society, disowning my own name, penniless, what would I become? Better submit to a prison, where, at least, I *cannot* yield to my besetting sin! No, I will not fly and leave disgrace behind only to rush into a fresh ruin; but you, dear Alice, have suffered enough for me, and shall suffer no more. No more! alas, what but suffering is there for you in a brother's ignominy, in being pointed at as a forger's sister? Oh! my father—my mother—I have dishonored your names upon the tombstone!"

Alice still continued her walk up and down the suite of rooms. Ever as she reached either extremity, she was confronted by her own image in the tall mirror—a pale, troubled face shadowed by the bonnet which she had not taken off, hands clasped tightly together, eyes which seemed to ask their perplexed reflection for the solution of a problem the answer to which must still be—"sorrow"—resolve it as they might.

It was at least an hour before the eyes gave her the required answer; then she stood before her brother, who had followed her light form with an eager, inquiring gaze.

"It is not to save our father's name from infamy, nor you from being an outcast; it is not that I fear that portion of the disgrace which will fall upon me; it is not even to save your young years from being wasted in a prison workshop, that I tell you that I am resolved to marry Alfred. All these things have their influence, of course, but I have already suffered so much on your account that I do not think they would have much power, but *I* cannot forget the last words of my mother. Ever since I have been walking here I have heard that dying voice—so precious, so beloved, saying, "Be faithful—love one another." I will be faithful, even to this extremity. I will do the utmost that can be expected from a sister; and if, through the grace of

God, my love be rewarded by your final reform, I shall be abundantly repaid for every sacrifice."

"It shall be—it shall be, Alice. Hear me swear that henceforth ——"

"Parke, you have made too many promises. I will not hear one; I do not require any; I leave the matter with your conscience, I am going home now; you may see Alfred and tell him that I wish him to call at our house this evening."

"After all, it is Alfred's great love for you which has caused him to treat me so illy," said Parke, whose fault it was to be too generous and forgiving.

She made no reply except the tears that dropped upon her cheeks. It seemed to her—she knew, that her brother could have no conception of the trial she was enduring for his sake. He went down stairs with her, and accompanied her part of the way to Mr. Crawford's. Here they parted on the street, she simply remarking that she wished him now to pursue such a course as his judgment and conscience should approve.

She spent the rest of that dismal March day in a vain attempt to become reconciled to her destiny. Mrs. Crawford was going out for the evening to visit with a small circle of friends; and an hour after tea, Alice was left alone to receive the expected call. She stood up as she heard Mr. Clyde come in, receiving him in the centre of the room. He held out his hand, and she placed her's, which was icy cold, in his clasp. He pressed it passionately, as if he would in that tender action express the feelings which had prompted his conduct, and at the same time make his excuse.

"Dear Miss Madison," he said, leading her to the sofa, and sitting by her side; "the depth, the truth of my love for you, is my only apology! — do I need a better?"

"If you truly loved me, Mr. Clyde, you would most desire that which would make me the happiest. Love is not selfish."

He almost smiled at those beautiful rebuking eyes.

"Human love is selfish," he replied; "I know not about divine. Show me the man upon earth who doted on a beautiful price of perfection like this, and yet would resign it, when, by any means not criminal, he could make it his own, and you will show me a triumph of self-denial which I have not yet witnessed. This peerless hand! to claim it as my wife's — the thought is enough to drive all other considerations away! But how am I selfish? what great sacrifice do I require of Parke, or you? If I thought it was a sacrifice I would not require it; but this fright will perhaps recall him from otherwise certain ruin; and as for you — why, Alice, what more of devotion can you ask? If it is love that makes a woman happy, then you will be the happiest of women, for you will be beloved beyond all others of your sex. If I did not think that I could make you contented — that after you are my wife you will learn to regard me with tenderness, I would say no more. But to give you up — impossible! That would be requiring of me a thousand times more than you are willing to do for a brother. Give you up, Alice, after you have once said that you would marry me?"

His eyes rested upon that bowed face as if it would be an impossibility indeed to resign that fair and trembling young creature.

"Is there no other way, then, of obtaining your mercy? Will not the whole of my fortune buy of you the few days' use of that miserable five thousand dollars?"

"There is none," he answered with a darkening brow. "Alice, you are to be my wife, and it will be better for both of us — for your happiness as well as mine, that you betray no more coldness or reluctance. Come," he added in a softer voice, "let us talk about Parke, and what we can do for him, to protect him from his own follies."

He proceeded to give such excellent advice, and to display such good judgment and apparent kindness, that Alice felt almost grateful. She wondered why a man of such reason and discretion had not exercised a more powerful influence for the right over her brother's easily governed mind. Clyde knew very well that hitherto his efforts had secretly been the other way; but now, made generous by the certainty of his own success, he was willing to undo the past and make, if possible, some amends for it.

When he arose to go, he again took the young girl's hand.

"Alice, will you not give me a kiss in token that I have now some small portion of your good will? You will soon be my wife; but even now I would think more of a smile than a kiss."

She held up her face with what she endeavored to have a cheerful expression, but she succeeded only in wearing a resigned one; and the moment he had left the apartment, she brushed her cheek with an involuntary motion, as if she would have brushed away the unwelcome kiss.

"It will never do to indulge such feeling," she murmured, sorry at herself; "if I am to be his wife, I must school my thoughts as well as my actions."

So pure was her mind, so humble her religion, that from the moment she was pledged to Alfred Clyde, she endeavored to exercise as firm a control over her very dreams as over her outward behavior. If he was to be her husband, she must not even *think* any ill of him. Alas, poor child! what a hopeless task was that, when the more intimately they were associated, the more did her true spirit shrink from the hardness and selfishness of his.

In a few days, Parke Madison had disposed of his bach elor's hall and its extravagant furniture, his horses, carriages, jewelry; dismissed his groom and *valet de chambre*, and with only the faithful John and his library of books reserved from his dashing establishment, he retired to the farm. This farm belonged to Alice, but she sold it to him for the sum of five dollars, that when she was married he might still have something from which to secure a living, his own fortune being almost dissipated. This Alfred proposed himself; and it was through his energy and good management that the sales were effected, the removal made, and Parke once more somewhat removed from temptation.

It was not an idle life that Parke now proposed to spend. His health was very much impaired, but what strength he had left, he wished to expend in personal oversight of his large and highly-cultivated farm.

He boarded in the family of the man who worked it on shares, and who permitted him the control of a portion of it. Here he occupied the room which used to be his mother's, and in which she died. After a day of activity he would return to this hallowed apartment, and with books, music, writing letters, and rude attempts at sculptury, while away the now brief evenings.

Alice's engagement was to be short. Alfred desired an early day to be appointed for their marriage, urging the length of time for which he had been a suitor, as one reason why his wishes should be considered. In the latter part of May they were to be wedded. Early in April, Lucy came to stay with her friend until after the ceremony. She was surprised when Alice told her of the engagement, for she had long come to the conclusion that if her friend did not dislike Mr. Clyde, she did not at least love him; but as no confidence was given her any further, she was not so indelicate as to hint her suspicions or to force her way to the truth. Besides she knew of no compulsion, and could frame no device why that good and beautiful girl should cast herself away upon one who did not have her affection.

Mrs. Crawford was in her element during the times of preparation. She occasionally rallied her adopted daughter's pale checks into blushes, but she had not discernment to discover any sadness deeper than a bride's pensiveness beneath that quiet, gentle manner. Even Lucy was not certain that the sadness was other than that subdued reserve into which a young maiden retires who is so soon to change her position in life. There is something then with which a young girl veils her hopes and fears which is sacred from the acquaintances of friendship. The sadness at parting with home and freedom, the doubt when thinking of the increased care and importance of the new life, the hope of untried happiness, keep her thoughts in the sanctuary of her heart, from the observation of others. Alice would sometimes look up from the pretty stitching she was doing and find her companion's eyes fixed upon her face with a grave and dissatisfied look, when she would smile and shake her head as if denying the mute question.

"It is a very serious matter, this getting married," she would say, as if in apology for her own abstracted demeanor.

Lucy had changed not less than Alice, who saw more plainly into the reason of *her* melancholy smile and drooping eye-lashes.

"How much misery one victim of intemperance can bring upon the hearts of others," was her thought. "Had Parke not 'tarried long at the wine' I should not have been this unhappy creature that I am, nor poor Lucy be pining her life away in a vain endeavor to stifle an unwise passion, and conceal a wild regret."

It was not long until the twenty-third of May. Mrs. Crawford had wished for the show and splendor of an evening wedding. The fashion, the season of the year, and the wishes of the parties were against her, and twelve o'clock of the morning was the hour appointed. The day was as fresh and fair and beautiful as the bride herself — more fresh, for its roses were of the brightest, and the bride's cheeks were pale.

Quite a party of friends, among them Mrs. Van Duyn, were assembled in the parlors, where, as Mrs. Crawford had so long ago determined, there was no lack of camelias. Lucy and Parke were the attendants. Finding that Parke had once more abandoned his reckless habits, and had been living industriously in the country for some time, Mr. Crawford had invited him to be present at his sister's wedding.

Colder and colder grew the heart of Alice in her bosom as the hour drew nigh that was to unite her with one whom she did not and could not love. Her fortitude would have given entirely away had she not been encouraged by the improved appearance of her brother. As it was, although she exercised the greatest vigilance over herself, she knew that Alfred was displeased and dissatisfied. It was true that he need not then have compelled the marriage; but since he did compel it, she must try to please him, let his injustice be great as it would. She was dressed, even to the typical vail; the bridal party stood in the room at the head of the stairs ready to descend; when in arranging some trifling part that was to be performed, she fretted the already moody temper of Alfred, and he spake to her sharp and quick. The tyrant was already beginning to manifest himself. A thought of the life to be led with one who could speak in that tone in the very hour of their union, rolled over her soul like a cold and drenching wave. But she smiled when she saw that the attendants look surprised, as if her smile was to excuse his hastiness, and taking Lucy's arm she said something about having forgotten to wear her pearl bracelet, and drew her into the adjoining apartment. Here the mastery of her emotions gave way; the tears rushed forth in a sudden torrent; leaning against the wall, she shook with terrible emotion.

"Lucy! Lucy! I wish that I were dead!" she cried in a low voice, with white and writhing lips.

Her friend stood, frightened and pale, not knowing what to say or what to do.

"It is not too late, dear Alice, if you feel in that manner," she ventured to suggest.

"Oh, yes, it is too late! there is no help for me now — but in heaven. Mother — mother — I implore your aid! oh, heavenly Father, I know thou wilt be my comforter."

She sank a moment upon her knees, and when she arose the spasm of agony had passed. A holiness and sweetness came over her demeanor, and with this look she went out again to the rest, and the party descended, took their places before the hushed gazers, and in a few brief moments she was the wife of Alfred Clyde. Wife! strange, sweet name, when heard for the first time! even to her it sounded inexpressibly soft and solemn. The looks of the bride were admired, and yet people were sure that she did not appear precisely as it might be expected a bride should appear. Beautiful she always was; and now their admiration was mingled with a wonder at the exquisite and almost saintly style of her beauty. She did not seem sorrowful nor glad. There were a few blushes, but no tears. In her aspect were resignation and sweetness; in the faint smile she gave her husband there was forgiveness. He had recovered from his transient anger, and strove to conceal his mortification by a show of reverence and devotion. Passion and worship he felt; yet as the thought had lately chafed him that even a husband could not compel answering love, and that a wife might be his as a marble statue was his, and yet he have no more control over her affections, her intangible spirit, her will, than over the moveless beauty of the statue: as this thought had forced its truth upon him, for the first time, he had hesitated in his selfish pursuit. But pshaw! he had no idea of relinquishing his object, for such a trifle as her happiness, or even his own future comfort. If he should tire of her, he could neglect her.

Of course some of the guests said that the groomsman would soon marry the bridesmaid; and others said not. Some, that she was a noble girl, and would make too good a wife for such a wild young man; others, that Parke Madison would never choose a poor wife with nothing but her lady-like manner and fine looks to recommend her; and still others, that a woman like Lucy Van Duyn would have a great influence over him in keeping him out of bad habits, and they hoped it would be a match. What the two themselves thought was known only to their own bosoms, and certainly not spoken to each other. There was some embarrassment in Parke's manner, and some sadness in Lucy's. After all, it was a grand wedding, and made the same stir that the announcement of Miss Madison's marriage with Mr. Clyde would make anywhere.

The two were gone a short time upon their bridal tour.

Upon their return Mrs. Crawford, despite the lateness of the season, gave a large party. None of the elegantes had left town, as it was yet June, and the weather continued delightfully moderate; so the lady's parlors were thronged; and as she looked around upon the gay people and beheld the attention bestowed upon the bride, she had only to wish that she had a dozen daughters yet to be married.

A week or two after, Mr. and Mrs. Clyde went to the farm to spend the summer with Parke. This was the wish of the brother and sister; and as Alfred was for the present contented wherever his wife was, he made no objections. Alice began again to enjoy the society of Parke, whose health was rapidly mending, and whose conversation and thoughts began to flow in nobler channels. His gratitude and love to her made him tireless in her service. No effort was too great that was rewarded by securing any pleasure to her. He hung upon her words and smiles with a devotion that called forth the ridicule and wit of Alfred; and at the same time his jealousy. He could not bear to be rivaled even by a brother, and his vexation so often made itself apparent, that Alice grew afraid to express her affection with the old freedom. Parke was innocent of this, for she blinded his eyes with the rosy sweetness of her temper, and allowed him not to suspect but that all was prosperous.

His loving, dependent disposition rested itself fondly upon his sister and contentedly upon her husband's judgment and strength of mind. The summer was to him as happy as it could be with the past no more atoned for.

He dreaded the approach of winter, for then he was to be left alone with his books, dog, gun, and sculpturing.

Alfred Clyde and his wife were going south to remain until spring. Alice gave her brother plenty of good advice, of love and prayers at parting; she was afraid to leave him so long, lest in the meantime some temptation should occur too strong for him to resist unaided.

They spent the winter in Cincinnati, and St. Louis, where Alfred had acquaintances and distant relatives. Alice would have been very happy had she been married to a man whom she respected and loved; but her husband gave her a small chance to cultivate either her affection or esteem. Highly displeased at not meeting with the warmth and tenderness which he could only have expected from a willing wife, he began early to exercise that tyranny which flourishes and grows to full size in an indolent, self-loving, passionate, luxurious nature.

Alice had not grown rosy or brilliant during her sojourn at the south. When they returned in April, her air was languid; her aerial figure seemed to have acquired more airiness of outline, and her step had a weariness in it, as if mind or body had lost its youthful buoyancy.

Her joy at finding Parke a better man than he had ever been before revived for awhile her drooping spirits. His health was excellent — his affairs prosperous — and on the anniversary of his sister's wedding-day Lucy and himself were to be married.

Alice hastened to the cottage to see Mrs. Van Duyn, and to wish happiness to her friend and soon-to-be sister. What a soft light there was in Lucy's brown eyes, and what a changing glow upon her dazzling cheeks! How prettily she blushed — how brilliantly she smiled! — oh, she could answer for herself now whether the hope was not stronger than the fear, the bliss greater than the sadness. While she busied herself with adorning her not too costly wardrobe, any one regarding her might observe the hurried brightness gathering beneath the silken lashes, the flitting color of her cheeks changing with the beating of her heart, and sudden gleams of joy stealing over her thoughtful face.

Oh, it almost maddened Alice to look upon her and think of the desolate, dreary waste of her own life. But she was goodness and sweetness personified; patiently repressing the bursting regrets which she could not but feel, she tried to be happy in her friend's happiness, and to find in her brother's reform a consolation for her own trials. Contrasting his joyful independence with a convict's doom, and Lucy's happiness with a broken heart, she thanked God and was silent.

"O, she that hath a heart of that fine frame
To pay this debt of love but to a brother,
How will she love, when the rich, golden shaft
Hath killed the flock of all affections else
That live in her!"

To the heart of Alice Clyde came never an answer to this impassioned inquiry. Loneliness came to it, and yearnings which drowned themselves in tears, wild wishes, unutterable pangs! for the most part, her life was a struggle against her own lovely nature, to bow it to the rude will of a capricious and obstinate ruler.

How lovely a picture was the cottage upon the wedding-morning! There was nothing but tasteful simplicity. The roses breathed their fragrant congratulations, and the birds warbled the bridal anthems. In Parke's frank and beaming face and proud carriage there remained no trace of former sin. One there was though who could not forget, and who trembled with secret forebodings. What mother ever gave a beloved daughter into the care of another, for weal or woe, without some trembling? Mrs. Van Duyn could not banish the reluctance she felt. She loved Parke as a son, yet she knew the weaknesses of his character; and had they obeyed her wishes they would have waited another year before they were united. She left a tear on the bride's cheek when she kissed her; and in the look she gave her daughter's husband as she grasped his hand, she seemed to implore of him a promise to bring no shame or sorrow upon that innocent brow.

"She is my wife," said Parke, in a tone deep with feeling, as Alice came up to him, and they stood a moment apart from the rest; "my wife and I owe this happiness all to you. Oh, my sister, even in the lowest depths of my degradation how I loved that noble girl. Her perfections only made my faults the blacker, I saw that she loved me, unworthy as I was, that she pitied while she loved, and faded beneath a sorrowful regret. I longed to throw myself upon her compassion, and beg her to save me from myself. But I knew that if you, if my mother, could not restrain me, that even Lucy could not, and I dared not approach her with the mantle of my guilt upon me. Through you, dearest Alice, I have been able to come to her, saved and redeemed, with the humble offering of my love; and now she is mine! You have made two happy hearts — hearts brimming over with happiness. God forever bless you!"

Could Alice regret the offering she had made of herself? There sat her husband moodily regarding her, as if inventing what new torture he should inflict upon the patient soul of the woman whose fault and injury was, that what force, tyranny, pride, and ill-humor demanded, her shrinking spirit did not give. She had never failed in becoming respect or in silent endurance. But endurance was not what he wanted in a wife. He wanted sympathy; and more, he wanted her soul to be in subjection to his will. No matter; she was his own; and she should feel his power to the inmost fibre of her quivering heart. He smiled at the thought.

As she turned from Parke's fervent blessing, she met that smile, sinister and threatening.

"No!—no! I will regret nothing," she cried silently. "Surely I can find some recompense in the joy of others, and after a time it may be that unresisting gentleness will soothe this tiger into less ferocious moods."

Mr. and Mrs. Madison were soon established in the old country-house. He now had half the farm under his own management. A comfortable house was erected for his tenant, who boarded all the men employed. An excellent superintendent of the kitchen and dairy relieved Lucy from all care as to those matters. With long visits from little Katy and short ones from her mother, she grew to be so contented in her own home, as to lose those pinings after the mother-home which disturb a young wife's joy.

Mr. Clyde purchased an elegant residence in the city, and surrounded himself and wife with a golden halo of splendor. Although he was so indolent, there was a strength and power of his mind which could not be smothered in ease, and this directed itself to the difficult study of how he could most delight his senses and gratify his luxurious tastes with the least exertion, and to make the greatest impression upon others. Art and science, genius and beauty, were called into requisition to give a finish to his heartless epicureanism. The more he lapped it in the sensuous softness of indulgence, the harder did his soul become. The tact, judgment, and intrigue of his character, which applied to the lever of some noble purpose might have lifted him into enviable fame, were dedicated to giving a polish and certain distinction to his known extravagance of living. To be the slave of this self-lover was Alice's fate. As a slave, he would not set a value upon her, for she was something upon which to exercise his refined tyranny; further than that, he hated her. Like the devotional nun, who binds the thorny girdle over her bleeding heart, and conceals it with a garment of white, she concealed her sufferings under a calm and sweet demeanor.

CHAPTER IX.

THREE years of prosperity rolled over the dwellers at the farm. A baby, with flaxen ringlets and blue eyes, sat upon Lucy's knee, or tottered with mighty baby ambition across the floor. The whilom library was turned into a nursery, where sat Lucy, one October evening, in a little, low rocking chair, having a great frolic with the darling Carrie. Carrie, of course, was the baby; and by the way, she had gained her name through much tribulation. The mother wanted her called Katy, after her own mother, and sister Katy of the golden curls. The father said the name was too German, and Alice must the little one be called. But Alice wanted no child named after her, lest, as she said with a smile and sigh, it should not be a gift which would bring happiness. Finally, an old bachelor, who lived alone on an adjoining farm, proposed that if they would call the pretty creature Caroline, he would stand god-father, and make an heiress of the wee lady by deeding her a city lot.

Every one liked the old bachelor, and suspected that

Caroline was the name of his lady-love who died in her youth, leaving him a faithful mourner and a solitary man. They would have pleased him with gratifying his wish without the offer of the city-lot; but as he was rich, and had no children of his own, they allowed the unconscious baby to accept his gift. No attention was paid to Miss Katy's suggestion that she should be called Olive Olivia; and at last, after all these important undecisions, she rested safe with the noble appellation of Caroline, abridged for short and sweet to Carrie.

"Will you have your tea served now, Madam?" asked the house-keeper, looking in good-naturedly at the gay mother.

"No, Hester, not until Mr. Madison comes home; he said he should be back by half-past seven."

Hester shut the door, and Lucy went on with her frolicking.

"Now, baby, now — say papa! look at mother —— pa — pa!"

But baby was pulling at mamma's dress and would say nothing.

"No, lady Carrie, you are not old enough to wear jewels yet; let the brooch be. Now — pa - pa!"

"Ga! Ga!" said lady Carrie, and laughed at her triumph in achieving such a wonderful speech.

"You little darling! if father had only heard *that!* will Carrie say 'papa' when he comes home? pa - pa."

"Ga! Ga!" repeated the little genius; and if she had

been the "fairy who spoke pearls," her mother could not have been more delighted. She half smothered her with kisses.

Then they had such a play-spell! Baby's fat fingers would dive into mamma's hair, and pull down one of its shining braids; then mamma would give a pretended, pretty cry, which would set the baby into an extasy. Then the dimpled hands would be made willing prisoners, and patted together in tune with the wonderful ditty of

> "Rock-a-by, baby, upon the tree-top."

Next the chubby feet were made to illustrate the ballad of

> "One foot up and one foot down—
> That is the way to London-town."

Presently Carrie grew tired of play; when she had had her supper, been attired in her night-gown, and fell to sleep in her pretty crib, it was eight o'clock.

Hester again presented herself at the door, and told Mrs. Madison she had better have her tea, for more likely than not, Mr. Madison would not be at home that night.

"John's at home an hour ago, and he says there's going to be great doings with their speeches and processions; and some of Mr. Madison's friends were going to have a supper at the Astor, and their candidate for Governor was going to be there and make a speech."

"Oh! I hope he will not stay!" was the young wife's thoughts, as a thrill of apprehension ran through her.

It was a time of great political excitement. Parke,

now developed into the full grown man, with established views and active purposes, was not contented with devoting all his energies, talents, and education to farming. Though his farm was a model, exhibiting all the latest improvements, and cultivated upon scientific principles; though it was the admiration of the country around, and though it brought him an income amply sufficient for a generous and elegant way of living, he was not content. He had plenty of leisure, since he was only the head, not the hands, of his farm, to turn his attention to other pursuits; and the Senator's son, following in the path marked out by his father, was fast becoming ambitious of political distinction.

His wife had a dread of this. To her, who had always lived in the country, there seemed no life so free, so happy, so virtuous, so healthy as country-life; no occupation so pleasant as the cultivation of land. She did not see how there could be any tameness, any want of variety in avocations which brought one continually to observe the changes and endless industry of nature. The budding of the tree, the ripening of its fruit, the gathering it into the winter-stores — the springing of the grain, the forming of the heads, the harvesting, the thrashing out, the carrying to the mill — all the seasons of the year were full of beauty and interest to her. The blessing of the deep, warm snow, clothing the planted wheat, or the evil of the biting frost killing it in its tender infancy, were things which called for her gentle sympathy. She felt a grateful solicitude for the comfort of the sleek cows so richly contributing their flowing bounties to the universal plenty. She had a tender affection for the pretty lambs, a kind care for the broods of chickens, a great respect for the sturdy oxen, and a love for the noble horses. Her heart and mind expanded while contemplating the broad stretch of land with whose features and peculiarities she had become as familiar as with those of a friend. She knew what soil was greedy for food, what tired with successive years of labor, what thirsted for more drink from the abundant stream, and what plead for relief from its too bountiful supply. She knew what ground had a fancy for feeding, with summer luxuries of clover-blossoms, the cattle — and what was willing to devote the warm weather to growing a golden store of corn for their winter uses. The earth to her personified one who conferred great favors and required a few in return. The plums had a dulcet voice, beseeching aid to free themselves from the tormenting curculio; even the cucumbers looked coolly up and pointed to their yellow-backed destroyers.

The peas reached out their arms for ladders to aid their climbing — the peaches turned their crimson cheeks lovingly towards her, and the rosy apples nodded and blushed as if saying — "we grow for you!" And that grove of maples! was there ever a moment when it was not useful and beautiful? With the first sunshining days of March, their veins, overflowing with sweetness, were yielded by the stately trees to the farmer's lancet. Then came the time for a woodland frolic with her; while the farmer and his boys went about among the buckets, emptying the contents of each into a common receptacle in the shape of a hogshead, and from thence replenish the singing kettles, she loved to find her a seat on some inverted trough under a tree close by. The blazing fire, the bubbling cauldron, the mystic smoke, the grim workmen, were objects which her fancy did not hesitate to turn into sorcery and its accompaniments, or at least into the romance of gypseying. She took a curious interest in the skilful abstraction of the natural contents of an egg-shell, and the filling of the same with sugar-wax; and delighted in bringing her husband's talents at sculpture, to the carving of various fanciful hollows in pieces of wood, for the moulding of this wax into tempting cakes for Kitty and her other juvenile visitors. A bit of frozen snow hid away in a hollow or corner of a fence was eagerly searched for, to make a moulding-board, upon whose cold surface the syrup might quickly obtain the wished-for toughness. After the sugar-making days were over, she could mark from the windows of her room, the soft green gradually breaking from the swelled buds; and when the days grew oppressive with heat, there were the full grown leaves, offering their fair shelter and murmuring of refreshment to be found in the shadowy alleys which they roofed. In autumn the grove was past all description beautiful — a tossing, waving sea of splendor, which every breeze changed in aspect and color, lifting up sprays of crimson, edged with scarlet, dashing down billows of gold capped with purple and green. Even winter could not disrobe the maples of their charm, for the sprites came down from the mystic north on silent nights, and behold! in the morning sunshine, there they stood, so many crystal towers, of an architecture rivaling the Gothic, the pride of man; delicate in structure and profusely ornamented from column to spire with glittering yet chaste decorations.

Yes! Lucy found enough in country-life to interest, instruct, and ennoble. She thought that no one could accuse her husband of an inactive or useless existence if he employed it only in such occupations as their present position suggested. She had reason to dread his being drawn into political whirlpools. She was suspicious of the strength of his resolutions; and had no cause to think but that the country would be just as safe if her husband took no part in its debates. Feverish, unhealthy, and dangerous seemed to her the ambition which was coming over him; the country was safer without him than he was with it. Therefore, by all the tact and power of affection, she endeavored to divert his mind from its tendencies. But Parke was determined not to be satisfied with a wife, a baby, a home, and a farm. Politics seem in this country frequently to take the shape of a fever, which disturbs the quiet operations of the physical and mental powers, exciting the brain to a kind of delirium which for the time destroys its finely-balanced qualities. Mental blindness; a strange inability to discern truth from falsehood; an insane conception that our institutions are tottering into the gulf of their opponent's treachery, and will soon fall unless *they* rush to the rescue and make columns of support out of themselves; an itching at their fingers-ends to dabble in the spoils, and a burning desire for office, are some of the symptoms apparent in many of the victims of this disease.

Parke Madison had not the fever in such a violent degree. He did not care about the emoluments, nor think the sudden dissolution of the Union at hand; but there were some principles he desired to see advocated, some more he wished to uphold; and as he felt himself competent to speak on certain questions, he was bound to make himself heard. The honor paid to the talents of his father encouraged him to believe that he could achieve eminence in the same path.

Upon the day which is introduced in the beginning of this chapter, he had gone to New York to join his party in a great outbreak of enthusiasm; he spoke, and was loudly applauded; the excitement of the day was followed by a supper given by the leaders to one of the great men, and to which Mr. Madison of course must remain.

The supper at the Astor was faultless, the wines were such as great men may drink without doing injustice to their taste, the remarks were profound, disinterested, and logical. Under the influence of the champagne and the speeches the country came very near being saved! But, alas, for one of its eloquent friends! Parke Madison, the generous, the witty, the earnest, the well-meaning, could control others better than he could himself. Forever striving after the right, and forever falling! That fatal weakness of resolution broke down this evening as it had done in days gone by. Not more surely will a moth always flutter into destruction when a lamp is by, than he would be tempted to excess by a scene like this. He knew it before he placed himself in the way of temptation; but his ardent temperament was already excited beyond prudence by the events of the day. He attended the feast given to the great man, and became intoxicated in his honor.

Lucy followed the suggestion of her house-keeper, and drank her tea, but it was with very little relish. She then returned to a charming employment, which was that of sketching little Carrie as she lay asleep in her crib. She was intending to surprise Parke with a birth-day present of the picture, painted on ivory, and handsomely set. The dimpled arm tossed up beside the rosy cheeks, the golden lashes, and the still more golden curls, the pouting, parted lips, made a fine subject for the mother artist. She drew the outlines and drapery, after which she laid her work aside in order to do the coloring by the nicer light of day. It was the usual hour of retiring; she no longer expected her husband that night, but she could not go to bed as long as there was a possibility of his returning. She hemmed a little on a piece of cambric, she played a short time on her guitar, she tried to get interested in a book, but her mind was uneasy, and she could not amuse it. At twelve o'clock, weary but nervous, she retired to short slumbers and disturbing dreams. It was her first night of watching for a dissipated husband, but it was not her last.

At noon, of the following day, Mr. Madison came home.

He thought that his secret was safe from his wife. He greeted her gayly, and with many excuses for not sending her word that he should remain in town over night, he kissed Carrie, sat her upon his knee, and proceeded to astonish and delight her with the gift of her first doll-baby. But the quick eye of affection detected the lurking shame in his glance, its ear pined with the nervous hastiness of the first greeting; and in his kiss, despite of the frequent confection he had been eating, remained the feverish complaint of an ill-used stomach. Lucy kept her wretched discovery to herself, and abated nothing of her gentle welcome. She would not humble the pride of her husband, by allowing him to know that she was conscious of his error. But when she found him more absorbed than ever in politics, and bent upon walking right into the net — that he was restless until the next day came for a public excitement, and that he spent more than half of his time in the city, she was obliged to remonstrate. Such remonstrance might rather be called the very gentleness of entreaty. It was with threads of silver and gold that she endeavored to keep him within the sacred circle of home, where the evil genii that surrounded him in the outer air could not intrude.

The worm of the still, when its eye is once fastened upon a victim, must exercise a fascination more alluring than the dreaded enchantments of the rattle-snake. Else how could it draw Parke Madison, held back as he was by past experience, by a wife like Lucy, a sister like Alice; how could it draw him from the holiness of his hearth-stone, downwards to the old desperation of excess?

Upon that birthday, when Lucy designed to surprise him with the exquisitely-finished portrait of Carrie asleep, he came home, for the first time, in a disgraceful condition. Hitherto he had carefully remained away until in a fit state to return to his family. It happened that Mrs. Madison had company. Mrs. Van Duyn was out, with an old friend from Philadelphia, a lady of such mind and attainments as secured for her the love and respect of whatever circle she adorned with her presence. She had always made a pet of Lucy, who, in her girlhood, had once or twice visited her in her own city. Now she had come to see what kind of a home the fair girl had to boast of, what kind of a husband, and what kind of a baby; for she had heard a great deal about all of these, but she had not beheld with her own eyes the prosperity of this beautiful branch of the fatherland vine.

When they first arrived Mr. Madison was not at home. Lucy gave them a cheerful welcome. There was not even a shadow upon her brow that day, for Parke had been so good for the past week, and she had so pleased herself with thoughts of the present she had as a surprise for him, that her brown eyes were seldom brighter, or her cheeks more glowing.

"I think you have chanced here to keep Parke's birthday, she said, as she drew chairs for them close to the grate in the large parlor.

It was a cold day for October, and they had rode from Mrs. Van Duyn's on the other side of New York.

"Dear mother, I am so glad to see you; why didn't you bring Katy or Willy with you? too cold! but they would have been so delighted with Carrie, now that she can run alone. It is an unexpected happiness to have you for a guest, Mrs. Smythe; I am so much obliged to you for coming. I wish Mr. Madison was at home. But he will be, before tea; and of course you will not stay less than a week, so a few hours will be no great robbery."

How musically the tongue of the young wife ran on. The mother and friend smiled at each other to witness her fine spirits. As soon as they were warmed, and had partaken of the refreshments welcome after their chilly ride, Margery, the maid, was sent after Carrie, who was taking her afternoon siesta. Margery led her into the parlor with triumph, walking in her own tiny shoes, and not tumbling down once all the immense distance from the door to her mamma's arms.

"This only 'leven months old," the maid informed Mrs. Smythe, who, eager as she was to get the little creature on her lap, must wait for 'grand-ma' to have done with her caresess.

"Aye! she's not a year old yet, and she walks, and says papa, and does a thousand such pretty things. Don't you think, Mrs. Smythe, that she is the greatest baby of the age?"

"I have not had very extensive opportunities for judging," replied that lady with her genial smile. "I am not acquainted with over thirty of her size, but I think that she compares favorably with the most of them. Come here, little one! Carrie is your name? let me look at you — soft, fine hair, curling up like golden grape-tendrils around your head — pure complexion — clear, full, violet eyes — those are father's eyes, are they not? — a mouth so beautiful in its rosiness that I cannot tell yet whether it will be a beauty's mouth or not — mother's neck, slender and peerless, as if the 'blood of all the Howards' had taught it its queenly mould — yes, Madam Madison, you may be forgiven for pride in your baby's looks. But as for her talking and walking, she isn't a bit more precocious than the rest of the thirty; and you do not want to be, do you, Carrie? You do not want to die of smartness in your infancy? nor to be a little wonder, in order to grow up a great dunce?" Probably Carrie did not, for she shook her head and laughed. "That is right. You shall not be if I can help it. You shall know nothing for a good while yet except to love papa, mamma, and sugar-plums. Here is a sugar-plum with which to engage your affections; it has hidden itself in the depths of my pocket as if on purpose for this occasion. Do not look so gravely, Mrs. Madison, there is nothing poison in this confection; it is pure sweet and will do no harm."

"I shall be jealous," said Mrs. Van Duyn, "of my grand-motherly rights, if Carrie is to take to you so contentedly. She is perched on your knee too quietly."

"The babies all like me — I am their aunt-in-general."

"Like your sweet gifts, perhaps," said Lucy.

"No, they like me. It is seldom that I purchase their love with sweets. I want them to love me on the sympathetic principle that I love them."

"And I know that they do," said Lucy, looking affectionately into that countenance which beamed with kindness and intelligence. "It isn't the little folks, alone, either."

"I am not ungrateful," replied Mrs. Smythe, gently.

That was the charm of her character. To give as much as was given, and more, of affection to all. Her sympathies were always ready to be enlisted, and her heart overflowed with that christian charity and good will to her fellow-creatures, which secured her in return their confidence and love.

Lucy brought the picture of Carrie, which she had caused to be set in gold and pearls the last time she was in the city, and showed it to her visitors. They were warm in their praises, and admired the design exceedingly.

"What does Parke think of it?" asked Mrs. Van Duyn.

"Ah! I should like to know what he *will* think of it, when he sees it!" replied Lucy. "It is his birthday gift; and you shall see the manner in which he receives it. I hope it will please him!"

"It cannot fail to do that. He ought to be enraptured," said her friends, and she put it in her bosom for safe keeping until tea-time.

The three ladies had such a social and happy afternoon, as confidential chit-chat among a kindly friend, a proud grand-mother, a joyous mother, and a good-natured little one ought to make. Lucy inquired minutely into every little circumstance of the life at the old home. That sister to whom she was teaching German, the eventful day upon which she introduced herself to her future husband, as he lay, regardless of elegance at her feet — that sister was now a blooming young lady, who had taken her place in the household circle. Katy was growing into a slender maiden, with a sentimental turn of mind, who read a great deal of poetry, and had been known to scribble romantic verses under the old oaks in the meadow. Willie was begging sturdily to go to his uncle Nold's in Philadelphia. This uncle was a forwarding merchant, who having not a boy, although blessed with five girls, desired to adopt this of his sister's.

The lamps were lighted before the sound of a carriage rolling up to the door, and of steps in the hall, told Lucy that her husband had returned. A rich color rushed into her cheek, and her dark eyes lighted up. Mrs. Smythe smiled secretly to observe the unconscious pride and brilliancy that came over her demeanor. Lucy was indeed proud of her husband, not only of his beauty and accomplishments, but of that eloquence of conversation and grace of manner which he had inherited from his father. She arose as he came into the apartment, but hesitated as she was about to advance to meet him.

"Lute, my love!" he began, in no very dulcet voice, "how do you do? Gen. Taylor will be President as sure as —— ah! Mrs. Van Duyn!" he shook hands with her gaily.

She was astonished at his flushed face and disorderly air; but as Lucy made no move to do so, she presented him to her friend.

"Mrs. Smythe — Smythe! you are not the person who makes shirts for me, by that name? ah, no! I remember now — from Philadelphia? I beg your pardon — how well you are looking — extremely well! I think I never saw you looking so finely, Madam."

"I presume you never did," replied that lady, not daring to glance towards the young wife, whose face had grown pale, and who stood motionless as if from alarm.

He took a chair and sat down confidentially near her.

"Would you ever have thought Old Whitey's prospects were so favorable?" he asked, in a muddled tone. "I've a bet of two thousand against one thousand that he will never sit in the Presidential chair."

"I dare say you will win," replied his guest, a flash of humor breaking through her gravity. "We have never elevated horses to that dignity yet; though it has been aspired to by a still inferior animal."

"'My horse! my horse! a kingdom for my horse!' says Hudibras. So there, Madam, was a man who was willing to give his horse a kingdom, if we are not. But you are right, I intended to speak of Old Whitey — not his master."

"Ah?" was all his companion ventured to say.

Mrs. Van Duyn was sitting opposite, her face burning with indignation and surprise. Poor Lucy retreated into the nursery, where she sank down upon the bed, and burst into tears of mortification. Was this the husband she had arisen in such a glow of pride to present to her old friend? Bitter was her humiliation; but humiliation is not the worst suffering of a drunkard's wife; and if we pity her now, we shall have more to pity her for bye-and-bye.

"It seems to me that you are hardly yourself, Sir, this evening," observed his mother-in-law, coldly.

"Why — no — I am not. At least I thought that I was not a short time ago," he replied, looking at her comically. "I imagined that I was a bottle of champagne which the Whigs and Locos were playing a game of 'brag' for. As I was only a bottle of wine they thought nothing of my looking over, and from where I sat on the table, I could see the Old General cheating furiously: I tried to inflate myself enough to get the cork out of my mouth, so that I could cry out 'fraud! treason!' and in trying to do it I upset myself — crash! fizz! — I was a bottle of spilled champagne, not worth quarreling about. I had no hopes of ever getting myself together again, when John picked me up and put me, not in the broken bottle, but on my seat. You see, the roads were so confounded rough, and he had driven over a stone and jostled me off!"

He told this little story with great spirit. The two ladies glanced at each other as if not knowing whether to laugh or cry.

"Are you satisfied now of your identity?" inquired Mrs. Smythe, after a pause. "I suspect that you hold more champagne now than a steady, respectable bottle should do."

"You wrong me," Mrs. Brown," he replied, with an air of dignity that would have been superb upon a sober man. "There no doubt appears something peculiar in my manner, but it is owing to the excitement of the times. I have taken a glass once or twice to-day with a few of my friends — but the condition of our party demanded it. When the interests of the country are at stake a man must not stand ——"

"Nor fall —" suggested Mrs. Smythe.

"There you have me again. You are witty, Mrs. Brown," with an admiring bow: "no, he must not fall, as I did once to-day; but he must not stand upon trifles. It is against my principles to touch any kind of intoxicating beverage. I swore to my dear Lucy, before I was married, that I never would 'toy with the dangerous flame;' did I not, my love?" he turned to where his wife had stood, but she was gone; "and I am bound to keep my promise sacredly after the first Tuesday in November. Excuse me, my dear mother — pardon me, Mrs. Brown — I must leave you a moment 'to the society of your sweet selves' — I haven't had a kiss from Carrie yet."

He made another princely bow, and retreated to the nursery in search of his baby.

"Poor Lucy! my prophecy has come true!" cried the

mother, as he disappeared, "woe and wretchedness are in store for you, I fear."

"Displeasure and pride for a time kept back her tears, and then they flowed accordant with her daughter's.

"I am more than surprised! I had no suspicion of this," said her friend. Poor Lucy! indeed! He looks like a splendid man though, what a pity—pity—pity!"

"It is the first time that I have known him to touch wine for more than four years. I had began to lose all my old apprehensions; but I had reason for them, I could read his character better than those young people who thought that a few months of trial had proved him sufficiently. 'Unstable as water, thou shalt not excel,' is written upon his destiny. It mars the brilliancy of his gifts, it makes of no account his good resolutions. Yet how could I blame Lucy for loving him—or for determining to share his fortunes, be they good or bad? For if his character is unstable as water, like water it is fascinating—sparkling with evanescent hues and shades, lit up by every gleam of beauty, musical with depths that excite curiosity, and tones that are strangely pleasing."

"I should judge as much of him. But, alas! of what avail are these excellencies, if all to be darkened in this manner! Probably though, this is but a rare excess, and will never lead to confirmed intemperance. Surely the influence of a strong-minded and warm-hearted girl like Lucy ought to prevent any man from becoming a brute."

"I pray heaven that it may! but I have no confidence

in him. With him it has always been to take one step and then look back no more, until dragged by some powerful effort of others into comparative safety."

Lucy interrupted them by coming to lead them to the tea-table.

"It is the first time I have seen him so — but he has been drinking for two or three weeks," she said in reply to her mother's question.

Traces of tears were upon her cheeks, but she said nothing more upon the subject. Mr. Madison was at tea, but as the stimulus he had taken subsided in its exhilarating effects he grew silent and sleepy. Immediately after the uncomfortable meal was finished, he pleaded fatigue, and politely withdrew. The ladies gathered around the centre-table in the parlor with their knitting, and tried to pass a cheerful evening, but tried in vain. Lucy was proud as well as affectionate; so that whatever her secret fears were, or however much she felt disposed to blame, she would not touch upon her feelings, even to her mother. She remembered that mother's warning; and with a swelling heart she resolved that the prophecy should not be realized if everything that a truthful and patient wife could do should have any effect.

Of course the presentation of the portrait had to be delayed until morning. Something of the mortification which had tortured Lucy the preceding evening was now endured by Parke, as he, with a faint recollection of his yesterday's absurdities, was obliged to be present at breakfast. He would have given half his farm to be a hundred miles away from the reproachful glance of Mrs. Van Duyn's eye, as she took his hand at meeting. He felt that he had wounded the mother through her child's heart — that beloved child whom he had taken from her, to cherish with a husband's fondness. Lucy was all kindness; and Mrs. Smythe appeared to have forgotten the manner in which their acquaintance was made. The remembrance to him was intolerable; hearing that the guests designed returning home that afternoon, he made an errand to town, that he might be relieved from that society which would have been so agreeable but two days ago; resolved not to return until they had departed.

There was a silent language in the embrace Mrs. Van Duyn gave her daughter at parting — unutterable love, the wish to avert danger, to protect from coming sorrow. It brought the quick drops to Lucy's eyes, but she bravely drove them back.

"Mrs. Smythe," she said, "you must forgive Mr. Madison for my sake. It is his first offence, and I am determined that it shall be his last."

She smiled, but it did not hide the quiver of her lips.

That night, again, Parke did not return home.

From that time began for Lucy Madison the untold miseries of an inebriate's wife. It had been hard and bitter for a sister to wear out the midnight hours in waiting — to wear out her hopes in watching — to wear out her heart in sorrow; but a sister's wretchedness cannot be that of a wife's.

She looked upon her child with mingled feelings; it was her consolation and her trouble. Its pretty ways wiled her of many a weary hour; but thoughts of its future, as cursed by an unhappy father, gave her many another sleepless one. It was with no tender thrill of joy that she found, before the winter was past, that she had the promise of again becoming a mother. Ah, no! why should she desire children? that they might grow up ashamed, with an inheritance of vice? Her spirits ebbed to the lowest tide, but she never for a moment gave up to despair. Parke, wavering and unsteady as he was, could not have had a companion more purposed for his good. With all her affection, Lucy had her mother's indomitable soul, her noble pride and persevering energy. When she saw that he neglected his farm affairs, and that his carelessness was taken advantage of by his men, she, herself, stepped forward to the rescue of their falling fortunes, and made their people feel that there was still a head at work, if it was a woman's head. One third of their beautiful estate went immediately after election into the hands of those with whom he had betted. This loss was not sufficient to diminish any of their comforts — it only foreboded troubles that were yet to come.

A few months of dissipation produced their usual effects upon Parke. His nerves, unstrung by excess, grew irritable, and as a natural consequence his temper grew harsh and fretful. His remorse did not tend to sooth them, and the result was coldness and unkindness towards his wife. In vain she tried now to wile him back to his former self with the sweetness of her guitar, and the still softer music of her voice. In vain that she strove to keep him at home by making their artless daughter the pretty pleader. His every-day stimulus was brandy now; and it eat into his heart and brain as well as his stomach. It preyed upon those nice perceptions and glowing imaginations which once added such spirit to his character; it gnawed ceaselessly at those heart-strings once so finely strung to the lightest touch of love, until they mouldered one by one, and when Lucy would have wakened their melody as of old, there was silence where once was sweetest sound. It inflamed the coarser passions of his nature, those which could endure the fiery lash; but his more delicate sensibilities fell and perished under the infliction. There grew less and less in him to love. It was not only that harshness and moodiness repelled her affection; when Lucy looked for those qualities which had won her passionate regard, they were gone. Gone the soul-beaming glance — gone the glory and purity of intellectual gifts — gone the gentleness of manner — gone the playful fancy —gone the tender and reverential admiration of her wifely excellence! In their place, the sullen and abashed look, the dull and diseased mind, the reckless hardness of actions, the senseless gayety startling at times out of stupidity, the cowardly coldness on the maudlin caress.

It takes more than a few months of trial to wear out a woman's endurance. Lucy's devotion was more than ever, if her affection was somewhat less. She loved him for what he had been and for what she still hoped he would yet be. She loved him as the love of her youth, her husband, and the father of Carrie. A protector he had ceased to be, and had become instead a persecutor.

The days came for maple-sugar making. Lucy allowed the fires to glare, the smoke to struggle with the leafless trees, the kettles to bubble and sing, without going out to enjoy this little piece of domestic romance. She thanked the farmer's boys when they brought her hearts, and doves, and eggs of new sugar, with a smile that sent them off happy, but she neglected her old seat among the gnarled roots of a maple; and giving the sweet devices to Carrie, who could best appreciate them, she turned with a sigh to other employments.

Dear little Carrie! playing a fairy's part in the drama of home, with a wand of sunshine, whose power fell brightly upon all. She was too little to fear the shadows gathering around the hearth; at last, they began to fall even upon her. Her father, in his irritable moods, would let his ill-humor rest upon her — a scowl, an impatient word, a cruel shake of that tiny form, was enough to grieve her to the heart, and send her sobbing to her mother. She did not run, as she was wont, to lead him by the hand the moment she heard his step in the hall; but shrinking close to her protecting mamma, she would wait until she had read his face before she ventured to intrude her innocent affection upon him. Whenever he observed this it displeased him, and he would accuse Lucy of teaching his child to dislike her father! There was another subject upon which he took it into his disordered mind to be uncontented. They were getting too poor, he said, to afford to raise a family, and he did not see what Lucy was such a dunce for as to be troubling him with the prospects of more children, when they could just manage to live now! Well might her mother exclaim, "Poor Lucy! woe and wretchedness are in store for you!"

The warm weather was trying to her health. Her mother, Mrs. Crawford, and Alice, all endeavored to induce her to spend a few weeks with them; but she refused, because she was afraid that in her absence her husband would feel still less restraint. It was "for better, for worse," that she married him, and she was not going to desert him even for a little while. In these dark days of his trial and temptation, if *she* did not cling to him, who would? If he had no patience, she must have all; if he had no dignity, she must have more; if he had no prudence, she must exercise double vigilance. God, who knows the heart, knows that Parke had hours of deep repentance, of mental agony; and that Lucy knew of these, and pitied while she blamed, and loved while she pitied. To others and to herself she urged, in extenuation, his inherited defects of energy and passion for stimulating drink, and they were good excuses as far as they went. She cried out as Parke's mother and sister, as he himself, had done—

"Since he cannot control himself, why is there no power that can be brought to bear to prevent this worst of self-murders?" In her anguish there was evidence that no sophistry, no policy of state, could refute. If any one had asked her in such moments "if the traffick in intoxicating drinks was an evil?" she would have gazed at him in astonishment. If he had went on with his questions and enquired "whether it was right to prohibit evil by law?" she would still have regarded these simple propositions, already decided in the hearts of every drunkard's wife and child and friend, and of every drunkard himself, as so established in the affirmative as to require no answer. She would not have stopped to enquire, "Will it add to or take away from the income of this Government?" but she would have stretched out her hands to the nation and cried,

"Give me my husband! give me back my husband!"

One pleasant day in September, Lucy sat by the window in that west room where Parke's mother had died, and which was always the pleasantest of summer rooms. In her lap was a variety of Carrie's out-grown baby-clothes which she was preparing for the expected little stranger. A tear would occasionally steal slowly down her cheek and drop upon her work, as she mused upon the past, and with what different and happier emotions she had first fashioned those fine cambrics, soft flannels, and dainty embroideries.

Carrie sat on a footstool by her side, with a huge needle, a long thread, and a wee-bit of cloth, taking her first lesson in the womanly-accomplishment of sewing.

Suddenly she hushed her childish prattle, for she heard her father coming around the portico with hasty steps.

"Curse it!" he was swearing to himself, "that dog Dixon has cheated me out of five hundred dollars — I know he has; and he's so cursed impudent about it, too! I'll not have him on this farm another year — no! he shall leave, if he goes to perdition!"

He came into his wife's presence and commenced his complaints. He was not intoxicated, though he had been drinking some. She ventured a remonstrance, when he swore that he would discharge his farmer; for she knew that Dixon would do better than anybody else, even if he did not always do right, and she told him so.

"What do you women know about that? he asked, with contempt. "Here, Carrie, come to your father!"

Mrs. Madison thought that she had had good opportunities for learning something of his affairs, but she said nothing. Carrie was hiding behind her chair, regarding her father fearfully, one eye just visible through Lucy's net-work of braided hair. She hesitated to obey his command, which was spoken in no gentle tone.

"What are you skulking there for? are you afraid of me? This is some of your work, Mrs. Madison, teaching our child to dislike me! I will have no such actions in a daughter of mine. When I call her, she shall come; and without turning white, either."

He was terribly out of humor, and as he approached the trembling little girl, Lucy was afraid that he would lay violent hands upon her. She stood up, and pushed Carrie behind her.

"Parke! what do you mean? I have taught your child no disobedience. You know very well that she has reason to be afraid of you. It is you who have taught her this fear."

"Is she to witness your disrespect, Madam, and to think that you are going to interfere with my commands?"

He put out his hand, not to strike, but to thrust her rudely to one side. In her present condition she was not strong; she staggered and dropped to the floor, bruising her temple against the window-casement. Ashamed and alarmed, her husband raised her, and found that she had fainted. At that moment his sister Alice confronted him. She had rode out from town upon horseback to enquire after Lucy's health, and coming silently up the greensward had dismounted and entered the house without being perceived. She stood in the door during this brief scene. When she stepped forward to the wife's aid, her face was colorless, and her eyes flashed with a fire that had never been kindled in their depths before.

"Go!" she said, in a clear, ringing voice, "leave her with me! You are unfit to render assistance here."

She took the sufferer from him, as if she had the strength of a giant, laid her tenderly upon the lounge, dipped her handkerchief in a pitcher of ice-water which stood upon the table, bathing that bruised forehead and wiping the blood which trickled slowly from the temple. He lingered until Lucy opened her eyes, and then retreated from the room. With mechanical composure, Alice continued her efforts, until consciousness had fully returned and Lucy made an effort to sit up.

"I am not hurt," she said, "I was only stunned for a moment. He did not intend to hurt me — I know he didn't — but I was so weak. Now, Alice, do not tell mother."

Alice turned away her eyes from that pleading face — she could hear no more — rising abruptly she went from the room. She entered the parlor and closed the door. Parke was there, moving restlessly about the room. He paused and gazed at her as she stood before him. Despite of his shame, he could not but look at her in wonder. She seemed two or three inches taller than usual. Her wasted, delicate figure expanded and heightened with the inward force of her emotions. Her face and lips were hueless — only those dark, large eyes burned with the flame that was kindled within.

"Oh, wretched man! will you have another victim?"

Was that his sister who was speaking? Something in her changed voice compelled his confused faculties to gather into one clear sense of hearing.

"Will you add murder to your crushing responsibility? Look at me, Parke; is this the eye, the brow, the cheeks of twenty-two? I am one of your victims; I gave myself a sacrifice to keep you from that prison where it were better you now were. I have inflicted upon myself more misery than a life of imprisonment in a dungeon could bring. I am the wife of a man who esteems himself a god, and worships himself accordingly. I am the slave of a heartless voluptuary. To save you, I overcame that terror with which my purer nature shrank from his, and stood beside him at the altar. I lived with him, and found that I had linked my earthly fate with that of an infidel, a hater of man and a scorner of God. I could not love him. He did not demand my love. It was enough for him to feel that I belonged to him; he made no demand for those tender fancies and yearning affections which form so large a part of a woman's nature. He laughed at my religion. I lived on with the heart of youth growing cold in my bosom, and its warm pulses declining to a weary slowness; associated with a tyrant, wrapped in luxurious indulgences, who took all that he could secure of pleasure in this world with no fear or expectation of another. At last he has grown tired of me. That coldness and resignation which he once delighted in, because he could torture it, has become too cold and too resigned for him. He will have no more of me. To-morrow, Mr. Clyde goes south, and leaves me behind. He never intends to see me again; but he does not wish the world to think it a case of heartless desertion, for he lives upon the honey of the world, and would keep its good opinion. So he has instituted an understanding that business calls him him away, and will leave people to discover in the course of time what his real motives are. He leaves me alone, exposed to misrepresentation and calumny. He leaves me without sufficient means for my support, for my fortune and his own are not too much for his pleasure. I must either become dependent upon the kindness of the Crawford's or give lessons in music for a living. Parke Madison! this is your work. In being faithful to you as my mother demanded, your own follies have led me into this bitter and neglected state. What is my reward? Have I a brother who will step forth like a man and demand the rights of his sister? Instead, I see before me a brute, who has just stricken the wife of his bosom to the earth. I see two hearts breaking. I see a little child, learning in its infancy the language of curses, frowns, and blows. And seeing this, I am tempted to renounce you, I think that I am absolved from that dying injunction, since I have beheld you strike your wife prostrate — and such a wife, and in such a condition. I wronged Lucy when I permitted her to marry you, without vowing to her that it would be her curse. Now I am going to take her away from you until she is in at least a less dangerous situation for enduring the blows of an enraged husband. I shall take her back to her mother, this very day, whether she wishes to go or not, and there she shall remain until you are worthy to claim her, or until her health permits her to return to you. Oh! my mother!" she laid her hands together and lifted up her eyes; "if thou canst look down from thy walks in Paradise, my sunken cheek, my dreary brow, my lingering step, my blighted heart, shall be to thee the assurance of my faithfulness; thou canst require no more of me — thou wilt not blame if I now forsake him!"

Had she ceased to speak? — Parke stood shivering before her, thrilled through and through by her voice, as by a blast of cold mountain wind. He half expected to hear the tones of his mother in response floating down through the sky and sealing his condemnation.

"My God! Alice!" he cried with a sudden burst of despair, "*are* you going to forsake me? then I am indeed lost!"

It seemed as if he had some idea that as long as so pure and etherial a creature as Alice clung to him, that the angels and their Lord might have compassion upon him and consider him kindly for her sake.

She made no reply, but glided like a shadow out of the room.

By her directions the family carriage was prepared as comfortably as possible, and Lucy placed therein. Carrie and a trunk of clothing followed. Lucy was loth to go. She felt as if she ought to go, out of consideration for her own comfort; but she could not endure to leave her husband to his own unhappy society. Parke saw them depart from the parlor-window; Alice riding her pony close by the carriage, looking in and talking to its occupants. Should he let them go? it was his right and privilege to recall his wife and child and compel them to obedience. The terror which came over him when he saw Lucy lying senseless before him, recurred to his mind; how should he answer for himself, that to-morrow he might not again be as much of a brute, or perhaps a murderer? How could he give surety for the conduct of a madman? and did he not make a madman of himself every day?

He turned from the window, as the carriage slowly rolled away, and walked rapidly back and forth, such fire scorched his brain, such red shapes swam before his eyes, such hideous images thronged his mind, that he was seized with a fear of the drunkard's mania. Was *that* madness coming upon him, too? with a cry between a groan and shriek he rushed out of the house and ran towards the grove. Anywhere, anywhere, out into the open air where no eye could behold him, nor ear take note of his distress. He fled along; in gaining the grove, he had to cross the stream which wound through the meadow. Late rains had swelled it to quite a little river. As his foot lingered on the log which spanned it, a new sound confused him — "Anywhere — anywhere *out of the world!*" rang through his ear; he obeyed the cunning suggestion and sprang into the stream. He fell face downwards, sank, and rose again struggling. He struck out his hands, but they clutched not even a straw. Demons were shouting in his ears and sitting upon his breast. Off! off! would they not release him from their dreadful weight upon his bosom? no! they laughed and roared, and their pressure grew intolerable. Then they slowly swam away, leaving him floating upon a cloud airily through the sky, and Lucy singing her cradle-songs to Carrie, close by his side. Then * * * *

It was scarcely more than a week after Lucy was settled in her mother's home before her baby was born. She was very ill, and the baby, a boy, was a feeble, tiny little creature. She had the best of nurses in Alice and Mrs.

Van Duyn. The slow-spoken Doctor, who once attended upon Parke's broken head and arm, was exceedingly interested in his patient and anxious to have her recover. For some time her life was in danger, but in the course of two or three weeks she began to amend. Every comfort and kindness surrounded her sick bed; every blessing except that she most pined for, the presence of her husband. He was the father of a boy; and perhaps he did not even know of it; he had never taken the little fellow in his arms, kissed its puny face, nor thanked her for the peril she had endured, nor the son she had given. For long hours she would lay with closed eyes, her whole being absorbed in an intense yearning to look upon her husband, to feel his lips upon her forehead, and to nestle her hand in his. She spoke to her mother about it every day; but the mother-in-law could not forget, as her daughter had, the wrongs of the sufferer. She was not aware of how powerful Lucy's feelings were upon the subject, until the physician told her that, as long as the cause for such nervous excitement existed in his patient, he could not hope to see her get well.

Katy was very much disappointed because the baby was not a girl. She had a name ready for it, but it would not sound well to call a boy 'Jane Eyre,' and she was obliged to relinquish the idea. She puzzled her brain to decide between 'Herbert Gray' and 'Vivian.' Poor little thing! it needed no name. After a brief month of pain and pining away, it closed its eyes upon a troublous earth. The children wept over the corpse, tiny and white in its pretty coffin, for 'the baby' was a precious thing to them. Carrie cried because 'brother' was so cold, and because they took him away and put him in the ground beneath the oak in the meadow and left him alone in the dark.

Lucy mourned deeply over its loss. It was all the dearer to her for being so surrounded by tribulations. Its sickliness and feebleness had awakened strange feelings of tenderness; and it was born, and dead, and buried, and its father had never beheld it. What to her now were his cruel taunts when he had declared himself too poor to be burdened with a family? nothing; she forgave him all and felt that she should die if she should not see him. She sank again so rapidly that messengers were dispatched with the news of her danger, and her desire to see him, to Mr. Madison.

When Parke left the house with that fierce cry, he had startled the house-keeper from her quiet seat in the dining-room, where she sat reflecting upon the wickedness of men, and wondering when her mistress thought of returning.

"Mercy sakes! I believe he's gone crazy!" she ejaculated, as she saw him flying across the meadow. "Here, Dixon, set down that milk and come and see what's the matter with Mr. Madison."

Dixon was in the kitchen helping himself to a bowl of bread and milk; he did not stir at her bidding.

"I don't care what's the matter with him, I'm sure. He called me a liar and robber not three hours ago."

"Lord a'mercy! if he hasn't jumped plump into the

creek! He's drowning; Dixon, you fool, aint you going to start?"

The farmer's resentment did not extend as far as to wish death for his landlord just then; so he threw down his spoon, and started on a lumbering run to the rescue. The drowning man was insensible when he dragged him out. Hester prided herself on her skill as a doctress as well as house-keeper; her strong arms and rude remedies were of good account. She threw over the first barrel she came to, which chanced to be the swill-barrel, and helped Dixon to bear him to it, and left him with injunctions to roll him desperately every minute while she hastened after blankets, and hot ashes, and the bellows. Their united exertions were crowned with success. Parke recovered his breath, with a portion of his senses, and passed a sick night with only Hester to sit by his couch. But the demons were driven away for the present. Hydropathy had cured him of incipient delirium-tremens.

The next day, haggard and weak, he rode on horseback to the city, to give Alfred Clyde a warning not to ill-treat his sister! but that gentleman had already left on the boat, and Alice was out at Mrs. Van Duyn's.

"After all," he muttered, turning from the Clyde residence, "what could I have said to the villain, when my own wife has taken refuge in her mother's home from my ferocity?"

Truly he could have said nothing; for Alfred with cool sarcasm, polished and sharp as steel, would have defeated him, and left him powerless on the field. As Alice accused him, he was not fit to be a brother or protector.

This reflection was so humiliating that he called at the first saloon for something to exhilarate his self-esteem. Another week of intoxication ensued, from which he was aroused by hearing of Lucy's danger. This appalling news brought another of those seasons of repentance, when the tempter was nearly overcome. Not daring to intrude into the house, he haunted the vicinity of the cottage day after day. Several nights he set under the window of the sick-room, as if there he could hear that feeble breathing which might so soon be suspended. His suspense was such that he always contrived to be somewhere near when the physician took his departure, and from him he was informed of her condition constantly. Had Hebe then offered him a goblet of nectar he would have dashed it to earth. He knew when his boy died; he saw the grave hallowed and the tiny coffin lowered; that night he lay upon the mound, with the bible Alice had given him in his school days, clasped in his hand, praying God to listen to his prodigal prayers, to strengthen his renewed resolutions.

The messenger had not far to go, who was sent for him. The doctor had informed him that he should order Lucy's wishes attended to. He, with Mrs. Van Duyn and Alice, sat in the outer room when Parke passed through to the sick-chamber. He did not look at them, but passed with a quick, light step to his wife's bedside.

"Parke!"

"Lucy!"

He bowed his head upon that thin hand and wet it with his tears. A faint pressure of her attenuated fingers and a wan smile was all the welcome she could give him.

"You are not going to die?" he asked, gazing eagerly into her face.

"No—I feel better this noon," she whispered.

In ten brief moments the physician separated them; but Lucy knew that her husband was under the same roof, and she sank into a refreshing sleep.

It was many weeks before she recovered strength so as to return to her own home. In the meantime Alice had found a refuge, pale and weary dove! with Mrs. Crawford As Mr. Crawford was gone, to be absent a year in the west attending to extensive agencies, she was delighted to get her adopted daughter back again. Not even to her did Alice confide the truth that she was deserted. Comparatively happy to escape from daily persecutions, she made an effort to regain some portion of her youthful vivacity. But her spirits had been too long strained to an unnatural tension; they would not spring back with the old buoyancy.

With no one who was meet to be her companion, Lucy and Parke absorbed in each other, and no one of her own age, in whose society to recover herself, she drooped, growing more silent, lily-like, and fragile every day.

CHAPTER X.

In a small dwelling, upon the outskirts of a western village, a lamp burned late at night. Snow was heaped about the steps, and upon the casement, which rattled to the tune of a disconsolate wind. Within, a woman of twenty-five, her chair and table drawn close to the stove, was busy with some motherly employment. A box of water-color paints, with brushes and drawing utensils, occupied a portion of the small table, but these were not now in use. A pair of small stockings, that had been darned for the fiftieth time, lay beside them, and the solitary worker, shivering over the stove, which contained only the pretence of a fire, was busily sewing up the rents in a pair of shabby shoes. A little girl, about four years of age, lay asleep in her crib, the clothes tucked warmly about her; unconscious, during the blessed rest of childhood. of the care her mother was giving to her humble apparel. She had placed the patched shoes beside the stockings, and was proceeding with a weary air to wash out a couple of aprons in a kettle of water that stood upon the stove, when the sound of an unsteady step, and a hand feeling for the latch, arrested her. She hastily hid the painting materials in a drawer of the stand, before she unfastened the door.

"What the deuce do you keep a fellow standing all night in the cold for?" grumbled a cross voice, as a person, who had once been a gentleman, stumbled over the threshold.

"I came as quickly as I could."

"No, you didn't come as quickly as you could. Do you call this a fire? a pretty way to treat a man when he is out until midnight, to come home and find no fire, and the weather cold enough to freeze the ———."

He sat down and commenced rubbing his hands to warm them, glaring half angrily, half stupidly at the hearth; while his wife wrung out the aprons and hung them upon a chair.

"I say, Lucy, where's that five dollars you got to-day?" he suddenly exclaimed, lifting up his head.

"What five dollars?—what do you mean?" she asked, with an endeavor to look unconcerned, but a slight flush arose to her care-worn cheek.

"Now, don't pretend ignorance in that style. I mean the five dollars that you got for painting little James Kinney. I know that you have it, for his father told me to-day that he had just paid it to you."

"Mr. Kinney is a villain!" burst from the indignant lips of the wife.

Mr. Kinney was a grocer, whose little boy's miniature she had done for the contemptible sum of six dollars; and when she called for her pay he had the heartlessness to tell her that her husband owed him nearly that for liquor. Perhaps the arrows of scorn and resentment which shot from the lips and eyes of a woman like Lucy Madison had wounded him in the only tender part of his heart, his vanity; for he doggedly paid her the money she had earned, except one dollar which she took in sugar, coffee, and tea. But you injure the self-esteem of such a man and he will be revenged. The grocer's casual mention to his customer of the picture his wife had painted, and the sum he had paid for it, was not so carelessly done as it appeared to be.

"I say, Lute, I want that money!"

"You cannot have it. I have imperative use for every penny."

"And so have I. Confound it! I've drank nothing but whiskey for a month. And to-morrow I am bound to have a high; on genuine brandy, too, such as a gentleman ought to drink."

"Wouldn't it be better to spend it for the children, Parke? Carrie has no shoes; nor stockings either, for that matter, that are fit to wear. Besides, we are out of wood, and yet you complain of the fire."

"Oh, nonsense, Lute, let me have the money."

"I must not, and I shall not," she replied firmly. "It is after one o'clock, and you had better go to bed."

A baby, lying in its parents' bed, awaked at the sound

of their voices, and began to cry. Lucy went to it and was soothing it, while its drunken father stumbled around the room, searching in drawers, cupboard, and corners, for the coveted five dollars. He could not find them.

"If you don't tell me where it is, I will beat you to death," he said, stamping his foot upon the floor, when he found his search to be in vain.

She laid down her child and turned towards him.

"Parke, if I give it to you, it will do no good, and the children will suffer. I will not do it for their sakes, nor for your own. You are better without it."

"Where is it?" he demanded, with increasing fury, regarding that slender woman with a threatening air which might well make her secretly tremble, though she tried to be brave, at the thought of her little ones. She folded her arms over her swelling heart and stood silent and pale.

With an oath he seized the kettle from the stove and hurled its contents towards her. The fire had truly burned low, but the kettle was placed immediately above the wasting embers and retained enough heat to be dangerous.

It was the instinct of self-preservation — she forgot her child — she stepped aside — and the scalding water fell into Carrie's crib. The piercing screams of the little sufferer startled the midnight echoes. The mother snatched up her darling, and ran wildly about the room, holding her to her bosom, too distracted to think of any means for her relief At last she sank into a chair, and tore the night-slip from that quivering form. One side of the face, neck, and chest, and one arm, were dreadfully scalded; as the dress was removed, the blistered skin came with it, leaving the flesh exposed and inflicting such excruciating agony that the child went into convulsions.

"Will you go for some one — will you do something?" cried the wretched mother to the man who stood like a stone, sobered by those shrieks of pain and appalled at his own deed. "For a doctor — a doctor!— there is one upon this street, quick!" He went out with so stupid a look, that gazing upon those spasms of pain she hesitated whether she should not leave the poor child alone, while she, herself, ran for aid. Fortunately the physician was returning from a very sick patient whom he had been called up to visit, and encountered Mr. Madison, before he had taken six steps. He returned with him.

"How does this happen, Madam?"

He looked around upon the drunkard's home and needed no other reply. He took the little girl, and gave such directions as Lucy had gained composure enough to follow. The wounds were soon dressed, in as soothing a manner as possible, and the exhausted child laid carefully on a prepared bed where her mother sat by her side the rest of the night, listening to her feeble moans with an aching heart. Overcome by heavy sleep, the author of this misery lay before the stove, drawing long and noisy inspirations, and filling the apartment with the odors of his corrupted breath. The physician had assured her that the burns were not deep enough to be dangerous, unless that upon the chest proved more serious than he anticipated.

"I am almost tempted to vote for the Maine-law men, after the scene which I have witnessed to-night," he told his wife, as he returned to the comfortable bed from which he had been roused. "I can't do it very consistently, either, for there are not three of them who belong to our party; and, after all, if men will make fools and beasts of themselves, I don't know who has a right to interfere."

"The heart knoweth its own bitterness," and none may know what bitterness filled Lucy Madison's during her watch that night.

Within less than a year after the birth of their second child the farm had gone from Parke's hands. His sister Alice could furnish him with no further means, and Mr. Crawford did not feel bound to do it. After gathering together the small remnant of their property, he found that there was enough to take them to some western village, within whose thriving precincts he was sure some employment could be found. And so there could have been for a steady and energetic poor man. But what was there for him, or what would he do if work was furnished, Lucy asked herself and him. There was no living for them in the city, however. Finding him bent upon going, and thinking it the best that could be done, Mr. Crawford offered him some business, which his knowledge of the law made him peculiarly competent to transact, in the village of

A———, in a western State. Lucy was urged by all her friends to remain behind with her mother, at least until it was seen whether Parke met with any success. She was strongly tempted to do so. She felt homesick at the very thought of parting with the scenes of her youth; and both terror and loneliness at the idea of going into a strange place with a husband who she well knew would bring mortification and disgrace upon her, instead of procuring for her and himself that position which she was, and he had been, entitled to. Duty as well as affection whispered, "for better, for worse." Striving nobly to overcome her repinings, she bade a tearful farewell to all endeared associations, and with beautiful little Carrie for her consolation, went with him to sojourn in a strange land. For a short time, pride restrained Mr. Madison from his worst excesses. His reputation as the son of the late senator Madison, the known excellence and fame of his family, procured for him a cordial welcome in the limited society of A———. His wife was esteemed as a most accomplished and dignified woman. They took a small house and furnished it plainly. Lucy's guitar and their books was about all that they retained of their former splendor; but good taste and refinement presided over their poverty, and all would have been well had Parke continued in respectable habits. His restraint soon wore off, and where he had been regarded as a dissipated gentleman he soon found himself a wretched debauchee.

Although Lucy had anticipated severe trials, hundreds that were unlooked for pressed upon her. Parke's situation was a sinecure; a respectable income and nothing of any account to do. Every dollar though, which he received, was wasted in self-indulgence. As long as he had the means, he got drunk bravely and fashionably upon wine, with cards and friends, and dishes of oysters. Want intruded its pinched face within their doors. Lucy advertised as an artist, and for a time received considerable patronage. Upon these earnings she supported the household expenses. She secluded herself entirely within her humble home. Ashamed of her husband, she felt unpleasantly to receive respect and attention which was no longer shown to him. Friends and well-wishers she had, but they were strangers. They pitied secretly, though they dared not condole. She shrank alike from pity and condolence. Her wardrobe began to grow shabby, and she had no purse from which to replenish it. Her health, too, became poor; so that in solitude and loneliness the days passed away. She would have sunk under her afflictions had not Carrie been a constant source of diversion, something to love, to live, to hope, to work for. With her own hands Lucy performed the household labor until nearly the time that her third child was born. She was attended through her illness by kind neighbors, who watched and nursed her, and brought numberless delicacies to tempt her dainty appetite. She was grateful for their attention and care, without which she would have suffered much more than she did; but they were not to her like her mother and Alice and Mrs. Smythe. He who should have made every effort to lighten the tediousness of her invalid hours, was passing the time in saloons and grog-shops, careless of her comfort and forgetful of her loneliness. Great drops would roll down her cheeks and fall upon her little baby's face, as he lay upon her bosom, while with a sigh the words would break from her lips as if they could no longer be repressed —

"Oh! if I could see my mother once more! oh, if Alice was only here to stay with me!"

When she recovered so as to go about the house, she found a sad lack even of the necessities of life. With an infant in her arms, little Carrie to do for, and the family work to perform, she had no leisure for painting. That source of income was cut off; besides, those who were pleased with her work, had nearly all employed her before this, and she had but few opportunities of profiting by her talents.

During the summer, it was the second summer of their stay in A———, these privations could be endured. A fire was not necessary, nor warm clothing; and she and the children could fare content upon simple food. With cold weather, matters grew infinitely worse. As Parke neglected what little business he had to do, his receipts thereupon grew less. Bad liquor — mean, contemptible stuff (not but that the best is bad enough) — was his food, drink, and clothing. He took it from a dirty glass, at a dirty bar, and then lounged in dirty attire upon a dirty bench. *This* was Parke Madison! The dwellers of the town of A———, who passed one of its numerous grog-shops, might cast careless glances upon the shabby man, sunning his rusty broadcloth in the door or upon the vagabond's seat, without a suspicion that he had once been the Count D'Orsay of New York. A lingering of gentility there was about him, a nicety of language, a courtliness sometimes in his drunken dignity; and some remains of his former beauty; but nothing else to distinguish him from the lowest sot who laid his sixpence upon the bar and swallowed his abominable whiskey.

Lucy disposed of her guitar — she had no heart to touch its strings to sweetness now — for money to buy a couple of cords of wood and a barrel of flour. From her own worn-out attire she could still fashion comfortable garments for the children. The first part of the winter passed until at the time when we have seen her in her miserable home sitting up until after midnight, to await a brutal husband, and to eke out the means of a wretched subsistence. There were some chairs, a pretty sewing-stand, a carpet, and some knick-knacks in her little sitting-room, which pride had forbidden her to dispose of, and which prudence suggested her to reserve against a case of actual starvation.

When the grocer had come to have his boy's miniature painted, she was not aware of who he was. She kept her work concealed from Parke, for she knew that he would possess himself of the proceeds; and was carefully calculating in what manner the money could be most judiciously distributed among so many wants. She was indignant to find that she had been employed by one of those vampires who preyed upon the weakness of her husband; and when Mr. Kinney would have reserved her dearly-earned dues to pay the score of his most constant customer, her resentment had taken some words and looks which smarted his small soul with a sting which would not be appeased until he had applied the balm of his characteristic revenge.

Here were some of the consequences. The mother watched by her suffering child. Bitter feelings arose. Her sense of duty transferred itself from her husband to her children. *He* had chosen his own lot — *they* were helpless, and she was their natural protector. She blamed herself for so long exposing them to the dangers of their father's presence. She resolved that the coming day she would write to Alice, and implore her to seek from her friends the means for her return to them.

Circumstances had changed in the old home. The sister next younger was happily married, residing in the cottage, and having her mother and Katy with her, while Willy had gone to his Uncle Nold's. But Lucy knew that somewhere they would cheerfully find a place for her and her little ones. She did not despair of being able to support them well, if left unmolested to her own resources. For the first time, she saw plainly that she was under no farther obligations to live with one who was no longer a man, but a something worse than brute. This was not the person with whom she had stood at the altar — the man, endowed with intellect, reason, judgment, heart, and those attributes which distinguish the immortal from the beast.

This was a sot, with whom it was an outrage upon refinement or decency to live — this was a madman with whom it was dangerous to be associated — this was an animal who had nearly drowned all indications of soul or mind in the burning bowl.

Her resolution was taken. If God spared poor Carrie's life, she should never again be the victim of a father's insanity. She counted up the weeks until she could return by the lake. It would be an impossibility almost to travel by stage, with two such small children. It was nearly the first of March. Courage — courage! she whispered to herself. "If it be necessary, I can at least claim the protection of the law, and have him imprisoned. Anything to save my children."

Even with the moans of the sufferer setting her nerves in a tremble, she felt a sense of relief. A crushing burden seemed lifted from her shoulders — that feeling of 'duty' which had weighed upon her heart and prevented her taking any steps for her own comfort or her babies. The thought that she could leave this disgusting companion — be free from his foul breath, his curses, and hateful caresses, and yet do him no wrong, came over her with a thrill of strength and hope. Her love had departed. She loved the Parke Madison of old with a passionate, regretful love, as one mourns for a friend who is dead; but this Parke Madison she could not love. Soul and sense refused to be enchanted with such loathsomeness.

When day dawned upon them, it found Lucy shivering

with cold, wrapped in a large shawl, Carrie sleeping under the influence of an opiate, and Parke rousing from his heavy slumber. Grumbling at the freezing state of affairs, and rubbing his shoulders, which ached with their repose upon the floor, he arose and stared at his wife.

"What are you up for? you look as if you had been sitting there all night."

She pointed to the bed; he approached and gazed at the poor little form lying there swathed in bandages. As recollection of the scenes of the night broke upon him, some thrilling screams rang again in his ears, his lips trembled as he spoke with an effort—

"I suppose this is some of the work of that cursed whiskey."

"It is a work which will bring you more sorrow than it has your victim. As sure as there is a God in Heaven, such things as these will bring retribution!"

"I know it—they will!"—he shook with cold and fear.

"Have you no fire?" he asked, to turn the subject; shall I build one up?"

"There is no wood. This is no place for you, either, Sir; I shall not complain of you this time, though the neighbors will probably see fit to have you placed in safety; but, if you dare to enter these doors again while Carrie lies here in this condition, I will no longer forbear. You shall have a home in the county-jail, where it will be impossible for you to beat your wife or burn your children."

"Why, Lucy! I never heard you quite so bitter before. But I suppose I deserve it. I shall see first if I can get anything for a fire, and then go, if I must. Where do you expect me to sleep? at the tavern? You might at least then give me a little money to pay for a bed, since you know I cannot get trusted."

Her look of contempt would have blasted a man in his senses; he only continued in a whining tone —

"Come! do be a little generous with your husband."

As she made no reply, he went out into the wood-shed, looked up a board, split it to pieces, and with some barks that were lying about, kindled quite a cheerful fire. He also filled the tea-kettle and put it on the stove.

"Hadn't you better get us a little breakfast first?" he next inquired, lingering by the fire, while Lucy took up her baby and nursed him.

As she made no move to do so, he ground some coffee in the mill, and had just got it finely boiling, and was slicing some bread and butter, when the doctor's step at the door arrested him. As Lucy opened it, he dodged into the sitting-room, afraid and ashamed to be seen. As the physician's call promised to be a long one, and as he began to feel the need of his morning bitters, he helped himself to a handsomely-bound volume of Longfellow's poems, which he hid in his coat and crept out the door, provided with the means of obtaining a day's whiskey.

Doctor Browning was a humane man who visited his poor patients almost as cheerfully as he did his rich ones.

Familiar as he was with poverty and distress, he was touched by the noble demeanor of Mrs. Madison, so superior to the station in which he found her. In a kind and delicate manner, he informed her that if she was in want of any comfort, she must not hesitate to let him know it. She smiled sadly as she went to the Bible which lay on the mantel and took from between its leaves five dollars.

"You see I am not quite destitute," she said. "If you will do me the favor to take two dollars and send a load of wood here; I cannot go out to look for it; and, as you see, I have none."

"Ah!" he gave a little sympathetic shiver at the thought of a February day and no fire. You shall have it in less than an hour, Madam. And if you will consent, I will speak to my niece — she's a pleasant, warm-hearted girl, and will be glad to come — to stay with you this afternoon and evening. She will be very gentle with the little girl — a good nurse is Miss Mary."

Mrs. Madison thanked him gratefully. He lingered with his hand upon the door-latch.

"And, my dear Madam, if you wish to get rid of your troublesome husband, we have a place where he will have a quiet chance to reflect upon his conduct. I will have him taken care of, if you say so; it is my opinion that it had better be done."

"I have warned him not to return here," replied Lucy, a faint blush mounting to her temples. "If he does, I will inform you, and you may take what steps you please."

"Very well. But remember your children, Mrs. Madison, and do not be too merciful."

He bowed respectfully and went away. A load of wood, and a man to prepare it, were soon at the door. It was hardly noon, before the niece of Dr. Browning, Miss Mary Browning, made her appearance, prepared to stay through the day and night. She was an amiable, rosy-cheeked girl, to whom the baby took immediately, laughing and crowing back answers to her smiles. Her hands were skilful in holding and soothing the little sufferer; and she let more than one tear fall amid the golden curls fastened back from that poor, tortured neck and cheek. Perhaps the mother saw these compassionate drops, for Mary had not been with her an hour, before she felt both love and gratitude towards her. As for Mary, she had conceived a kind of girlish worship for Mrs. Madison from the first moment she beheld those beautiful brown eyes and heard those sweet, touching cadences in her voice. She would follow every movement of that elegant figure with secret attention, wondering from what circle of brightness this star had dropped to so forlorn a sphere. Bits of poetry would come into her head — romances of a princess in disguise — all the stories she had ever read of fallen fortunes and the inebriate's home. Hitherto she had thought that only low, ignorant people became drunkards — at least *such* drunkards as Mr. Madison was a specimen of — and that their wives, although to be pitied, were somehow incapable of very sensitive feeling, and that sympathy would be somewhat wasted upon them. She had entertained a dim idea that when drunkards' children had their limbs broken, or fell into the fire, or had hot water thrown upon them, that the limbs undoubtedly ached and the burns smarted, but not with any such pain as would set the whole village in commotion had it chanced to her own pretty cousin, or to Lawyer Harris' beautiful little boy. Here, however, she saw a child, whose shining ringlets and fair complexion, whose violet eyes and dimpled hands, might awaken the pity of these fastidious people who were insensible to other distress than that of refinement and beauty afflicted. She saw a woman, born to queenliness of station, dragged down to share her husband's disgrace. She would have done just as much for the most ignorant; every fellow-creature had claims upon her attention and kindness; but what she often did out of pity she now did out of love.

Several people were in during the day. Numberless little gifts accompanied their visits; a pitcher of milk for the baby, a basket of pippins, a large paper of sweet crackers for Carrie to eat when she got well enough, and the like. Doctor Browning dressed the burns again in the afternoon. Mary ironed the aprons, played with the baby, brought in the wood for night, made her bed while the mother held Carrie, and did all that there was to be done. Mrs. Madison was enabled to set out a very well-spread tea-table; and had not her child been so injured, she would have felt a glow of comfort in her heart as she sat opposite to her bright-eyed friend.

There was something so caressing and genial in Mary's manner, that she was almost unconsciously led on to speak of things long past and obscured by the darkness of the present. As they were putting away the tea-things, their conversation chanced upon music. Miss Browning listened with delight to the description of those rare singers and great performances which her companion gave her; she sighed to hear an opera and see a prima donna; to sit in the midst of a wilderness of jeweled glasses, bouquets, and light, and behold a splendidly-dressed cantatrice come out upon the boards and thrill an audience with the wonders of her divine execution; while the lorgnettes were all leveled in that direction, ditto the bouquets — then an exciting murmur of applause, and the brilliant prima donna bowing low and more lowly, smiling, dropping deep courtsies and retiring.

Mrs. Madison could not help laughing, as the fanciful girl, who had read and imagined so much, but seen nothing, ran on with her voluble wishes. Mary, who played the piano tolerably, was anxious to take lessons on the guitar; and she promised when Carrie got better to give them to her if she remained in the place any time.

Speaking of the guitar, they came to talk of Germany, and from that, the older lady spoke of her own family, and of her mother being German in birth, but American in education. At ten o'clock that evening, Mrs. Madison was telling in tremulous tones something of her history, while

Mary sat at her feet, with her head in her lap, sobbing in sympathy with her new friend.

"This will never do to sit here disconsolate all night," she said, with a return of her natural gayety. "You must go to bed, Mrs. Madison, and sleep as securely as you have a mind. I will put on my dressing-gown and lie here upon the lounge, where I can hear the slightest moan that little Carrie makes, I will take good care of her."

"Are the doors fastened?" asked Lucy, trying them all before she ventured to undress. She was worn out, and needed rest so much, that she willingly obeyed the dictates of her companion, and was just in bed by the side of her baby, when she heard her husband's knock at the door.

"He has come," she whispered, slipping out of bed and putting on her dress; "but we must not let him in."

"Of course not," responded Mary; "he must find other lodging this night, as sure as I am Mary Browning."

A thundering rap at the door set the baby awake and crying. Its mother hushed it at her breast, and her friend went to make sure that the other door was secure.

"Can't you hear a fellow knock when he's knocked his knuckles off?" they heard him muttering outside. "Its a pretty pass things have come to, when a gentleman's wife locks him out on a night as cold as the Dickens. What's the use of having a wife? Lucy!" raising his voice, "Lucy — Lucy, let Mr. Madison come in, that's a lady! if you don't I shall go back to Kinney's and sleep with old

Peter, and he's as dirty as the swine — got the measles too, I suspect."

Finding that this threat produced no effect, his temper rose like a gust of wind, as he rattled at the door.

"You'll be sorry, if ever I do get in there!" he mumbled, giving a kick at the panels, which startled Lucy into a faint shriek.

"He will burst the button off!" she cried, clasping her hands. The door was only secured by a wooden button.

"And if he does, we will be a match for him," returned Miss Browning, taking up a stick of wood. "Two women ought to conquer one drunken rascal."

There was a short silence, and they heard him going away from the steps, but it was only to frighten them by crashing in a pane of glass at the window. The curtain protected them from sight.

"Oh, dear, what *will* he do," ejaculated Lucy; for her experience of the preceding night had made her cowardly. Another assault upon the door sent the button so nearly off that they saw their defence was nearly gone. Mary was a courageous girl and not to be subdued.

"Stand here, out of sight, Mrs. Madison, I am going to hold a parley with the enemy."

Laying her stick close at hand, she opened the door.

"What do you mean, Sir, disturbing your neighbors at this late hour, and breaking their windows? You will be fined to-morrow for this tumult."

"My neighbors?" said he, putting a foot on the threshold, and winking at her with one eye, "perhaps this is not my house, and you are not Lucy Madison, Esquire?"

"Well! am I?" she asked, turning her face so that the lamp shone full upon it.

"Really, I *do* believe it isn't you, after all," he said, drawing back; "but that's Carrie's crib, I'll be sworn," catching a glimpse at it, "and that's our bed and stove. "If you are not my wife, whose are you?" he inquired, gazing at her with a mixture of suspicion, astonishment, and incredulity.

"You will learn to your satisfaction when Mr. Brown gets his boots on, Sir. Come! are you going away quietly to the tavern where you belong, or will you wait until Mr. Brown is ready to accompany you?"

"Well, I guess I'll go back to Kinney's, since I can't find my own house. I was certain it stood here, and it did this morning; but I'll be bound it isn't anywhere in the neighborhood now. I beg your pardon, Ma'am, and Mr. Brown's. He need not trouble himself to see me home. But, really, I was sure —

While he took a puzzled survey of the premises, Mary shut the door, with a word of warning against stirring up Mr. Brown's indignation by making any more noise at their door. As they heard him mutteringly depart, Mary laughed over her stratagem — honorable in war — and Lucy again retired to her couch.

There was no further disturbance that night. The next day Mary, with Mrs. Madison's consent, informed her uncle of the affair, and Parke was arrested, and remained in the jail for the next three weeks.

Carrie slowly recovered from her injuries; but that dear cheek and once lovely neck and arm were so cruelly scarred, that the physician would not promise that they should ever regain their smoothness and beauty.

CHAPTER XI.

A 'MAINE-LAW' banner had been hoisted in the principal street of the village of A———, giving its blue and white folds to the sultry breezes of a summer's day. A party of men were gathered around the staff from which it floated, and as the flag had just been placed there, their conversation was of course upon the subject.

Lawyers, politicians, merchants, mechanics, and, as it chanced, three notorious drunkards, were of the crowd. Some listened in silence, but the most of them expressed their opinion for or against the Maine Law, and its adoption in that State. One or two of the politicians made short speeches, explaining the grounds upon which they stood in its defence or condemnation.

"I propose," said a gentleman who warmly advocated the law, "that we listen to the opinion of these three persons, whose approval or disapproval will be valuable, since it is their 'rights' which are to be 'interfered with.'"

He pointed to the trio of sots who disgraced the village with their long-continued excesses.

"Aye! let us have your opinions, gentlemen," cried another, thinking the proposition vastly amusing.

"Yes!" added a non-advocate, pleased with the idea—"You, Peter Greene, speak first; you are the oldest, the drunkest, and the worst of the three. Come, man, rouse yourself, and tell the people what you think of their forbidding you your privilege of taking a dram when you want it."

The old creature got upon his feet, but being already considerably intoxicated, although it was but the middle of the day, he found it difficult to keep there.

"We'll sustain you — opinions and all," laughed some of the young men, taking hold of his arms, and keeping him up. "Speak out boldly, Peter Greene, for your rights, or perhaps we will take them away."

"I don't know much what you're talking about," he began in a weak, high-pitched voice, looking at the non-advocate with red eyes, which were nearly hidden in a bloated mass. "But if its about getting drunk, or not getting drunk, why, drink as much whiskey as you can get; and when you can't get it any longer, die, and go to the place where I am going next week! I'll tell you how I know. Last night, as I lay awake, feelin' mighty unwell, I saw the door open, and a real gentleman, dressed all in black, came in — he looked like a Doctor. I was just a going to ask him — 'Doctor, what do you think is the matter with me?' when I sees his foot sticking out, and a pair of horns on his head. I knew the rascal by them, and sat up in bed, while a queer kind of shiver went all over me.

"I am not just ready to go yet," says I, thinkin' he had come for me. "I'm owing Stuck's widder for making me these pants as much as two years ago, and I'd like to settle up my affairs first."

"Very well," says he, with a polite bow, and speaking like a gentleman, "I didn't expect you to go along to-night; I only called to let ye know that I'd be coming for you next week."

"Its very good of you to let me know," says I.

"Where's your bottle of rum?" says he.

"Its in the closet," says I; "won't you step in and take a little? you're welcome."

"Thank ye," says he; and goes into the closet after the bottle, and I up like a streak and shuts him in and kept him 'til mornin'. I could hear him all night a-beggin' me to let him out, and a promisin' to let me off and take Gus Elliott in my place. But I allers' knew him for an liar, and I jist kept the key turned on him till mornin'. When I went to let him out, about sunrise, he wasn't there! I suppose he'll be along again at the time appointed; so I expect to have one more 'high,' and then bid ye all farewell."

He sank back, a loathsome object, upon his bench, amid the rather curious applause of the crowd.

"Now, Gus Elliott, let's hear you."

The second person addressed was the youngest son of one of the finest families in the State. His brothers, one in the Navy, one in the Army, were ornaments to society, and highly respected men. He had sank so low that they could no longer uphold him, and although still sharing a corner of the hearth-stone when he chose to claim it, the largest part of his time was spent upon the grog-shop settle. He had just taken a glass of brandy, but was not intoxicated.

"Friends! if that law had been passed twenty years ago, I should have been the richest man in this State. Many is the night I have spent my three hundred dollars on a champagne supper," he said, looking round as if some of those gentlemen might have shared his prodigality in years gone by. "What I am, and what my brothers and sisters have tried to make me, you all know. All that I can say is, that I wish it had been passed before I was born, I wish it could be passed this year — it might do for others what it is too late to do for me."

After closing his brief speech, he sauntered down the street, trying to look less miserable than he felt; his hat battered down, his cloth coat bearing the marks of the gutter, and two or three little scamps of boys amusing themselves by throwing dust at him.

"Now, Mr. Madison, will you be as kind as your compeers and tell us whether you are going to vote for the Maine Law?" The last of the trio had eagerly regarded Gus. Elliott while he spoke. Something in the similarity of their circumstances might have attracted him. His countenance had a pallor and ghastliness unlike the bloated red of his companions. He was leaning against an awning-post when they addressed him; he straitened himself up and advanced a step or two; a flush came into his haggard cheeks, and he spoke in a clear, round tone which startled them.

"I am no longer fit to address gentlemen; but if you wish to know whether I intend to vote for the Maine Law or not, I answer that if I live to go to the polls again, I shall vote for it. Do you want to know my reasons? I, too, have spent my three hundred a night on champagne-suppers — I say it to my disgrace — not boastingly. I was intended to be a pretty fine man! God gave me talent, an eloquent tongue, and a generous, affectionate heart. He gave me, too, a christian mother, and a sister! — a sister worthy of the best man that ever lived. My father bequeathed me wealth and a good name. But he bequeathed me, too, that weakness which made him "tarry long at the wine," and which, at last, led directly to his murder, as some of you may have heard. Well! what has this inclination led me into? After years of ambitious study it sent me disgraced from college — it led me into all the accompanying temptations of a city, and destroyed my mother's health with anxiety and sorrow. Upon that beloved mother's dying requirement I vowed to never again taste wine, and it led me to break that vow. It led me to commit forgery; and that beautiful, that angelic sister of whom I scarcely dare speak, to save me from a prison, made the sacrifice I demanded of her, and married the villain in whose power I was. I wooed and won a noble, true-hearted and lovely woman, and it led me to blast her happiness, to inflict upon her poverty, disgrace, and wordless wretchedness — it led me to nearly murder my only and innocent little daughter; she wears upon her once charming face the scars which tell of a father's fiendishness. This passion has made a pauper of me; it has caused me to break the most powerful chains that were ever woven by the love of friends, the pride of position, the desire to be a good man; it has brought me days of anguish, such as I pray God none of you may ever feel; it has gnawed my heart out with remorse, and yet drawn me on with its burning fascination into this depth of degradation. It has killed my pride — destroyed my intellect — hardened my heart — ruined my soul! In my extreme youth, when I lifted the sparkling goblet to my lips, I laughed and said — "I can take care of myself! — it is nobody's business but my own!" *Now*, I would go down on my knees to the world if it would stretch out its hand and save me. I ask of the law, of you who make the law, to save me from this monster which preys upon human hearts. Hercules was sent out to slay the Namean lion, and to kill the dreaded boar of Erymanthus, but what were their ravages to that of this passion for strong drink, that such thousands of your fellow-creatures have to struggle with! Will you aid them? will you send out the Hercules of the law to protect them? or shall they all perish, as I am perishing? Heaven knows I have fought until I have fainted many times, and yet I am a victim. You may throw a class of men out of employment, but if they make their living out of the blood and tears of the hearts of wives and children, why should they not abandon the unholy work, and turn to more righteous gains? The serpents prey upon frogs, the frogs upon spiders, the spiders upon flies, but need man to prey upon the weaknesses of his brothers, in order to find food? If you throw this grog-shop across the way out of business, and in return gain three honest, industrious, and peaceable citizens, who are now its patrons and the pest of society, can you answer whether you gain or lose? You may say that rich men can procure their costly wines and privately poison themselves, and teach their children to do the same, even if you should have this law. The rich are not the largest class of any community; and if they refuse to be benefited, shall the other classes all suffer for want of that protection which their need demands? When they have sunk as low as I, they will not refuse this rope which is thrown to keep them from drowning. If every man in this State, who could not pay five dollars for a bottle of wine twice or thrice a week, was to stand up with steady hand, undimmed eye, clear voice, and dignified demeanor, before the rich, free from all marks of this vice, those who now grow pompous over their costly decanters, would be ashamed of the wine-odor in their breath and its flush upon their cheek.

"Speak! gentlemen, I cannot speak what I feel! My

mother is dead — my sister's heart is broken — my wife has gone from me to struggle alone against poverty and woe — my children are afraid of me — they tremble at the mention of my name — they too are gone, and I am left to my fate. My fortune is gone — my health is gone — my religion, my talents, my happiness. It is this passion which has stolen all; now that I am weak and forlorn, incapable of taking care of myself, have you not the heart of humanity enough to try to obtain for me my rights? I charge you to do it! in the name of all the misery I have inflicted and endured — in the name of christian charity — in the name of a DYING SOUL! — will you serve me? Will you save my soul? I know that Satan is bound to obtain it; he has visited me as plainly as ever he did the disordered fancy of Old Peter; but if you do your best you may cheat him of his gains. Will you do it?"

He stretched out his hands for a moment.

As a lamp that has burned nearly out suddenly lifts itself into temporary brilliancy, after it is apparently extinguished, his mind had once more startled into life. The group regarded him with astonishment. He had not made exactly that expression of his sentiments which they anticipated. The flame blazed up a moment, betraying the shattered and ruined condition of the lamp, and sank back into darkness. His strength was overtasked by the sudden excitement, and, as his arms fell to his side, he dropped fainting to the ground. After the little tumult attending his recovery had subsided, the crowd dispersed, satisfied for that day with what they had heard about the Maine Law.

"I wish that *I* had a voice to speak with or a pen to write with," said Mary Browning, with sudden energy, after listening to her uncle's narrative of the above incidents.

"What would *you* have to say, Miss Mary?" asked he, smiling, as the roses brightened in her already glowing cheeks.

"Well! I should say — that — you know I am not accustomed to public speaking! uncle — that though I spake with the tongue of a denouncing angel, from now till the day of retribution, I could not depict all the evils of the liquor traffic; that though I wrote with a pen inspired with terror and winged with lightning, I could never write out the half of its abominations. I should say that a poor and virtuous nation was more secure of immortality and dignity than a rich and wicked one; and that if it was going to impoverish this country to abolish this traffic, it had better be honorably humble, than magnificently wicked; and I would refer my hearers to those often quoted examples of the cities of the Plain, of Babylon, and Rome. But I would further affirm, that so far from decreasing agricultural and commercial prosperity, it would increase both, just as certain as the wretched inebriates who support one rummery would invest the money which they there throw away on food, rent, and clothing. I would say that if there are ten thousand men supported in this State by the trade, that they are supported by the entire ruin of thirty thousand, and the injury of three hundred thousand. I would ask if that was political economy. I would state a very simple proposition, and let them multiply the answer by as many drunkards as there are in these United States. If a man instead of eating twelve bushels of grain, drinks eight and eats four, will the farmer have any larger market for his produce? — and by the loathing of food which liquor produces, the wasting of strength, and the shortening of life, will he not lose ten years of that man's custom? while the producers of clothing lose almost entirely his support, his employers lose what might be a profitable workman, and the man himself, and those whom he would have benefited by it in honest exchanges, loses almost the whole of that comfortable income which his wasted strength and industry would have achieved! The farmer sells ten dollars' worth of grain; to support the distiller and rumseller, both needless and useless members of society, the consumer pays thirty for it — the thirty dollars is all that he could earn under the influence of the distilled grain, where he would otherwise have earned ninety — the hatter, and shoemaker, and landlord, and merchant are robbed of sixty — and the many lose that the few may gain. Then there is another loss in the diminished demands of his starving and naked family; another in his requiring a police-officer or sheriff to attend to him, a prison or workhouse to put him in — a coffin and six feet of earth, at the expense of the community. Another loss in his premature death. So much for the political economy. Of some other losses I might not have the courage to speak; the loss of health, of peace of mind, of reason, of friends, of domestic prosperity, and the loss of future happiness. I am afraid my woman's voice would fail if it touched upon such losses. Perhaps I should regain my courage, however, if I had little Carrie Madison by my side, and could hold up her injured form in my arms and point to the cruel proceeds of a shilling's worth of whiskey."

"Of course — of course — you women try to prove everything by an appeal to our sympathies."

"Well, what better part of you is there to appeal to? Reason, of which you men are so boastful, forever and forever runs away with itself unless restrained and directed by the heart. Take those greatest and most subtle reasons, and let them run the rounds of their mighty intellects, and to what have many of the most brilliant returned? — to a lower point than the humblest heart could ever fall to — to a belief in their own brutishness and materiality.

"Pooh! my dear niece, what are you talking about?"

"I hardly know, uncle," replied Mary, a little confused. "But is it not a principle in all good governments to adopt those measures which will secure the greatest good to the most people? You know that the Maine Liquor Law, or even a more stringent one, would do this. I tell you what it is, dear uncle, there are a large class of people demand this law, who have yet no voice in the matter. They are the wives, sisters, mothers, and daughters of those who support the distillers and rumsellers. Not that I wish women to go to the polls," with another blush, as she saw Dr. Browning opening his eyes; "but if every man, this coming autumn, would ask the female portion of his house who to vote for, those men would be elected who would not fail to give us this law."

"A pretty way that would be to place the reins of government in the hands of women! —

"We'll even let them hold the reins,
But we'll show them the way to go!"

"Oh, you ladies are so crafty and so ambitious that I should not be surprised to see some one of you stealing her way into the Presidential Chair before ten years. In that case, farewell to Liberty and the American Eagle! the chair would become a throne in less than three weeks, and there would be an end of our 'glorious Republic.' Of all tyrants, women are the worst! no more to be trusted with power than a child with a candle in a barrel of tow!"

"For shame, Uncle Browning! that sentiment is not original, I know. You have caught it out of some crabbed book, and you don't believe it yourself. However, if you wish *me* to play the tyrant, I will begin now and exercise my power over your favorite — that talented, promising young student of yours — and not one word of encouragement shall he ever receive from me, unless he approves of, and gives his influence to, securing for our State the Maine Law."

"In that state of affairs, I should like to know who would do the voting? for his views lead him just the other way; and if he is weak enough to become your waiter, to carry *your* vote to the polls, then I shall no longer extend to him my approval. Ha! what did I tell you? that you were slily working to get the reins into your own hands!"

"Mrs. Browning, I do wish you had educated my good uncle to be a little more sensible! I do not care who votes, nor for what men, nor who induced them, only that we get absolved from this terrible liquor-traffic. *There* is where I have set my foot down, and I have a thousand excellent reasons for keeping it there.

"And yet reason has a tendency to ——"

"From what I have observed of your student's convivial inclinations, there may yet come a time when he will gladly wear the 'arbitrary' chain of this law, and I am going to compel him to forge one of the rivets himself. You, aunt, can do as much for your struggling and ill-disposed partner, and will have them both under wholesome restrictions.

"I wonder if you don't think we need restriction," spoke up the good Doctor, a little tartly, for he never drank anything but his cherry-bounce in the morning, his currant wine for dinner, and something warm, in the shape of a punch or hot toddy, before going to bed.

"No," said Mary, lightly touching her pretty finger to her uncle's ruddy nose; "not until *this* is twice as rosy as it is at present, will we make any complaint against you."

The Doctor was very sensitive about the peculiar glow upon his nose; he could not imagine why it should be redder than the noses of other people who took their brandy-and-water daily, whereas he only took cherry-bounce; starting after his mischievous niece, he caught her and pinched both her cheeks. The effect was to make her look prettier than ever; but being tired of her attempts at 'public-speaking,' she sat down demurely to a paper. Suddenly she lifted up her head, —

"Here is something in point of fact, uncle. Not a bit of romance:

"'If England would sign the temperance-pledge, and devote all the money now spent in intoxicating drinks to its liquidation, she could pay her debt of four billions of dollars in fourteen years. What a fact! And we have calculated nothing but the mere money spent; not the waste of time, labor, strength, health, and life.'

"Now if the temperance-pledge would do so much for that little island, what would not the Maine Law do for these United States? And when we add to the saving of money, the saving of tears, of broken hearts, of midnight watching, of neglected children growing up to ruin, of wasted happiness, of lost souls, what a saving is that! Ah, Uncle Browning, what economy is there! political, domestic, religious economy! I declare," here she threw aside her paper and started to her feet, "I am going to lecture on this subject. It is getting fashionable for ladies to lecture; and I have chosen my theme. I can't keep still any longer — my heart and conscience won't let me! I would write a book were it not for three reasons. Firstly, I cannot; secondly, no one will publish it after it is written; thirdly, no one will read it after it is published. But a lecture! people will come to hear a woman speak when she is as young and as beautiful as I. (Quoted, uncle, quoted from that truly reliable source, the young medical student). So you must have the advertisement in the next number of the A—— Republican; for I shall commence in this village, and from thence my eloquence shall diverge in widening circles until bounded by the Atlantic and Pacific."

"It would not be for the want of a 'gift of tongues,' if you did not succeed. About the advertisement — we will see — we will see! we will have to consult our younger partner about that."

So saying, Dr. Browning composed himself for a siesta upon the settee, which occupied a cool place on the back portico.

It is improbable that his niece, Miss Mary Browning, carried her sudden resolution into practice; though she would fain have studied out some method by which she could have made her enthusiasm felt on more hearts than those of her worthy uncle and his gay protagee.

One or two of her youthful opinions, having been shaken like unripe fruit into this book, may be gathered up a moment and cast down again; but no wider range will ever chance to her ambition, notwithstanding that allusion to the two great oceans which bound our continent.

To her honor and wisdom be it said, however, that the medical student, whose predelictions for the doctor's cherry-bounce had prevented her giving any decided encouragement to his otherwise pleasing attachment, was converted to her way of thinking before autumn, and became willing to resign his own especial inclinations for the general good; so that at the polls, his voice was heard, not for men against measures, but for "men *and* measures."

In the meantime, Parke Madison, while Dr. Browning reposed in comfort upon his settee, reclined also upon a settee, seeking his afternoon's repose. His couch was the lounger's bench before the grog-shop, which stood opposite to the liberty-pole, from which floated the newly-made banner. It was not as cool as the doctor's portico, for the sun shone down upon his face, but poorly protected by a rimless hat of straw. An awning would have made too comfortable a refuge for his customers, and taken from the respectable look of the place by encouraging loungers, and so Mr. Kinney had no awning before his shop. The August sun beat, therefore, upon the inebriate's face and head in cruel power. When he had recovered from his fainting-fit, nothing but a glass of brandy could restore him to his feet or overcome the trembling of his limbs. Mr. Kinney, to whose tender mercy he was left, furnished him with the restorative for which he pleaded. When he had drank it, he crept out and stretched himself upon the bench. His blood-shot eyes, shaded somewhat by the rimless hat, were fixed upon the blue and white folds of that graceful flag. His mind was confused, his memory was gone; but an idea, vague, phantom-like, dim, swam in his brain, that that banner was the precursor and proclamation of some great good that was coming to him. He would fall partially asleep; the heat would waken him, or the flies, or the step of a passer-by, and his gaze would rest upon the flag, following its undulations with dull dreaminess in which there was the shadow of a speculation. What good it was going to achieve for him he did not know. Whether it was going to bring his wife back, with some angelic power, to restore him to his old prosperity; whether it was the spirit of little Carrie hovering there on blue and white wings to bear him up and show him the forgotten way to his mother, he could not think. Once, opening his eyes upon it suddenly, he thought that his mother was leaning out of heaven with the banner in her hand, waving it gently to and fro. Presently he fell into so heavy a slumber that passing objects no longer aroused him. The hot sun had retreated from the sky, and the calm moon was shining in his place when the inebriate awoke again. He awoke with a cry. He felt a huge serpent creeping and crawling over his breast; he put his hand there and tried to thrust it off, but it would not go. He endeavored to fling it away, but it writhed and twisted itself around his hand in slimy folds, while its fiery tongue pricked him in his breast a dozen times. With another cry and a furious effort, he plucked at the noisome thing. A hiss was the only answer, so loud, so threatening, that he sprang to his feet in terror. His eyes fell upon the banner, hanging against the sweet, blue sky, the moon just shining over its softly-fluttering edge. He fell upon his knees and raised his hands; the serpent glided down his limbs and ran away. It came back no more that night; but the unhappy man's nerves were too keenly awake for him to slumber again. He crossed the street, and leaning up against the liberty-pole, watched its long, slender shadow down the street, and listened to the sighing, fluttering spirit in the folds that rustled above his head.

"It is Lucy's voice," he whispered tremblingly; "she is charming the serpents, to keep them from stinging me. She was always kind — but why is she 'way up there beside the moon? — perhaps she is afraid of that reptile — ugh! how cold, how horrible it felt."

The moon sank behind the horizon; poor Parke sank too, to the friendly ground at last, pillowing his swimming head upon the soft, fat side of a kind old porker, which animal is not denied street-room in the most of our western villages.

From that time forward there grew upon his side a strong attachment, if it may be so called, for that banner which waved its azure folds against an azure sky. He had a dim perception that it hung there for his benefit — *him* whom nobody in the world cared for except to misuse, who slept with swine, who had no father, mother, wife, sister, child, or friend. In his most lucid moments he understood its meaning; how it could advance his good, what principles it advocated, in what manner its friends might save him. But the most of the time, unsubstantial fancies thronged his disordered intellect; the banner became, by turns, his old-time companions, one or another to whom he muttered unmeaning jargon, on Kinney extending a glass of champagne, inviting him to drink and be merry. His favorite seat and couch was the bench upon which he could recline and follow those playful folds with his half-idiotic gaze.

Oh! most wretched, most forlorn of lives! what fate is there so wholly miserable as that of the inebriate when he is wearing out the last few months or years of his life, forsaken by heaven and earth, tormented with glimpses of that punishment which is to overtake him at the close of time? Leaning above my paper, with the pen dropping idly from my hand, I have fallen into a reverie over the fate of Parke Madison, who has thus become a victim to an inherited passion which has taken from him all and bestowed upon him nothing. I see that a mother and sister have done all for him that they could do — I see that his wife was compelled to leave him by a higher duty than prompted her to remain — I see that society has abandoned him — that he is left alone with the robber. I see that the robber has taken already everything but the base remains of a base life; but while there is life, there is hope. Hope is calling in piercing tones upon the law to rush to the rescue of the dying; to chain and throw into prison, aye, and execute this highwayman, who has cast his dead victims by every road-side in the land.

Election day came, Parke understood that an effort would be made to place such men in power as would give him and others the protection they demanded. He endeavored to keep his senses enough about him to vote for these men. But his friend Kinney had motives and designs the opposite; he did not begrudge a few glasses of whiskey, if it would make one vote the smaller the chance of interruption to his profitable employment. Parke was not the only poor fool to whom, that day, he proved himself generous; nor his the only vote he secured by this dishonest means.

The Maine Law banner hung at half-mast, mourning for the defeat of those who would have waved it high and broad in triumph across the State. Parke lounged upon his bench, staring drearily at its drooping lengths. A chilly rain began to gather out of mist, and, dropping slowly from the gray sky, saturated the soiled folds till they clung forlornly to the staff. It saturated Parke's shabby clothing also — it chilled him to the heart. Dreary, desolate, shivering, miserable, he arose, and with one despairing glance at the lowered flag, he turned into the grog-shop, muttering —

"They won't do anything for me, this year, and next it'll be too late. I've given up doing anything to save myself long ago, and now I'll not wait any longer. I'm all in a shiver — I can't live without whiskey; its the only comfort there is left, and I don't see, after all, what they wanted to take it away for. How could I get warm if it was not for whiskey, when I've no fire of my own, and Kinney's always driving me away from his of nights? I shall never stop again. I shall take all I can get, and when I can't get it, the old fellow will be after me."

His bottle was filled with liquor; he took it and wandered forth, filled with a momentary pleasure.

CHAPTER XII.

A LADY came up in the omnibus from the cars one bleak November evening, and stopped at a hotel in A———. The best private parlor was placed at her disposal, and tea was served attentively in her room; for there was that in her appearance which demanded respectful consideration. She was young and beautiful; but her beauty was of a rare and touching kind, such as emanates from the spirit and is diffused over a fragile form for a little while before the earth closes over it and it is no more. A pair of large, luminous hazel eyes lighted up a pale face with a soft, smileless, melancholy lustre, giving it so sad and lovely an expression that the maid who brought up the tea lingered at the door, server in hand, lost in a maze of wonder. So fair an apparition had never brightened that dull parlor before; an apparition she almost seemed, so shadowy and yet beaming were her looks. The lady leaned back in her chair as if very much fatigued; she had just tasted the tea and toast which were brought up.

"Is there nothing else you'll be pleased to have, Ma'am?"

"Nothing at present; except you may ask the landlord if he will be so good as to come up here for a moment."

The girl disappeared; in a short time the proprietor stood bowing before the stranger. She motioned him to take a seat, and struggled a moment with some emotion before she spoke. As she fixed her eyes upon the fire, a hectic flush stole through the transparent whiteness of her cheeks.

"Do you know anything of a person by the name of Parke Madison?" she asked, after he had taken a chair.

He started at her inquiry, looking at her close. This was not Mr. Madison's wife, though; for he had seen her several times — was it a sister? who? what?

"Yes, Madam, I have seen Mr. Madison nearly every day for the last two years."

"I am his sister, Mrs. Clyde. I have come to A——— on purpose to visit him. Can you tell me where he can be found?"

The gentleman hesitated, giving a nervous hitch to his chair.

"He is in this house," he replied, presently.

"Will you ask him to come in and see me?"

"He will not be able to do so to-night, Madam. The truth is, he is ill — very ill."

"Then I must go and see him, I have come just in time to be his nurse."

"Indeed, Mrs. Clyde, he is in the best hands, now.

You had not better think of seeing him to-night — you ar tired."

"Oh, yes! I must. What is the matter with him?"

The landlord gave another twitch to his chair.

"Fever — dangerous kind. He would not recognize you, Madam, if you should go to him, and at present he is so raving that it might be unpleasant for you. You seem too delicate to endure much. After a night's rest you will have more nerve."

"I know what is the matter with him," she continued with a slight shiver — "do I not?"

He bowed a silent reply in answer to those melancholy eyes.

"Has he been sick long? is there any hope of his get ting well?"

"But litttle, I am afraid. He was brought here this afternoon by some benevolent gentlemen, who promised to see to the necessary expenses. I do not care for that; but he will disturb my guests some, I apprehend. However, I am glad he is here. We will do all for him that can be done."

"Thank you — thank you. You will be repaid here and hereafter. I must go to him," rising from her chair, "perhaps I can soothe him, or recall him from his delirium by the sound of my voice."

"Indeed, Madam, Mrs. Clyde, you have no idea — it will be too trying. It is enough to make *my* blood run cold, and I fancy that I have pretty strong ——"

A shrill scream, rising from a distant room, interrupted him. Alice sprang into the hall; before that shriek of agony had died in prolonged echoes through the house, she stood at the door of the chamber from which it emanated. Opening it she passed in. Her brother, at that moment, was lying quiet upon the bed, as if exhausted by the passion of mortal terror which had given rise to that loud cry. It was only a moment that his disease would allow him rest. Turning his eyes to the door at the slight noise made by closing it, they dilated with icy and staring horror, his teeth chattered, the hair rose bristling upon his head; pointing his finger at Alice, he spoke —

"It has come back! oh, my God! it has come back!"

So shivering was the sound, so dreadful the look, that the intruder dropped fainting into a chair. Three or four gentlemen were in attendance; one of them, Dr. Browning, advanced to her side.

"In heaven's name, Madam, what are you doing here?"

"He is my brother," sobbed she, recovering herself with difficulty. "I promised never to forsake him."

"You can be of no service to him here, dear lady; you had better retire; a few hours will close his sufferings."

"And he will die in such a state!" — she buried her face in her hands — "oh, mother, intercede with Christ for him!"

The Doctor lifted her gently from her seat and carried her into the hall.

"Should he have a lucid interval I will certainly call

you; but I cannot permit you to remain here," he said, and returning, he bolted the door.

"Doctor!" whispered his patient.

"What is it, my dear Sir," he asked, as he approached the bed.

"Do mad dogs *always* foam at the mouth so, just before they spring?" he pointed to a chair which stood in a corner.

The physician looked around involuntarily, as if he expected to behold the dreaded animal upon which that fixed and fascinated gaze was riveted.

"There is no dog there," he said decidedly, recovering himself.

"Yes there is, there—yes! hear him snarl and snap—now!—here he comes—keep him off! Doctor! keep him off!"

He struggled with the bed clothes desperately, until his strength was once more gone.

"Why didn't you turn him out?" he queried in a faint voice; "or at least let me have my pistols—I could have finished him with one of them, without getting half eaten up in this manner. Look at my arm! there isn't an ounce of flesh left on it—but I strangled him—the cursed cur!—I strangled him. He's dead—he's dead—he's dead!"

Suddenly his roving eyes were arrested and fixed upon the wall with a look of such inconceivable fear and despair that every one in the room turned theirs in the same direction; *they* beheld only the blank white wall, but what shape of horror *he* beheld, their frightened fancy dared not devise. It was enough reflected in his countenance — rage contending with an agony of terror.

"It was Satan's dog that I strangled," he shrieked. "He's here to threaten me about it. Hell and all the furies! what do you stand there grinning for?"

He seized a candle-stick which chanced to be on a stand at the head of the bed, and hurled it at the inoffensive wall. His companions wanted no more definite idea of the expression of the ruined angel than was stereotyped in his stony face, while he glared defiance at the foe.

It seemed that the missile did not overthrow his adversary, for the next moment he recommenced his struggles and began a succession of those long and quivering screams whose unearthly anguish curdled the blood of the remotest listener.

Alice heard them, as she paced with restless steps her apartment. The hotel-keeper's wife, who had kindly volunteered to stay with her, shuddered, and placed her fingers in her ears. Alice threw herself prone upon the floor. The next instant she started to her feet. Her quick ear had detected another sound. She rushed to the window — threw it up — and looked down. A dark mass, dimly revealed in the starlight, lay upon the pavement, beneath the window of her brother's room: two or three heads were thrust from that window, also looking down, and she heard exclamations of terror. She turned away and ran into the hall — down the broad stair-case — out the door — and fell with a cry beside that quivering but lifeless heap.

She was the first to reach the spot. They raised her from the dead body of her brother and bore her back to her room. She was indeed faithful to the last. If a sister's love could have redeemed an erring man from ruin, Parke Madison would not have died the drunkard's death.

The law refused to aid him in his great extremity — the last refuge of the lost was denied him — in what should have been the pride and vigor of manhood he fell, and was overcome by the Destroyer.

Alice was the only mourner at his funeral. A grave she gave him in a pleasant place, and a stone to bear his dishonored yet beloved name.

Poor child! her own grave is ready for the marble now. The sods lie fresh and chill upon it — the first light snow has covered it with a cold, fair drift. The most tender heart, the most beautiful form, lie fading in the coffin upon which the mourner's tears are scarcely yet dry. The pale and peerless dove has folded her wings over a breast that grew cold and colder under the pressure of earth's bitter cares; that voice which was the sweetest in mortal choirs has gained a more inspired sweetness in the land to which she has flown.

Alfred Clyde, having spent the most of his princely fortune in brilliant extravagancies, infests our southern cities, living splendidly upon the weakness and inexperience of those rich young men whom he can tempt to the gambling-table.

Lucy Madison has found a refuge for herself and children in her mother's home. By industrious application to her art, she will obtain for them a comfortable living; and she has friends who will see to the education of her boy. Sad and resigned, in widow's weeds, she moves about; that placid and noble expression which always characterized her, receiving a yet higher beauty from the touch of patience and sorrow.

Even if lightened by christian faith and sweetened by resignation, her future life will be one that claims sympathy —left lonely, poor, and unprotected in the summer and bloom of her youth, with two helpless little ones to cherish and provide for.

But what a joy and comfort are these little ones; Carrie is a gay and affectionate child, the sunshine and music of the house. The marks of the sad accident which so nearly disfigured her for life are fading out, as its memory has already vanished from her happy mind.

As for the boy, he is as promising as a boy of eighteen months dares to be; but if he should grow up with the inclinations which ruined his father, we have only to pray that, before *he* reaches the dangers of manhood, the law will have woven about him a protection too arbitrary for him to loosen. So prays his mother nightly as she lays him in his crib and joins his tiny hands together while she makes her mute appeal.

www.ingramcontent.com/pod-product-compliance
Lightning Source LLC
LaVergne TN
LVHW020245110826
845151LV00003B/1024

* 9 7 8 1 4 2 5 5 2 9 9 5 6 *